Robin Jenkins was born in Lanarkshire in 1912. He taught not only in Scotland but in Spain, Malaysia and Afghanistan. A prolific novelist, he is widely regarded as a powerful force in contemporary writing. He lives in Argyll, the setting for *Poverty Castle*.

Other titles by Robin Jenkins include:
So Gaily Sings the Lark
Happy for the Child
The Thistle and the Grail
The Cone-Gatherers
Guests of War
The Changeling
Dust on the Paw
A Very Scotch Affair
The Holy Tree
A Would-be Saint
Fergus Lamont
The Awakening of George Darroch
Just Duffy

Poverty Castle

Robin Jenkins

BALNAIN BOOKS

Printed and bound in Britain by Billings and Sons Ltd.,
Worcester.
Cover printed by Wood Westworth, Merseyside.

Cover painting by John Wilson
Photograph of the author: George Young
Designed by Balnain Books

Published in 1991
by Balnain Books,
Druim House, Lochloy Road,
Nairn IV12 5LF
Scotland

The publisher acknowledges subsidy from the Scottish Arts
Council toward the publication of this volume

British Library Cataloguing in Publication Data:
Jenkins, Robin 1912-
    Poverty Castle.
    1. Title
    823.914 [F]

ISBN 1 872557 05 8

For Alison, Trisha, and Emma, my grand-daughters

He had always hoped that in his old age he would be able to write a novel that would be a celebration of goodness, without any need of irony. The characters in it would be happy because they deserved to be happy. It must not shirk the ills that flesh was heir to nor shut its eyes to the horrors of his century, the bloodiest in the history of mankind. It would have to triumph over these and yet speak the truth. Since he would wish also to celebrate the beauty of the earth he would set his story in his native Highlands, close to the sea.

In his 73rd year, when his powers were beginning to fail, he realised it was then or never. From the point of view of the world's condition the time would never be propitious. Fears of nuclear holocausts increased. Millions guzzled while millions starved. Everywhere truth was defiled, authority abused. Those shadows darkened every thinking person's mind: he could not escape them. They would make it hard for his novel to succeed.

'Impossible, I would say,' said his wife Jessie, a frank · and cheerful Glaswegian. 'You've always been severe on your characters, Donald. I can't see you changing now.'

They were sitting in deck-chairs on the grassy patch — it was too rough and sheep-trodden to be called a lawn — in front of their cottage overlooking the Firth of Clyde, about fifteen miles from the Holy Loch. It was a warm summer afternoon. Red Admiral butterflies fluttered in flocks from one buddleia bush to another. From the safety of rhododendrons chaffinches mocked Harvey the white cat asleep in the shade. Making for the opening to the sea, between the Wee Cumbrae and Bute, slunk an American submarine, black and sinister, laden with missiles.

In his childhood, in the West Highland village of Kilmory, there had been black beetles of repulsive appearance to which he and his friends had attributed deadly powers. Whenever one was encountered everybody had to spit with revulsion and yet also with a kind of terrified reverence, to ward off its mysterious evil. When he had grown up he had learned that the creatures were harmless, but he remembered them whenever he saw one of those submarines.

Jessie noticed him turning away his head and pretending to spit. 'See what I mean!' she cried. 'You can't forget those awful things and you could never let your characters forget them either. So how could they be happy?'

'Many people seem to be happy in spite of them.'

'Like me, for instance? Like my friends? But Donald, if you put us in a book you'd make us pay for our happiness. You'd want to show that it was just our way of escaping from despair.'

He smiled. 'Well, isn't it? Country Dancing while the world burns?'

'It's not burning yet and with a little luck might never burn. What's wrong with being hopeful? You've always had too low an opinion of humanity, Donald: in your books anyway. I suppose there were reasons. An only child, brought up in that small-minded place by a dreary

8

bigot of a father. I'm sorry to miscall the dead but that's what he was. If your mother hadn't died so young I'm sure your books would have had happier endings.'

He had been six when she had died.

'Where would you set it? Not in Scotland surely.'

'Why not in Scotland?'

'But you think the Scots have lost faith in themselves, don't you? 'The only country in history that, offered a modest degree of self-government, refused it.' No inspiration to a novelist, therefore. The very opposite. A blight on his imagination. You've said it often, Donald.'

Yes, but because he had been born and brought up amongst them the Scots were the only people he felt competent to portray.

'Whereabouts in Scotland? For heaven's sake, not Kilmory!'

'Why not Kilmory? It's the place I know best.'

'What nonsense. You haven't been back there for more than ten years. From what you've told me you couldn't have been very happy there yourself, so how could you describe characters that were? Who would those characters be anyway?'

'I don't know. I haven't met them yet.'

'You must have some idea.'

'None at all. I'm looking forward to meeting them.'

One thing she had vowed never to be, and that was jealous of his precious characters.

'You'll just exhaust yourself.'

And for what? To produce a book that few would read and fewer still buy. Lack of appreciation didn't seem to have embittered him but it had her.

Writing her weekly letter to her daughter Morag in America she mentioned that Dad was talking about starting a new book. 'A triumphant valediction, he has the nerve to call it.' She didn't expect it to get far because he wasn't very well. He had become uneasy and strange. It had crossed her mind that he might be preparing himself for death. Though not very steady on his feet he went for a walk every day whatever the weather: in search of his characters, no doubt. She suspected he took tumbles for there was often mud on his clothes, but if asked about it he just smiled. He seldom looked at a newspaper or listened to radio or watched television: a sure sign that he was broody with a new novel. At such times he wasn't much of a companion, but then he had always been aloof and solitary, as Jessie well knew. After more than forty years of marriage she knew that there were barriers beyond which she had not been allowed to pass. At her age she wasn't complaining, she was just facing facts. He should never have got married. She had often accused him of having more interest in his imaginary people than in his wife and child. Here he was, proving it again.

Part One

They loved the house from the moment they discovered it, though sheep had to be shoo'd out of the ground floor rooms and ceilings had fallen in and Rebecca, four years old and very fastidious, slid on a cow-pat and made a greenish smelly mess on her knickers. They had caught sight of it from the beach and were eager to explore. The path up to it or rather the numerous paths, for cattle, sheep and rabbits had made many, lay first over a wide machair of turf and wild flowers, then among shrubberies of whin, broom, and rhododendrons, and lastly, in what at one time must have been the garden though the surrounding wall was broken in several places, through grass as tall as Africa.

Papa, his face under the Panama flushed with wine and sun, led the way, shouting encouragements and brandishing his arms, as if to chase off hostile natives or ferocious animals. Behind him nine-year old Jeanie pretended to be frightened, though if any fabulous beast had been encountered she would have greeted it with the least fear and incredulity:

she doted on all animals, even the ugliest creepy-crawly. Her twin Effie was as usual matter-of-fact and kept crying why were they all so excited, it was just an abandoned old house. Rowena, aged seven, always had to have a secret: now it was a small shiny green bug held in her fist. Rebecca who could see only grass, held on to Diana's skirt. Diana at eleven was the oldest. She was also the only one dark-haired, all the others being fair, especially Rowena, the beauty of the family. Diana had long ago appointed herself its guardian, looking after not only her sisters but her parents too. She kept turning to make sure her mother was following. Oblivious of sticky-willies in her hair and wine stains on her white dress and butterflies dancing round her head, Mama was singing. She loved her family and would have given her life for them but often, in their midst, she was absent. They had once asked her where she went. To elfland looking for your little brother, she had answered. They had been, with reservations, satisfied for the time being anyway. Elfland, which didn't exist, was as good a place to look for their little brother who didn't exist either, at any rate not yet.

It was July, about three in the afternoon, hot and sunny, ideal for blood-sucking clegs and pestiferous flies. The air was heavy with familiar scents: meadowsweet, mint and honey- suckle. There were others, ambrosial and elusive, not identified then or afterwards.

The picnic basket had contained two bottles of red wine. Behind their backs in the hotel Papa had slipped in the second one, thus breaking the agreement. To prevent him from drinking too much and falling asleep Mama had taken more than she could manage without becoming light-headed, and the girls had demanded share. As a result they were all reckless and rushed in through the open door, scaring sheep which had been lying on the floor. It was then that Rebecca had slipped on the cow dung and Papa, shouting 'Damn' put his foot through a rotten floor board and grazed his ankle for he was wearing no socks and his khaki shorts, though unfashionably long, were nonetheless no protection for his pale thin legs, as the clegs had found out : there was already blood where he had been bitten. Clegs, his daughters had decided must like wine, for they bit Papa more than anyone else.

All the windows on the ground floor rooms were broken. What glass remained was black with dust and cobwebs and dead flies. Ceilings had fallen and most of the plaster had come off the walls.

'Nobody's lived here for ages,' whispered Jeanie.

She and Effie ventured through the house to the back door or rather to the opening there, for the door itself had disappeared. There was a large courtyard overgrown with brambles and briers, to which stuck tufts of wool. 'Like messages left by somebody,' whispered Jeanie. Beyond lay a wood of elm, beech and ash, now silent in the sunshine except for the fervent moaning of doves. The twins smiled at each other. Here was a place of many enchantments.

Rebecca's knickers had to be taken off, they were making her uncomfortable. Diana helped her. Mama was still in a dwam. She looked lost and lovely.

Rowena opened her hand. The little green bug did not move. She frowned. It had no business to be dead. She had not squeezed it hard. She blew on it, in vain. She pretended to be overcome with grief: tears came into her eyes. Inwardly she was smiling.

Papa was testing the staircase. But for some loose or mouldy boards it was still usable, with care. It had been solidly built in the beginning, as indeed had the whole house. The walls were four feet thick.

'Why don't we buy it, Papa?' asked Effie

Diana was also the family's puncturer of wild ideas, its reducer of things to normal size. 'It's falling to pieces,' she said.

'But Papa's an architect,' said Jeanie. 'Well, he used to be, anyway. He could get it repaired. Couldn't he, Mama?'

Mama then came back, laughing happily and kissing them all at random. Heedless of damage to her dress she sat on a rusty can that had once contained sheep dip. 'Your Papa could repair the Acropolis in Athens if he set his mind to it.'

That was the trouble, they all knew. Papa never put his mind to anything for long. He had many glittering ideas that he ran after briefly as they did soap bubbles.

'It would cost a fortune,' said Diana.

'Well, we've got a fortune,' pointed out Effie.

Yes, and Diana sometimes wished they hadn't. She thought she preferred the old hard-up but settled and sensible life in Edinburgh, where Papa had gone to his office every day and the girls, except Rebecca, had attended St Mabel's School which they had liked except for the uniform of silly hat, itchy grey stockings, and navy-blue knickers. Since then they had wandered about the Highlands like rich gypsies, living not in caravans and tents, which might have been fun, but in hotels and freezing furnished rented mansions, seeking a permanent home where Papa would be inspired to proceed with his book on the characters in Sir Walter Scott's novels. He had got stuck after only eighteen pages.

An uncle in Canada had died and left him nearly three hundred thousand pounds.

'I don't think you should venture upstairs, my love,' called Mama. 'It might not be safe.'

They knew that Papa attracted accidents they way he did clegs. It wasn't just that he was often befuddled with wine, it was also that he had too much faith in the appearance of things.

'If we do not venture what do we ever achieve?' he cried.

His daughters always felt most protective and loving when he was in this rash and defiant mood.

'I'll go first,' said Effie. 'I'm lighter.'

They all cricked their necks gazing up the stairwell. They hadn't realised the house was so high: three storeys, plus attics. If the roof or one of the upper floors collapsed they could all be killed.

Papa tweaked his moustache, first the right side and then the left: it was his way of crossing himself. Then he ascended the stairs, very cautiously. Diana came close behind, ready to yell a warning or grab him. The twins followed her. Rowena and Rebecca stayed behind with Mama. Rowena, who hated unnecessary exertion, pretended to be aggrieved and tried on various expressions to indicate it.

Sheep had not managed up into the rooms on the first floor, but birds had, and children: there were feathers and sweetie papers among the sand blown in from the beach. Cobwebs were everywhere. There were remnants of wallpaper. People had lived here once. They could live here again.

'Look at those skirting-boards and cornices,' cried Papa. 'The best materials were used in the building of this house. Nothing shoddy or skimpy. I wonder why it was allowed to go derelict.'

'Perhaps there was a murder,' said Effie, 'and now there's a ghost.'

'It's too bright and sunny for ghosts,' said Diana.

'What about at night, when the wind's howling?'

Jeanie shouted down. 'It's all right, Mama. It's quite safe if you want to come up.'

Intrepidly Papa led the way up to the second floor.

'This is the style in which many old Scottish castles were built,' he said, 'very high and narrow, with thick walls and small windows.'

'But this isn't a castle,' said Effie. 'It's got no turrets.'

'With all these stairs and all these rooms we'd need a servant,' said Diana.

'Well, we could afford a servant,' said Jeanie. 'Couldn't we, Papa?'

But, Papa on his knees almost, was peering out of a window, ecstatic about the view.

Jura's great lumps of stone shone in the blue sky.

'You can almost see the deer,' said Jeanie.

In the distance, southward, across the river, was the little harbour with boats in it; and on a hill above it people played on the nine-hole golf course. Walking over it that morning Papa had picked what he claimed to be mushrooms. To prove it he had eaten half of one while the girls shrieked in alarm and waited for him to turn black and die.

'What's that over there?' asked Effie, pointing.

Northward, beyond the wide machair, was a dense wood out of the heart of which rose chimneys and parts of a roof.

'That'll be the big house where the laird lives,' said Papa.

'Who's the laird?' asked Diana

'This is Campbell country so I suspect he'll be a member of that clan.'

'Was it him put up those notices on the beach?' asked Effie.

They were to the effect that the beach was private and trespassing was forbidden. The Sempills had not been deterred.

'Does he own the ruins of the old castle?' asked Jeanie. 'That said private too.'

'I expect his ancestors lived in it once, hundreds of years ago.'

'Is this house on his land?' asked Diana.

'It could well be.'

'I think he's too greedy,' said Effie.

'Who is, my dear?' panted Mama, arriving just then with Rowena and Rebecca.

'The laird. He owns all the land.'

'Look at that splendid rowan,' cried Papa.

They crowded round the window, looking.

'Do you mean that tree with the white blossoms?' asked Effie.

'That is not just a tree, my dear. That is a symbol.'

He quoted: "Thy leaves were aye the first to spring
  Thy flo'ors the simmer's pride,"
'Did Sir Walter Scott write that, Papa?' asked Jeanie.

The girls had all been called after Scott's heroines.

'No, Jeanie, it was written by a lady called Caroline Oliphant or Lady Nairne. A very moving tune goes with it. Mama, please sing us a snatch,'

'I'm still recovering my breath, darling.' But after a few more deep breaths she broke into song.

They loved listening to Mama singing. Sometimes she was out of tune or forgot the words but it never mattered.

'I know that tune,' cried Effie. 'Pipe bands play it.'

'So they do,' said Papa. 'It is one of the best known and best loved of Scottish songs. Some decry it as sentimental but in my opinion it expresses in a simple but moving way the sanctities of family life.'

They gazed again at the tree, more earnestly this time. It was, they agreed, like a gigantic white rosebud and had more than its share of magic that all growing things had, including toadstools.

'What are sanctities, Papa?' asked Effie.

Mama rescued her agnostic husband, not for the first time.

'Papa will explain later. In the meantime I think we should go down. We are tempting providence by remaining here.'

'Have no fear, my love,' said Papa. 'The rowan will protect us.'

'How will it do that?' asked Effie.

'In the old days people planted a rowan near their

20

home, to keep evil spirits away.'

'That's superstition,' said Diana.

'It didn't stop the house from becoming a ruin,' said Jeanie.

'It is not yet a ruin. Restoring it would be costly but quite practicable. Perhaps we were sent here for that purpose.'

'Are you going to buy it Papa?' asked Diana.

'It may not be for sale.'

'Aren't we going to live in Spain?' asked Rowena.

A friend of Papa's had offered to sell him a villa in the province of Alicante, beside the sea. Papa had pointed out the advantages: sunshine all the year round, which would help Mama's arthritic little finger; cheap wine and fruit; miles of sand and a warm sea; orange and almond groves; a swimming pool in the garden.

The girls had been learning Spanish.

'Que hora est?' asked Jeanie.

'Uno, dos, tres,' sang Effie.

'Olé,' piped Rebecca.

Papa clapped his hands. 'Muy bien. It does seem a pity to throw away such accomplishments.'

Mama was not keen on their exiling themselves. 'Do you really think, Edward, that this house could be restored?'

'Indeed I do. It would be a challenge but it could be done.'

'It would make a beautiful home. Don't you think so, girls?'

'Too many stairs,' said Diana.

'That doesn't matter,' cried Effie. 'None of us is fat

or stiff or old.'

'Granny Ruthven's old,' said Rowena.

Mama's mother was nearly eighty.

'She could climb a mountain if she wanted to,' said Effie. 'Couldn't she, Mama?'

'Indeed she could.'

'Carrying her handbag,' said Papa.

They all loved him for saying it. It showed how kind and forgiving he was. Granny Ruthven often made fun of him, rather cruelly. She called him fushionless. Her handbag was a family joke. It weighed a ton, they said.

'Why don't we go and make enquiries?' cried Mama.

'Ask the laird, do you mean, Mama?' asked Diana.

Mama laughed. 'I was thinking of asking the village shop-keeper, who is usually a source of information.'

'Good idea,' said Papa. 'We could have tea among the apple trees.'

Suddenly Rebecca burst into tears. 'I can't go,' she wailed.

They comforted her. 'Of you course you can, darling.'

'I've got no knickers on.'

They took care not to laugh. 'That doesn't matter.'

'Yes, it does. Look.' She showed how immodestly short her light summer dress was.

'You can have mine,' said Effie, about to take hers off.

'They're too big and you need them yourself.'

'So you do, my dear,' said Mama.

Papa and Diana saved the situation between them. He produced a white silk cravat and she two tiny safety pins.

Mama's eager hands quickly fashioned panties that Rebecca, to their relief, after much twisting and turning, accepted as satisfactory.

It was the kind of little incident that happened often and brought them all close in loving dependence.

Going down the stairs their feet were cautious but their minds soared.

'If we bought it we should call it Eagle's Nest,' cried Effie.

'Eagle's Eyrie, you mean,' said Jeanie. 'We could keep dogs and hens and rabbits and goats.'

'And pussy-cats,' said Rebecca.

'I would like a white peacock,' said Rowena. She imagined herself leading it about with a silken cord.

On their way back to the beach, where their things had to be gathered and carried a quarter of a mile over fences and through fields to the Daimler, Diana took it upon herself to warn the twins to hold their tongues while Papa was talking to the shopkeeper about the house. Blurters out of truth, in accordance indeed with Papa's precept, they sometimes gave away family secrets. Diana was old enough to know that if you were thinking of buying a house you shouldn't appear too eager, otherwise the price might be increased. She agreed with Mr Chambers, the Edinburgh lawyer, that Papa's money ought not to be wastefully spent. She and Mr Chambers had once exchanged winks to that effect, his amused but hers most serious.

2

Another of Papa's precepts was to be valiant in naming one's rights but not aggressive in seeking them: better to yield a little than cause strife. Like the nations of the earth Effie and Jeanie were not persuaded. On arrival at the village store, when they saw that only one table was vacant in the apple orchard where tea was served, and another family was making for it they dashed from the car to occupy it, and then, while Jeanie planted the flag, Effie went about hunting for empty chairs. Thanks to their efforts their family was soon accommodated.

Diana noticed, anxiously, how people at other tables were amused by her sisters and impressed by the whole Sempill family. It would have been difficult for her to explain why she was anxious, for nothing threatened her family then and nothing she could foresee threatened them in the future, except possibly Papa's fondness for wine, and she felt confident that she and Mama together could keep this under control. Perhaps it was because they were so fortunate, being healthy, happy, clever, handsome and now rich. She did not know yet whether she believed in God. Papa said that they all had to make up their own minds. She sometimes thought that if she was God and had made a family as lucky as the Sempills she would expect them in return to be humble, generous, and grateful; otherwise she might have to teach them a lesson. Often she lay in bed dreading that one of them would die. They were all generous, Papa so much so that he had to be restrained. Perhaps they were not as humble as they should be, especially Effie, but they weren't conceited either. Her sisters were too young to know about being grateful, but she knew and tried hard to make up for them.

She seemed to be the only one with these worries and doubts. For instance, at that moment a wasp was buzzing about their heads. She thought they had a right to kill it before it stung one of them, but the others, especially Jeanie, were making excuses for it and crying that it would go away if they didn't frighten it. Often she wondered why she was so different from her sisters, in appearance as well as nature. Once, when she was seven and Rebecca had just been born, fair-haired like all the rest except her, she had asked her mother if she had been adopted. She had been lovingly assured that she had not, and had been shown a photograph of Granny Ruthven, at the age of eleven, seventy years ago. But for the old-fashioned dress she could have been taken for Diana. She had the same dark hair and the same responsible frown, as if everything depended on her.

At last the wasp gave up and went off to bother people at an adjacent table. Almost immediately it was replaced by more welcome intruders. Two robins darted out of an apple tree on to the table where they helped themselves to crumbs. No one spoke or even breathed: such charming marauders must not be scared away. Jeanie held out her hand, palm uppermost. One of the birds hopped on to it, while the other perched on Rebecca's shoulder. Both bowed, as if acknowledging applause, like comics on a stage.

A big rosy-cheeked girl came up to wipe the table and take their order. She wore a tartan overall.

'Cheeky wee things,' she said, with a Highland lilt. 'They think they own the place.'

'They're delightful,' said Mama. 'Are all the inhabitants of Kilcalmonell so friendly?'

'I don't know about that. They're wee bullies actually. They chase away finches and sparrows. What would you like then?'

As if huffed by her criticism the robins flew off to another table.

'Tea for two, please,' said Papa, 'five lemonades, and lots of buttered scones.'

'Is that your car?' she asked, staring at the Daimler.

Diana had noticed before how possession of the big blue rich-looking car had gained them respect they hadn't really earned.

'Yes, it's ours,' said Effie, by no means humbly. 'It's got real leather seats.'

'I expect you know the village well,' said Papa to the waitress.

'I should do. I've lived here all my life. In October I'm going to University, thank goodness.'

'Congratulations, which university?'

'Glasgow.'

'We're from Edinburgh ourselves.'

'I thought that, you talk like Edinburgh folk.'

They weren't sure whether that was a compliment or not.

'When we were on the beach,' said Papa, 'we saw a very big derelict house.'

'That'd be Poverty Castle. You shouldn't have been on that beach, you know. It belongs to the estate. It's private. Didn't you see the notices?'

'Yes, we saw them. Poverty Castle? Is it a corruption of some Gaelic word?'

She laughed. 'It's because of the state it's in. It's been like that for ages, since before I was born.'

She went off to attend to their order.

'I wouldn't like to live in house called Poverty Castle,' said Effie.

'I'd like the castle bit but not the poverty bit,' said Jeanie.

'It's quite a large house,' said Mama. 'It must have at least a dozen rooms.'

'Fourteen,' said Effie. 'Me and Jeanie counted them.'

'Jeanie and I you should say, my dear.'

The waitress returned with the tea and scones.

'This house, Poverty Castle, who owns it?' asked Papa.

'Some old lady who lives in Edinburgh. She's about ninety, I think. If you're interested you should speak to my dad. He knows everything about the village. Will I tell him ?'

'Yes, please.'

A chaffinch hopped on to the table. It fled as the robins swooped. They did their version of a victory roll.

'Wee bullies is right,' said Effie.

'Robins are very jealous of their territory,' said Papa, a little uneasily. He often said that if human beings behaved with the natural decency of animals there would be no wars.

The waitress now brought through the glasses of lemonade. 'Dad will be out in a minute. Were you thinking of buying a house in the village ?'

'It is a very beautiful part of the world,' said Papa, warily.

'In weather like this it's all right. You should be here when it's been raining for weeks. Ugh!'

'It's the rain that makes everything so fresh and green,' said Papa.

'It gives people rheumatism,' said Jeanie.

'It doesn't give robins rheumatism,' observed Rebecca.

They all laughed. No creatures could be more agile.

'Frost will never be severe here,' said Papa. 'Because of the influence of the Gulf Stream.'

'What's that?' asked Effie.

He was saved the burden of explaining by the arrival of the proprietor, a chubby little man with a shopkeeper's ready joviality, tempered in his case with his Highland canniness. He too gave the Daimler a very respectful look.

'Good afternoon,' he said. 'Shona tells me you're interested in Poverty Castle. My name's Campbell,

Dugald Campbell. My father had this shop before me.'

'My name's Sempill, Edward Sempill. From Edinburgh. Yes I am interested. You see Mr Campbell, I'm an architect and it struck me as a great pity that a house of such character and situated so idyllically should have been allowed to fall into disrepair.'

'Aye, it is a pity, Mr Sempill. I've often said to Christine, my wife, that anybody with money to spare and with some knowledge of the building trade, such as an architect like yourself, could make the house fit to live in again, at no exorbitant cost either. I've no authority for saying so, mind you, but I wouldn't wonder if it could be got at a bargain price in the state it is.'

'Shona said it's owned by an old lady who lives in Edinburgh.'

'Mrs Braidlaw. She died a week or two ago as a matter of fact, in a nursing home, aged over ninety. Her family bought the house form the estate a long time ago. I believe it was built for a dowager lady. Anyway it's been lying empty for the past thirty years. Don't ask me why. Some family quarrel among the Braidlaws maybe. I hear Willie McPherson's cattle are using it as a byre.'

'His sheep too.'

'No doubt. There used to be a wall. I can mind as a boy stealing gooseberries there. The man to see, Mr Sempill, is Mr Patterson, lawyer in Tarbeg.'

'We're staying at The Royal Hotel in Tarbeg.'

'Are you now?' It was four star and its rates were steep. 'Well, it should be convenient to arrange an appointment with him.'

'What was the house called in the old days?'

'Ardmore, which means the big field. Were you thinking of settling in the neighbourhood, Mr Sempill?'

'It is a possibility.'

'You could do a lot worse and not much better. It's bonny here, summer and winter. Yet, do you know, our population's falling. They say that in St Kilda they had to give up when they didn't have enough able-bodied men to man the boat. Well, our golf club's in desperate need of members and the country dance club can't manage three sets any more. Our school's in danger of losing its second teacher. We need twenty-five on the roll to hold her and at present we're down to twenty-six. We could do with these five bonny lassies.'

'Who is the laird, Mr Campbell? Some member of your clan, I suppose?'

'Used to be, Mr Sempill, used to be. About twenty years ago old Sir Lochiel was forced to sell, to a Greek, I believe, whom we never saw. Since then it's changed hands twice. The present laird bought it just three years ago. A rich Englishman. Family made its fortune in pharmaceuticals. Sir Edwin Campton, a baronet. Wife's a daughter of Lord Marsley. We haven't seen much of them either. They come up for the shooting and fishing and sometimes not even then. To be candid, Mr Sempill, they have not so far anyway been much benefit to the village.'

His daughter called him from the shop. 'Dad, you're wanted to slice ham.'

'It would be a pleasure, Mr Sempill, and you Mrs Sempill, and all of you Misses Sempill, to have you members of our community.'

He did not touch his forelock as he left but he stroked his apron.

'He wants more people to buy things in his shop,' said Rebecca.

'Are you going to see the lawyer, Papa?' asked Diana.

'Do you think I should, my dear?'

'Yes, but just to ask. Mr Chambers said that before you decide anything you should always sleep on it.'

'Jeanie and me want to come with you, Papa,' said Effie.

'Yes, Papa,' said Jeanie. 'You always let Diana go with you but not us.'

'You're too young, my dear.'

'We're nearly ten and she's not twelve yet. Hands up those who think we should all go?' She made faces at Rowena and Rebecca, letting them know she wanted their votes.

She herself, Effie, Rowena, and Rebecca put up their hands.

'Four to three,' cried Effie. 'We all go. That's democracy. Isn't it Papa?'

'Mr Patterson might not welcome such an invasion of his office,' said Mama.

'You've said so yourself, Papa,' said Jeanie, 'that we give good advice.'

'Sometimes you do, my dear.'

'Sometimes it's very silly,' said Diana.

Effie put out her tongue at her.

3

After dinner when the girls were in bed Mr and Mrs Sempill sat in a corner of the luxurious residents' lounge, he drinking large brandies and she small creme-de-menthes. Of the two she, who had drunk so much less, was the more tipsy and also, for this was the way alcohol affected her, the more uxorious. She was wearing a long green dress with dangling earrings of jade. As usual she had put on too much too red lipstick, so that her big soft mouth looked still bigger and softer. She kept squeezing Edward's thigh.

He wore a black blazer with gold-coloured buttons, a pink silk cravat, and fawn slacks. Hair and moustache were artfully brushed and expensively perfumed. His pale blue eyes were moist and benign as he acknowledged her amorous homage.

She seldom disagreed with him, preferring to use wiles to bring his opinion closer to hers. Most of the time she succeeded but if she did not she gave up without sulking. She adored him, body and soul. In the children's presence — they were all little prudes — she had to damp down her adoration but when she was alone with him, even in such a public place as now, she let it blaze. That he accepted it with sultanic benevolence was, she thought, as it should be.

She was not sure that it would be such a good idea buying the derelict house in Kilcalmonell.

'We saw it today in warm sunshine, darling, but what will it be like in bleak December?'

'As I said to the girls, Meg, this is the West coast, under the influence of the Gulf Stream. You saw the palm trees in the gardens. Winters are mild here.'

'But very wet, alas. I am worried about your chest, darling.'

'And I about your pinkie, dear.'

Her left pinkie ached in damp weather but it did not keep her off her sleep as much as Edward's wheezings did.

According to his mother he had been at death's door, with pneumonia, when he was only eight: It had left him with a weak chest. According to Mama's own mother, Granny Ruthven, a sterner and franker lady, Edward was the kind 'that would hoast and splutter to a ripe old age.'

He wheezed a little now. 'You'd really like us to go back to Edinburgh, wouldn't you, Meg? God, when I think of the icy winds whistling down those precipitous streets! Small wonder R.L.S. took himself off to Samoa.'

Where nonetheless he had died when 44, only four years older than Edward was now.

She did not want to live in Spain but if it benefited Edward's health she would go anywhere.

'I was thinking, Meg, why not spend the winters in Spain and the rest of the year in Kilcamonell?'

'Could we afford that?'

'Bless you, of course we could afford it.'

'What about the girls' education?'

'As long as they can read and write they will educate themselves. They are very bright.'

She smiled proudly. 'Yes, they are very bright, thank God.'

'Thank me, Meg. Thank yourself.' He looked wistfully at his empty glass. He had promised it would be the last for tonight. 'My books, Meg, when will I ever produce them?'

They were already written in his mind: the difficulty was in getting them out. Could it be, he had asked, that he was too happy a person to be a writer? Perhaps writers had to be bitter and discontented. Encouraging him to persist, Meg had pointed out that the world had more than enough of gloom, violence, and hate: it longed for his gentle and optimistic philosophies. Really she agreed with her mother: Edward just did not have the necessary sticking power.

'If this fellow Campton is failing in his duty as benefactor to the village why shouldn't I take his place?'

Edward, she knew, yearned to be a philanthropist. To the horror of his lawyer Mr Chambers he had given ten thousand pounds of his legacy to charities. 'If you don't mind me saying so, Mr Sempill, such gestures are not the way to tackle the problem of the

poor and deprived. If the rich make themselves poor no one prospers.'

He had even talked about giving it all away. 'Whatever Chambers might say, Meg, it would astound the world.'

But, he had added, sadly, he did not have the moral greatness such an act would require.

Meg had been much relieved.

'They would look up to me as the laird, Meg, not to this Campton fellow. He's an interloper, after all.'

'So we would be interlopers, my dear.'

'Not at all. We're Scots. This is our native heath. Do you think I should have another, as a night cap?'

'No, Edward. What do you say to a stroll along the harbour?'

'You're forgetting the midges, Meg. You know how they go for me.'

'It's too late in the day for midges. I believe it's a lovely mild night.'

So, a few minutes later, they were at the harbour, hand-in-hand, looking at the fishing boats. There was a strong smell of fish. This, along with the creme-de-menthes and the misty moonlight produced in Mrs Sempill an access of love and desire: so much so that she dragged him into a nook among fish crates and kissed him ardently.

The result was not what she had hoped for. He philosophised, somewhat morosely.

'I sometimes wonder, Meg,' he mumbled, for her lips obstructed his, 'if I lack the iron to succeed in anything.'

'You have succeeded in making your wife the happiest woman on earth.'

'Am I a man of my time, Meg?'

'If you are not, my love, it is to your credit. You lack the vices of our age, envy and greed and violence.'

'Your mother laughs at me.'

So she did, but then Granny Ruthven often boasted that it was one of her clan who struck the first blow in the assassination of Rizzio, Mary Queen of Scots' effeminate secretary. It amazed and vexed her that her feeble son-in-law had managed to sire five beautiful children. She could not very well say that their being all girls was evidence of his feebleness, for she was formidably female herself.

'My mother laughs at everyone.'

It was then that he realised Meg had been over-sanguine in thinking it was too late in the day for midges. Some night brigades were about. Meg was not yet aware of them, though from the nature of her dress she should have been more accessible. Suddenly he was itching all over.

They hurried back to the hotel.

Meg went off to see the children were safely asleep. She found Diana still awake.

They whispered.

'Mama, is Papa going to buy that old house?'

'He hasn't decided yet. He has to see Mr Patterson the lawyer first.'

'I've been thinking about it. I think he should.'

'Do you, my pet?'

'Yes. The twins and Rowena think we should go to Spain because they've been learning Spanish, but I think we would be safer in that house.'

'Safer? What is going to harm us?'

'I don't know. I don't believe what Papa said about the rowan tree protecting the house — well, I don't think I believe it — but I did feel safe there, even if I was afraid all the time that the floor was going to collapse under us. Does that sound stupid?'

'I think I know what you mean, darling. Once the house has been restored it will be very safe and we shall all be very happy there, I am sure. Except that the dampness might be harmful to your father's chest.'

'Is there anything wrong with Papa's chest?' Sleepy though she was Diana she managed to sound sceptical. She was indeed very like her grandmother.

'You must have heard him coughing.'

'We think he does it when he wants us to pay him attention.'

Yes, sometimes poor Edward, the only male in the family, felt left out. With God's help that state of affairs would not last much longer.

'Goodnight darling.'

With difficulty she refrained from rushing out of the room. It occurred to her that Edward might have fallen asleep.

She found him wide awake and naked, applying lotion to midge bites. One, in a very tender place, itched abominably.

'Let me, my love.' Kneeling, she dabbed with delicacy.

Later they made love. No contraceptive device was used. Her love for her husband, she thought, would never have been fully expressed until she had given him a son. Often, at the outset, he would remind her fondly that if she did get pregnant again it might be another girl. That consideration, it had seemed to her, had caused him not to try as hard as he might. But not tonight. To her joy he performed with frantic zeal. Who was to say that it did not pass through her mind that she owed it to a midge? Conceptions could result from brief and cursory copulations. Therefore this love-making, fervent and thorough, was bound to be rewarded with the gift of a son. She was not aware of how many times she thanked him. It was four.

4

Next morning instead of blue skies and sunshine there were dark clouds and pouring rain. Undaunted the girls in their hats, oilskins, and Wellingtons, all pillar box red, went off to feed swans in the harbour, with rolls bought in the baker's. From the hotel Papa telephoned Mr Patterson and arranged an appointment at eleven.

The girls could not be persuaded to stay with the swans.

They insisted on accompanying him. Effie reminded him it had been voted on. Besides, said Jeanie, they had a right to have a say in where they lived. Other fathers would have told them not to be impertinent. Papa meekly acknowledged the justice of their claim.

Since it wasn't far, they walked. Papa and Mama shared an umbrella.

They had to stop and let Rebecca look at some small dolls dressed as Highland dancers, in a shop window. She wanted to add one to her collection.

Papa could not help saying, 'Made in Hong Kong, I'm afraid.'

'We ought to buy half a dozen then,' said Effie, 'for the people in Hong Kong are very poor, aren't they?'

'Those who made those dolls are very poor, certainly.'

'In Hong Kong do they sell Chinese dolls made in Scotland?' asked Rowena.

'I wouldn't think so.'

'Well, they should.'

'Why don't the Chinese make their own dolls and the Scottish people make theirs?' asked Jeanie.

'It's a matter of international co-operation.'

Papa smiled at his rueful reflection in the glass. He was used to having his utterances subjected to this ingenuous but rigorous examination. He took it very well, just as he did Diana's beating him at chess, the twins trouncing him at draughts and Rowena and Rebecca being twice as fast at doing jigsaws.

Beside his in the glass was Meg's face, still as radiant as it had been that morning when she had told him she was sure she had conceived and the child was male. Her breasts, look, were triumphant.

Her desire for a son had become an obsession. God knew what would happen to her if she did not get her wish. Those absences of mind weren't indications of mental derangement, the psychiatrist had said. But what if one day she never returned?

Meanwhile the girls were helping Rebecca to count her money. 'I don't think I've got enough,' she said.

'Papa will make it up,' said Effie.

They all marched into the shop.

The shopkeeper, a small thin woman with spectacles, peered at them suspiciously. She had reason to believe that children in groups, with or without their parents, were likely shoplifters. That they were all well dressed and spoke politely did not necessarily mean that they were honest. She had read in the newspaper of titled ladies being caught shoplifting.

The youngest girl had to be lifted up to inspect the dolls set out on the counter.

'Where were they made?' asked one who looked like a twin.

'In Scotland of course. These are genuine tartans.'

They all burst out laughing as if she'd made a joke.

'You were wrong, Papa,' cried the other twin.

He should have cuffed her ear. Instead he grinned sheepishly.

'How much is this one, please?' piped the youngest, whom they called Rebecca, a Jewish name surely.

'Three pounds fifty-five pence. This kilt is real silk.'

She put what money she had on the counter. Her father made up the difference.

The doll was put in a box.

As they went out the shopkeeper, assuaged by her three hundred per cent profit, decided that they were what they appeared to be, a handsome, well-to-do, and highly respectable family.

Out on the pavement Effie said: 'Did you see her looking at us as if we were thieves?'

'You mustn't say things like that, Effie,' said Mama.

Rowena took something from her pocket. It was a tiny white glass cat with green eyes.

'Where did you get that?' asked Diana.

'I took it.'

They were all shocked. They stopped.

'Rowena Sempill, you didn't!' cried Jeanie.

'I did.'

Papa and Mama stared at each other, appalled. A serpent had crept into their Eden.

'Good heavens, Rowena,' said Mama, 'do you know what you are saying?'

Rowena smiled. 'When she wasn't looking I took it.'

'But you had just to ask and I would have bought it for you,' said Papa.

'She'll have to take it back,' said Effie.

Rowena looked pleased at this suggestion.

At any moment, thought Papa, the shopkeeper and a policeman would come running towards them. The cat couldn't cost more than two pounds. He'd offer twenty to have the matter hushed up. Poor Rowena after all was only seven. She would have to be taken to a child psychologist.

'Say you took it by mistake,' said Jeanie.

Rowena shook her head. 'I wanted to take it.'

'Good God,' muttered Papa, as if she'd confessed to murder.

'In heaven's name, why, my pet?' asked Mama.

'I know why,' said Diana, calmly. 'She was pretending to be a shoplifter. She's always pretending to be different things.'

The twins confirmed it. 'She likes to act,' said Effie.

'Will I take it back now?' asked Rowena. She was looking forward to the part of playing the penitent thief.

Papa thought: I don't know my children. Would I, if they were boys?

Mama thought: Don't they say a child does naughty things as a signal that she is not being given enough love? But I love all my children, and of them all Rowena is the one who seems to want or need it least.

'I suppose I must take it back and explain,' said Papa.

'I shall come with you,' said Mama.

'I'd better go,' said Diana.

The twins nodded. They were sure Diana would handle it better than Papa.

'Give me money, Papa,' she said.

He gave her a five pound note. 'What will you say?'

'I'll say she's just seven and forgot to pay.'

Rebecca, in tears, was comforting Rowena, who was dry-eyed and still smiling.

'She'll ask if Rowena took other things as well,' said Effie.

That hadn't occurred to Papa. 'Did you, my pet?'

'Of course she didn't,' said Diana. 'She just needed to take one thing for her game. That's all it was, just a game.'

'Not a very nice game,' murmured Mama.

With the glass cat in her fist Diana marched back to the shop. She didn't hurry, but it wasn't because she was afraid. For her family's sake she would have faced a tiger.

They huddled under an awning outside a grocer's. Luckily it was still raining and few people were about.

Can it be, wondered Papa miserably, that my poor wee daughter is mentally retarded? Have we been so proud of her beauty that we haven't noticed the dimness of her mind?

Guiltily he glanced at Rowena. She was looking at him with eyes as bright and intelligent as they were beautiful.

'I'm sorry, Papa,' she said. 'It was silly.'

'She's still acting,' muttered Effie to Jeanie. 'Sometimes she doesn't know whether she's acting or not.'

They saw Diana come out of the shop, holding her head high.

The twins ran to meet her. 'What did she say? Is she going to tell the police?'

Diana did not speak until they had joined the others. 'It's all right. She said anybody could make a mistake.'

'That was generous of her,' said Papa. 'Did she

take the money?'

'Yes. She said it was three pounds forty pence. It shouldn't have been. I saw the price on one the very same: it was only two pounds eighty pence.'

'Maybe it was a smaller one that was two pounds eighty pence,' said Jeanie.

'The one I took was the smallest,' said Rowena, still unperturbed.

'We are living in a dangerous world,' muttered Papa.

It was now ten past eleven on the church clock.

'We are late for our appointment, Papa,' said Diana.

'Should we keep it, my dear? Do we want to live anywhere near here?'

'In Kilcalmonell, in that old house, when it is repaired, we shall be safe.'

With that defiant prophecy she walked across the road, threw the glass cat into the harbour, and then led the way to the lawyer's office.

Effie and Jeanie nodded. What could be safer, as far as collapsing floors and falling slates were concerned, than a house newly rebuilt?

They frowned too. What other dangers had Diana meant, and Papa too, and Mama as well, judging by her frightened eyes?

5

Mr Patterson was reading the financial columns of the *Glasgow Herald* when Miss McGibbon, his white-haired clerkess, came to announce that Mr and Mrs Sempill had arrived for their appointment.

'Nearly fifteen minutes late,' she said, grimly. 'They're gentry, or think they are. Scotch gentry,' she added, with a touch of scorn.

Mr Patterson smiled. Peggy — though he would never have dared to call her that, since she was a prudish old spinster — lacked humour and tolerance, unlike himself who had perhaps too much for a man in his profession.

'Have they come about a house?' she asked.

'I believe so.'

'Which one?'

'He didn't say.'

'It'll have to be a big one. I can't see her living in a three-bedroomed bungalow.'

Mr Patterson folded the newspaper and put it away in a drawer. From another drawer he took out an important-looking document and placed in front of him.

'You can show them in now, Miss McGibbon.'

'All of them?'

'How many are there?'

'Seven. There are five girls. Two look like twins.'

'Good heavens!'

'Dripping all over the place.'

'Well, it's a wet morning. Perhaps you and Mary could entertain the children while I talk to their parents.'

'How are we to do that?'

'Give them magazines to look at.'

'We have none suitable for children of their age.'

'Send them next door to Farino's for wafers. Take it out of the petty cash.'

'I'll let Mary deal with them. She's nearer their age.'

But when she returned to the outer office and said that Mr Patterson was now ready to see Mr and Mrs Sempill the five Misses Sempill made it plain that they were not going to be left behind. They did it politely but firmly. Miss McGibbon happened to believe that modern children were horribly spoiled. Now she saw that the gentry were no exceptions.

'You promised, Papa,' said one of the twins.

'We voted,' said the other.

'But Effie, my dear, it might not be convenient for Mr Patterson to have so many people in his office.'

'There wouldn't be enough chairs,' said Miss McGibbon.

'We'll stand,' said the oldest girl, with what child-lovers would have called dignity but to Miss McGibbon was downright impudence.

It was their mother's fault: a vague creature who scarcely knew what day of the week it was. Her

yellow raincoat with hat to match must have cost at
least a hundred pounds, yet the one was stained
with what looked like oil and bramble juice, while
the other had been pulled on any old way. Or was
that straggling out of her hair deliberate, to show off
its golden colour and to hint at its abundance? Just
as the raincoat was open, revealing a white jumper
of finest cashmere and white-and-green skirt of top
quality tweed, not to mention immodestly prominent
breasts. Her jewellery might be genuine but there
was too much of it. She was the kind of woman that
Miss McGibbon and her friend Mary McGill, schoolmistress at Kilcalmonell, over their drams, called a
Delilah. If men pinched her bottom she would not
resent it as a decent woman should but would regard
it as a tribute.

Her husband was hardly a Samson: he was tragic
in quite a different way. Like Bonny Prince Charlie,
after the battle of Culloden. His manners indeed
were royal. Miss McGibbon couldn't imagine him
being rude or coarse or unkind. She had no
hesitation in putting him on the list (not even God or
Mary McGill knew of it) of men she would have
welcomed into her bed. Some had won the honour
because of their hairy-chested virility, others for their
red-eyed passion, but Mr Sempill deserved it for his
gentleness. That he was twenty years or more
younger than she did not matter: in her dreams she
was ageless, like Cleopatra.

Mr Patterson was displeased when not only Mr
and Mrs Sempill but their five children too were
ushered into his office.

His displeasure lasted only for moments. The five
little girls in their red raincoats and with their alert

eyes reminded him of robins. He had three grand-daughters but he had to confess they had never lifted his heart as high as these Sempill girls did.

Their mother had his heart somersaulting. She was tall. (His Bessie was only five-feet-two.) Elegant. (Bessie was sturdy.) Her large blue eyes were soft with trust and innocence. (Bessie's were blue also but hard with scepticism.) She had a fine figure. (Bessie's stomach was large.) Her hair was fair and lustrous. (Bessie's was grey, stiff, and growing scarce.) If she had a fault it was that she doted on her wishy-washy husband, but as an elder of the Church of Scotland Mr Patterson should not have seen that as a fault but rather as another virtue.

The parents sat on the other side of the big desk. The girls stood in the background, in a row. They had taken their hats off. The eldest, the only dark-haired one in the family, looked more business-like than her father.

'Now, Mr Sempill, what can I do for you?'

'Yesterday, Mr Patterson, visiting Kilcalmonell, we came upon a house that took our fancy. We were informed that you were the person to consult. It is close to the beach. It has not been occupied for many years. It is therefore in a ruinous condition. As a consequence it is known locally as 'Poverty Castle'. I am by profession an architect, Mr Patterson, and it seemed to me a pity that a house which at one time must have had character should have been allowed to become a ruin.'

Mr Patterson was astonished but was too wily to show it. Calmly he took a file from a cabinet. Its most recent additions were letters from Mr Wrigley-

Thomson, nephew and heir of Mrs Braidlaw. For over thirty years she had refused to let Ardmore be sold or rented or kept weatherproof. Mr Wrigley-Thomson on the contrary was desperate to be rid of it. He had discovered that substantial rates were still having to be paid.

'The house you are referring to, Mr Sempill, is Ardmore. Is not your description of it as a ruin somewhat extreme?'

The girls spoke up, one after the other.

'It's got lots of slates off the roof.'

'It lets in rain in lots of places.'

'Some of the ceilings are on the floors.'

'It's got no back door.'

'Sheep and cows get in. Their dirt's, everywhere.'

'Rebecca slid on a cow-pat.'

'There are millions of cobwebs.'

Well-rehearsed wee lassies, thought the lawyer. Then he saw that he was being unfair. They had spoken for themselves. They always would.

'If you are interested in purchasing a property in the district, Mr Sempill, I have a number for sale, in what is known as 'walk-in' condition.'

'We are interested in this one. I understand it was owned by an old lady recently deceased. Who is the present owner?'

'Her nephew. He lives in Putney.'

'Is he prepared to sell it?'

'He may well be.'

'How much does he want for it?'

That was how gentry did business: brutally to the point. Mr Patterson had had working class clients who had shrunk from mentioning money, thinking it would be bad manners.

The girls were gazing at him like judges. They expected fair play.

'There is a complication, Mr Sempill. Ardmore was once part of Kilcalmonell estate. It was built for the mother of a past laird, before the family became impoverished. Indeed the whole estate passed out of the hands of Kilcalmonell Campbells years ago and is now in the possession of an English gentleman, Sir Edwin Campton. Sir Edwin wishes to buy Ardmore, to raze it to the ground. He believes it detracts from his privacy. Mrs Braidlaw refused to sell. Her nephew, as I have said, sees it differently. However, he considers that the offer made on Sir Edwin's behalf is unacceptably low.'

'Whatever it is,' said Mr Sempill, 'I shall double.'

Which would not amount to much really: for Sir Edwin, rich but thrifty, assuming that no one in his senses would want to pay a penny for a ruin, had offered only £3000.

'Something else I should mention, Mr Sempill. Since Ardmore was built in the estate grounds the road giving it access to the public highway necessarily runs through those grounds. It is stated in the title deeds that the owner or occupier of Ardmore is legally entitled to the use of that road, without hindrance of any kind, for perpetuity.'

'I should hope so, seeing that it is the only way by which vehicles can approach the house. We ourselves approached it on foot, from the beach.'

'In which case you were trespassing, but perhaps you did not know that.'

50

'There were plenty of notices warning us to keep out.'

Mr Patterson coughed. 'Yes, so there would be. This road, Mr Sempill, was never anything but a cart track. Like the house itself it has been badly neglected. I understand it is now hardly recognisable as a road at all, being completely overgrown. To make it serviceable and keep it so — it is half a mile in length — would cost as much as the repair of the house itself. In fairness I must point that out.'

'Thank you Mr Patterson. If I were to buy the property there would be no dispute. The road would be my responsibility.'

The girls were more circumspect.

'Shouldn't you see it first, Papa?' asked the eldest.

'If we mended it would it be just for us or would the people from the Big House be allowed to use it too?' That was asked by one of the twins.

'If it's on their ground they should pay their share,' said the other twin.

Litigation to settle that very point had been threatened in the past.

'Whose road would it be, ours or theirs?' asked the second youngest, the most beautiful child Mr Patterson had ever seen and, he had thought up to a moment ago, one of the shyest.

'It would not matter, Rowena,' said her father, 'so long as there is amicable agreement.'

There probably would be if it was left to Sir Edwin, who from all accounts was good-natured but was said to be under the dominance of his aristocratic wife. To be honest neither was well-known locally.

'I propose to put in an offer forthwith,' said Mr Sempill, 'through my solicitors, Chambers and Wishart of Edinburgh.'

Mr Patterson had heard of them. They were prestigious.

'In the meantime, Mr Patterson, we would like to rent a house in Kilcamonell. Do you have one available?'

'An excellent one, Bell Heather Cottage. Centrally situated. Handy for school, shop, church, and golf course. Four bedrooms, two public rooms. Large secluded garden.'

'How many bathrooms?' asked Mrs Sempill.

'Only one, I'm afraid.'

'We really need more than one.'

He could appreciate that. He could have sworn that one of the twins winked at him.

'It would only be for three months at most,' said Mr Sempill, 'and of course it depends on whether or not we acquire Ardmore.'

'Why not have a look at it?' suggested Mr Patterson.

They went off with the keys.

The telephone call from Mr Archibald Chambers came in the afternoon, offering £8000 for Ardmore. Disguising his gratification, Mr Patterson let it be understood, as one lawyer to another, that such an offer was not only acceptable but was accepted there and then: all that remained were formalities. Mr Chambers' tone conveyed that in his view his client Mr Sempill, though he had plenty of it, was something of a simpleton where money was concerned. Mr Patterson who would have gladly have accepted £6000 saw no reason to disagree.

Afterwards, though, he wasn't quite so sure. As an architect of even adequate competence Sempill could make a good job of restoring Ardmore. By spending, say, another twenty or thirty thousand on a house and road he could end up owning a property worth sixty thousand, if he ever wanted to sell. Mr Patterson hoped he would not. It was pleasant to think of the resurrected house on the machair ringing with the laughter of those charming little girls, and having as its chatelaine that sweet lovely woman.

H e had never let anyone, not even Jessie, see his work in progress. Nor had she ever asked. She knew how touchy and anxious an author was when working on a new book. All the praise in the world wasn't reassurance enough.

This time, however, since it would be his last, she subdued her pride and asked how his 'happy' novel was getting on. Would he mind if she had a look at what he had done? If he had declined she would have been relieved, because in fairness to both of them she would have to say honestly what she thought, even if it disappointed and hurt him.

He hesitated. He had only written five chapters, he said. A lot of revision had to be done.

Thus discouraged she should have said, 'All right. I'll wait till it's finished.' Except she didn't think it would ever be finished. But it was her duty as his wife to give him what support she could. If what he had written showed signs of enfeebled powers it would be up to her to try and dissuade him from going on with it, to the detriment of his health, physical and mental.

'If you like,' he said at last.

She waited until he had gone out for his daily walk before reading it. She did not want him moping nearby. Like Harvey the cat when a mouse he had brought in had been taken from him.

He was back in the house a good three hours before the subject was brought up. Out of pride he would not bring it up, and she perversely indicated that she had more urgent matters to attend to, such as the ironing and preparing the evening meal.

At table they listened to the six o 'clock news on the radio. As usual it was mainly about violence and death.

'About your book, Donald,' she said. 'You've cheated. By making them so well-off. So it's easy for them not to be envious or covetous, which I've heard you say are the greatest causes of bitterness and unhappiness. Rich too, through no effort of their own. Handed to them on a plate. I thought you objected to inherited fortunes. Why should a rich man's children have so many advantages over a poor man's?'

He was silent.

'I'm surprised you didn't have them give it all away. That would have been more your kind of book.'

'Perhaps I couldn't.'

'Do you mean nobody would have believed you?'

'A novelist can't make his characters do what's untrue to their natures.

'Nonsense. They're your characters, your creations. You can make them do anything you like.'

'It's not as simple as that.'

'Another thing, you said you were going to do without irony. Isn't calling the house Poverty Castle blatant irony?'

'Maybe.'

'How's it going to end? What's going to happen to them?'

'I don't know that yet.'

'You mean you haven't decided?'

'I mean I don't know.'

It wasn't the first time she had felt impatient at his implying there was something mystical about the relationship between a novelist and his characters.

'Usually you've got some nasty surprises in store for your characters, Donald, but you can't have for the Sempills. You think they deserve happiness. They don't know it but it's *you* who are protecting them.'

She was doing what she had vowed not to do. By showing interest in his characters she was giving them life.

'So you would like to know what happens to them?'

'I won't lose any sleep over it. It's real people I'm interested in, not phantoms. I know you have some kind of daft notion that the characters in your books have a kind of reality of their own. Where are they at the moment? If I was to visit Kilcamonell, or Kilmory, would I find that house? Would I see the Sempills?'

'In your imagination you might.'

She was unwilling to admit it, yet the next thing she said was itself an admission. 'That scene where Mrs Sempill — lovely sweet woman indeed! — thanks her husband for making love to her. What nonsense! No woman with a scrap of self-respect ever thanked a man for *that*! Four times, my foot!'

6

It continued to be a fine summer, with long warm sunny days. Brown as tinkers, scratched, bitten, stung, and pricked, the girls explored everywhere, on bicycles or on foot. If an expedition was to a place too distant, Rebecca stayed at home, to keep her mother company and help her with the baking and house-work. Rowena too sometimes, but her reason was that she hated being tired and dirty. They became kenspeckle in the village. They made friends with Mr Campbell's robins but were, alas, unable to teach them to share the crumbs with the chaffinches. They stood for hours on shoogly stones in the middle of Kilcalmonell river fishing for minnows while dragonflies darted past their heads. They gathered mushrooms on the golf course, heedless of roars of 'Fore!' They went to the harbour and watched the fishing boats unload their catch. They swam or paddled at their beach. Tutored by Mama they learned the names of trees and wild flowers. Smeared with oil of citronella they picnicked in midgy places, often in the estate grounds. Their hair was bleached almost to whiteness: except Diana's, out of which often had to be combed sticky willies, tiny flies, twigs and even caterpillars, because in all their adventures she took it on herself to go first, even to the tops of trees, though she hated heights.

Rowena went on practising acting. On one occasion she appalled them by expiring on the lawn at Bell Heather Cottage, her mouth stained with juice, feared at first to be that of the deadly nightshade but later discovered to be that of elderberries.

They did not have much contact with the village children. This was not snobbiness. They just found their own company sufficient.

To begin with their uninhibited inquisitiveness was regarded by the villagers as upper-class cheek, especially when they switched from their refined Edinburgh accent to the local bucolic lilt. But they proved so unquenchable and were so enthusiastically interested, even in matters quite unsuitable for small girls, such as the mating endeavours of Willie McPherson's white bull, that they were soon accepted as valuable acquisitions to the life of the village, even if they did not go to Sunday school.

They often went to watch the making of their road, especially when the tar was being spread. They came home with tar on their hands and even in their hair, and with their vocabulary increased. They talked to the workmen as equals.

They visited Poverty Castle to give Papa and the building contractor advice. They advised Papa to have three bathrooms, one for himself and Mama and two for them. They had seen how he suffered in Bell Heather Cottage having to wait to get into the one bathroom there, because they were washing their own or their dolls' hair or sitting on the loo reading.

They asked to be consulted as to which rooms should be theirs. They caused Papa to sigh and the decorators to curse under their breath by the number of times they changed their minds as to the colour of paint and the kind of wallpaper they wanted.

Sometimes the cost of it all worried them. What was the good of having a grand house and a private road, not to mention a private beach, if it meant that they would be too poor to keep animals or buy books? Mama reassured them, having herself been reassured by Papa. It seemed that, so long as you started off with a large enough fortune, such as Papa's, and provided you invested or spent it wisely, you could not help becoming richer. For example, Poverty Castle would cost about forty thousand pounds but in the end would be worth more than sixty thousand. Papa was of course pleased about this increase but for some reason he was also a little ashamed. Mama begged the girls not to pester him for explanations.

Effie proposed that they should go and take a close look at the Big House. As far as they knew there was no one there except a caretaker and his wife. Papa was consulted. He saw no objections as long as they didn't peer through windows.

One sunny afternoon they set off, cycling along the main road until they came to their own road that led to Poverty Castle. There was a new gate of wrought iron, to which Papa intended to have fixed a plate with the name of the house. Hiding their bicycles under bracken they took to the wood, stealthy as Red Indians. Coming upon some wood pigeons feathers Effie, Jeanie and Rebecca stuck them in their hair. Diana thought it was too childish for her. Rowena was wearing a white sunhat. It was to keep her face from becoming freckled.

They came to a small green field laid out with red-and-white hurdles for horses to jump over. Whooping, Effie and Jeanie climbed the fence and began jumping. Crows in the tops of trees made a great clamour, alerting any gamekeeper within half a mile. Diana refused to ask her sisters to make less noise. They were doing no harm and were enjoying themselves. Even little Rebecca was pretending she was a pony.

Rowena's hat and dress were still remarkably clean. She perched on a hurdle and imagined she was their mother. She shook her head at the antics of Effie and Jeanie but smiled at Rebecca's dainty and cautious jumps.

Suddenly they heard dogs barking. More interested than alarmed, for they all liked dogs, the girls watched and waited. Down a ride raced two big Labradors, one black and the other golden. Foaming at the mouth, they made for the trespassers.

'Aren't they beautiful?' cried Jeanie, but her voice trembled a little.

'Keep together,' shouted Diana as she ran in front of her sisters.

Rebecca was frightened. The dogs were so big and strong that they could easily send her sprawling.

Rowena assumed the part of a heroine about to die bravely.

Then they saw the lady. She was running after the dogs and yelling to them to come back. Two boys followed her.

'Good dogs,' cried Diana, shielding her sisters. 'Good dogs.'

Puzzled at finding that the insolent intruders were really harmless little girls the dogs snuffled and whimpered. Patted on the head they responded with slobbery kisses.

Being so small Rebecca had to be protected.

The lady arrived, red-faced and panting. She was not pleased to see that the trespassers, to save whom from being torn to pieces she had run harder than she had done for years, were patting and hugging their supposed savagers.

'Who the hell are you?' she gasped.

They weren't shocked, because Papa sometimes said 'Hell!' but they did show on their faces amazement that a lady so well-dressed and with such a posh accent (though her voice was a bit rough) should use such language. They guessed that she must be the lady from the Big House.

'Our name is Sempill,' said Diana, with dignity. 'I'm Diana.'

Her sisters gave their names.

'I'm Effie.'

'I'm Jeanie.'

'I'm Rowena.'

'I'm Rebecca.'

'Good God! Where have you come from? What are you doing here? Don't you know this is private property?'

'We apologise,' said Diana. 'We did not know you were in residence. Our father has bought Poverty

Castle. It's not far from here.' She turned and pointed. 'He's having it repaired.'

'So that's who you are!' Lady Campton was not readily embarrassed but she did not find it easy to meet those five frank critical gazes. They were such damnably good-looking children, though four of them were dressed like ragamuffins. The fifth, in a white hat, was a real beauty. She could not help glancing at Edwin, big-nosed like herself, and Nigel, small-eyed like his father.

The girls already decided they liked the older boy, who was about Diana's age. It wasn't his fault he had such a big nose, but there wasn't any need for him to be so shy. His brother was too sneery.

He spoke sneeringly too. 'Your father had no right to buy that house. My father wanted to buy it and knock it down. It's on our land so it should belong to us.'

His mother smiled at the rude little beast. 'What did you call the house?' she asked. 'I thought it was called Ardmore.'

Diana explained. 'The people here call it Poverty Castle because it was so derelict for so long. Papa likes the name. We're not sure why.'

'What does your father do?'

'He used to be an architect.'

'In Edinburgh,' added Effie.

'I say,' said Edwin, in a voice so posh that the girls thought it very funny though none of them so much as smiled, 'were your names taken from books by Sir Walter Scott?'

He must be cleverer than he looked. They nodded.

'Rowena and Rebecca are from Ivanhoe,' he said.

'Jeanie and I are from Heart of Midlothian,' said Effie, and Diana's from The Fair Maid of Perth.'

'Good God!' said the lady again.

'What are your names?' asked Effie.

'Sorry. I'm Edwin. This is Nigel.'

'Papa said if one of us had been a boy he'd have been called Nigel,' said Jeanie.

'From Fortunes of Nigel,' said Jeanie.

Nigel looked aghast at almost having been a member of such a family. He was also peeved that the dogs, Nelson and Drake, were ignoring him and showering affection on these strangers.

'Papa said he hoped we would be good neighbours,' said Diana.

The lady snorted.

'It was jolly brave of you facing up to the dogs,' said Edwin.

Nigel sneered. 'They've never bitten anyone.'

'Diana didn't know that.'

'She's always brave,' said Effie.

'She's afraid of nothing,' said Jeanie.

Diana blushed.

'I'm afraid of lots of things,' said Edwin, making them like him all the more. 'I say, do you play cricket?'

'Girls are rotten at cricket,' sneered Nigel.

'We play at everything,' said Effie, grandly. 'Badminton, rounders, football, marbles, croquet, *and* cricket.'

'Would you like to come and play cricket with us? That would be all right, wouldn't it, Mother?'

'I suppose so, Edwin, but perhaps they would have to ask their parents first.'

The girls conferred, not to consider whether Papa and Mama would give permission, they took that for granted, but to decide if they really wanted to go and play cricket at the Big House. It was four to one. Diana was the dissenter.

'When have we to come?' asked Effie.

'What about tomorrow at three? Would that suit?' Edwin couldn't keep his eyes off Diana.

'That would suit fine,' said Jeanie.

'Where are you living now? asked Lady Campton.

Diana replied. 'In Bell Heather Cottage. Poverty Castle won't be ready until September.'

'Is that really what your father's going to call it?'

'Yes.'

'He's going to put it on the gate,' said Rebecca.

'Good God!'

Courteously they withdrew. The dogs whined with disappointment at not being allowed to go with them.

'Shall we send a car for you?' cried Edwin.

'Thank you,' cried Diana. 'There is no need. We shall come in the Daimler.'

7

'I hope you didn't invite yourselves,' said Mama.
'Of course we didn't,' said Diana.

'Sometimes you do, you know.'

'Well we didn't this time. Did we?'

Her sisters shook their heads.

'The lady said 'Hell!'' said Rebecca.

'She said 'Good God!' three times,' said Rowena, who would remember to say it herself when acting the part of a lady with a title and a Big House.

'She made noises like this,' said Effie, and she imitated Lady Hampton's snorts.

'Good heavens, girls, I hope you weren't rude to the poor woman.'

'She's not poor,' said Jeanie. 'She's got a gold wrist watch with diamonds in it.'

'Her perfume was lovely,' said Rowena.

'I don't know how you could smell it,' said Effie. 'She was sweaty, like us.'

'The dogs were beautiful,' said Jeanie. 'When are we going to get dogs, Mama?'

'When we move into our new home.'

They had noticed how Mama avoided calling it Poverty Castle.

'We liked Edwin, but we didn't like Nigel,' said Rebecca.

'All he did was sneer,' said Effie. 'He said Poverty Castle should belong to them because it's on their land. It isn't on their land, is it?'

'Well, it's surrounded by their land.'

'The lady's got a very big nose,' said Rebecca.

'Rebecca darling, it's not nice to make personal remarks.'

'So has Edwin,' said Effie, 'but he's got good manners.' She mimicked Edwin's accent. 'Shawl we send a caur for you?'

Even Mama laughed. Diana did not, though.

'He fell in love with Diana,' said Jeanie. 'He said she was jolly brave facing up to the dogs.'

Diana's lips were tight.

'Quite a lot seems to have happened in a short time,' said Mama.

'Can we go and play cricket tomorrow?' asked Effie.

'I suppose so but you'll have to ask Papa.'

'He'll say yes,' said Jeanie. 'He always does.'

'He's not feeling too well-disposed towards Sir Edwin, whose lawyers have been sending letters.'

'If you say we can go, Mama, Papa will say it too,' said Rowena.

'Yes, Mama, he always agrees with you,' said Effie.

'Not quite always, my dear.'

They couldn't remember any such occasion. It

must have happened when they weren't there.

Papa had been on a visit to Tarbeg to see about a consignment of timber that was late in arriving. He had called on Mr Patterson who had shown him the most recent letter from London solicitors acting for Sir Edwin Campton. It stated that, according to the agreement drawn up when Ardmore was sold to the Braidlaws sixty years ago, the estate had to be given first option to buy back. It was hinting that Sir Edwin was contemplating taking the matter to court. 'Mere bluster,' Mr Patterson had said, cheerfully. 'Pique and bluster. The estate *was* given first option. Their offer was unacceptable. Legally they haven't a leg to stand on. Your right to the house, Mr Sempill, is unassailable. I have replied in those terms. We shall hear no more about it.'

The girls listened while Papa recounted all this to Mama. They had not yet told of their adventure.

'These bloody English, Meg, they think they have bought us, body and soul.'

'I hope Mr Patterson is sure of his ground, my dear. It would be a great pity if you were to make this house habitable, at much expense, only to find it taken from you by law.'

'I would blow it up before I let that happen.'

'But would not that please Sir Edwin? Doesn't he want to own the house so that he can raze it to the ground, as Mr Patterson said?'

'How could I be a good neighbour to a man plotting behind my back to undo me?'

'Perhaps he is not so vindictive. We do not know the gentleman.'

'He shall find me resolute. I tell you this, I shall

never go near that man's place.'

Effie could hold her tongue no longer. 'You'll have to, Papa, because you wouldn't let Mama drive the car.'

That was unfair, Mama had been given lessons. She had landed the car in a ditch.

Diana then described their encounter with the Camptons.

'Was *he* there?' cried Papa, purple with anger.

'No. Just Lady Campton and the two boys.'

'How dare she accuse you of trespassing.'

'But we were trespassing, Papa.'

'Ridiculous. Less than half a mile away from your home. If those dogs had bitten you I would have had him jailed.'

'They were very friendly dogs,' said Jeanie.

'Will you drive us there, Papa, or will we go on our bikes?' asked Effie.

'I'm not sure that you should go at all. How do we know that they haven't invited you just to humiliate you?'

'Please, Edward, give them credit for more genuine breeding than that.'

'Meg, tinkers on the shore have more genuine breeding than many so-called aristocrats.'

'It was Edwin invited us,' said Jeanie. 'We trust him.'

'If Nigel wanted to be nasty to us Edwin wouldn't let him,' said Rebecca.

'*I* wouldn't let him,' cried Effie, clenching her fist.

Mama sighed. 'If I thought you were going there to brawl, Effie, I would have to refuse permission.'

'We promised, Mama, so we'll have to go,' said Diana. 'It will be all right. We know how to behave ourselves.'

'Of course you do, darling. Do you know, Edward, I don't think we could send more persuasive envoys. Who would not want our girls as neighbours?'

'Very well,' said Papa, 'but do not let them patronise you.'

'As if anyone could,' murmured Mama.

'What does patronise mean?' asked Effie.

'It means making you feel you're their servants or at any rate beholden to them.'

Rowena smiled, scenting opportunities.

'We'll just act like ourselves,' said Effie.

'Do that, my darlings,' said Mama, 'and you will be invincible.'

8

Usually the girls liked to dress differently, each according to her taste, the twins often counting as one, but for the cricketing expedition to the Big

House they all wore white dresses, white socks, and white sandshoes. They still showed individuality by the ribbons in their hair, white in Diana's case, yellow in the twins', blue in Rowena's, and red in Rebecca's. They were freshly bathed: it meant Papa's exclusion from the bathroom for three hours. From the window they had seen him sneaking behind the garden shed, to listen to the birds he would have said, but they knew better.

Mama went with them in the car. 'Insist on playing with a soft ball. I hope they remember you're girls.'

Effie was indignant. 'We're girls, Mama, but we're not softies.'

The drive up to the Big House was weedy.

'Why did they buy this place if they weren't going to keep it in decent order?' grumbled Papa.

He stopped the car as soon as the house came in sight, about two hundred yards away.

'Couldn't we go a little bit closer, darling?' said Mama. 'I would like a good look at it.'

'What is there to see, Meg? It is merely an eighteenth century mansion of no great architectural distinction. It does not fit in well with its surroundings as you can see, unlike the house it replaced, a sixteenth century castle, bleak but dignified. It has two staterooms of fair size with painted ceilings (naked nymphs and gods, that sort of thing) but inside and out there is not much of particular interest.'

He was quoting from a book on the stately homes of Scotland. Kilcalmonell House merited only eight lines and no pictures.

The girls were curious about the naked nymphs and gods.

'We'll have to ask Edwin if we can get seeing them,' said Effie.

'You mustn't embarrass the poor boy,' said Mama. 'It may not be a handsome building, Edward, but it is certainly large.'

'No more than forty rooms, I assure you.'

'Forty!' cried the girls, astounded.

'Some stately homes have hundreds. Bear in mind that the Camptons, on his side at any rate, are no more blue-blooded than we are ourselves.'

'We read a story in which a boy had green blood,' said Effie. 'He came from an alien planet.'

'He ate daisies,' said Jeanie.

'But Lady Campton's family is aristocratic,' said Mama. 'Isn't her father Lord Marsley?'

'Who ever heard of the Marsleys? I have no objections to titles, provided the right people are ennobled.'

Mama smiled. He had once confided to her that he would have liked to be Sir Edward or better still Lord Sempill.

'You will see that Sir Edwin looks no more distinguished than the man who delivers our milk.'

He drove the car forward until they could see people on the grass outside the house.

He had brought binoculars. He looked through them. 'That's him, seated in the deck chair. Look, Meg. If you ask me an oaf, an arrogant oaf.'

Mama took the binoculars. 'I can't see his face for his hat.' She was more interested in Lady Campton. Alas, her face too was obscured.

'Drive right up, darling,' she said. 'Be bold.'

'We're late enough as it is, Papa,' said Effie.

'Princes are punctual,' said Jeanie.

Nettled by insinuation that he was timid Papa sent the car roaring up to the house.

In their deck chairs Sir Edwin was reading a newspaper, his wife a book. Both were smoking: in Papa's opinion a plebian habit. Sir Edwin wore a floppy white hat, she a wide-brimmed one. They raised their heads and stared at the visitors.

'He doesn't look arrogant, Edward,' murmured Mama. He did look rather oafish though, but she didn't say so. There were people who didn't think Edward looked very intelligent at times. One of them was Granny Ruthven. Her word for him was glaikit.

Wearing a cap of many colours and white shorts held up by a tie, Nigel was ready for cricket, with pads on and a bat in his hand. Edwin, also in white shorts and shirt, was holding the ball. It did not look soft, though he himself did, soft and nice, with his shy smile. Not only his nose was big, so were his ears.

'Where are the dogs?' asked Jeanie.

'Out you get girls,' said Papa. 'I'll come back for you at five prompt. Be ready. I would not wish to wait here a moment longer than necessary.'

He turned the car and raced it down the drive, making the gravel spurt.

The sun still shone. It was going to be a good afternoon for cricket.

The girls walked over and presented themselves to their hostess.

'Good-afternoon, Lady Campton,' they said.

She hardly looked up from her book. 'Good afternoon.'

'Who was driving that car?' cried Sir Edwin.

They turned and faced him. They were not going to let him or anyone else say anything bad about Papa.

'Our father,' said Diana.

'In a devil of a hurry, wasn't he? Did he want to get to the public house before it closed?'

They looked at one another and agreed by signs that that was meant to be a joke. It wasn't a good one but it wasn't a mean one either. Sir Edwin laughed at it himself. He was the only one who did, but it was quite jolly if rather silly laughter. They did not think it likely that he knew about Papa's fondness for wine. In any case his own cheeks were as purple as Papa's, probably from the same cause. He had piggy eyes and a fat face but he was cheerful and friendly. It could have been his lawyers who wrote the nasty letters about Poverty Castle.

'Come and let me have a look at you,' he cried.

They went and stood in front of him.

'So you're the famous Misses Sempill?'

'We're not famous,' said Effie, modestly. She meant, not yet. They were all going to be famous one day.

He was greatly taken with Diana. Her sisters weren't surprised or jealous. When she was upholding the honour of her family Diana could be formidable, like Granny Ruthven.

'How is it that you're the only one with dark hair?'

Effie answered. 'Granny had dark hair when she was young.

It's white now. She's my mother's mother. One of her ancestors was the first to strike David Rizzio, Mary Queen of Scot's secretary, in Holyrood Palace hundreds of years ago. There's a brass plate on the floor telling where it was done.'

'Grandfather Ruthven was a surgeon in Edinburgh Royal Infirmary,' said Jeanie.

Rowena joined in this parade of her family's credentials.

'Grandfather Sempill was an architect.'

'Like Papa,' said Rebecca.

'You're a damned handsome lot of girls,' said Sir Edwin.

'Aren't they, Molly?'

They could hardly believe he was addressing Lady Campton. They hadn't expected her to have such a common name as Molly. Somehow it made them like her a little more.

She didn't say yes or no, she just grunted.

'Where are the dogs?' asked Jeanie.

'They were sent off in disgrace,' said Sir Edwin. 'They kept running after the ball and picking it up in their mouths. It got all slavery, you see.'

They liked him for using such an unaristocratic word but were sorry that the dogs had been banished. Nigel approached impatiently. 'I thought you had come to play cricket and not to chatter.'

His mother who should have didn't reprove him. So Rebecca did.

'We are being polite,' she said.

'You're putting it off because you can't play,' he sneered. 'You're afraid of the ball. It's a real cricket ball. Show it to them, Edwin.'

Edwin held it out it. 'Feel it,' cried Nigel. 'Go on, feel it.'

'Don't get so excited, Nigel,' said his mother, fondly.

'I would like to bang him on the head with it,' whispered Effie.

They all felt it, as part of their politeness.

'Isn't it hard?' yelled Nigel.

It was, alarmingly, but they would have died rather than say so.

'Come on then,' said Nigel. 'We've wasted enough time. I'll bat first.' He waddled off to take up position in front of the stumps.

'Please excuse us,' said Diana.

Lady Campton glanced up. She grudged showing admiration for the upstart's daughter but could not help it.

'A girl with style, wouldn't you say?' said Sir Edwin.

'A bit too brazen for my taste,' replied Lady Campton, but she was telling a lie. She would have been proud to have a daughter like Diana Sempill.

On the cricket pitch Nigel had taken charge. Since there weren't enough of them to pick sides, he said, they would play a game of one batsman against the rest. The one who scored most runs would be the winner. Edwin or himself would do all the bowling. Everybody knew girls couldn't bowl. He implied that they couldn't bat either or field or catch or run or throw. It was only right that he should bat first because he was the best batsman.

This display of reckless bragging interested the girls. It showed that Nigel was just a child after all. He hadn't learned yet that boasters had to prove themselves extremely good, otherwise they looked ridiculous. Someone, such as Edwin, should have knocked sense into him long ago. But Edwin, the softie, wouldn't even hurt a fly if he could avoid it.

'Who told you girls can't bowl?' said Effie, aggressively.

Nigel sneered. 'They can only bowl underhand.'

'What's underhand?'

He demonstrated.

'What's wrong with that? Is it against the rules?'

'Of course it is.'

'No, it isn't,' said Edwin. 'It's not often done but it's not against the rules.'

'I suppose it's all right for girls,' said Nigel.

'Diana's a jolly good bowler,' said Effie.

Nigel laughed. It wasn't an improvement on his sneering.

'Let her bowl if she wants, Edwin.'

Mumbling apologies, Edwin handed the ball to Diana. Briskly she placed her field. Effie kept wicket, wearing gloves much too big. Edwin fielded on the off-side, Jeanie on the on-side. Rowena and Rebecca were stationed where the ball was not likely to reach them.

Diana bowled, overhand, slowly but straight. The ball trundled along the grass. Nigel rushed forward, swiped, and missed. The ball hit the stumps. A bail fell off.

'Out!' screamed Effie. 'You're out. Bowled.'

'Well done, Diana,' cried Edwin.

Rowena and Rebecca clapped their hands.

In a rage Nigel stamped the ground with his feet. 'I'm not out,' he yelled.

The girls were fascinated. To show that you were a bad sportsman by sulking, say, was bad enough, though forgivable; to do it in this extravagant way was awful.

'It was a no-ball,' shrieked Nigel. 'You can't be out from a no-ball. Father, can you be out from a no-ball?'

'God knows,' said his father.

'I don't think you can,' called his mother.

'It wasn't a no-ball,' said Edwin.

'Yes, it was. She stepped over the line. I saw her. You stepped over the line, didn't you?'

'I did not,' said Diana.

She remembered they were guests.

'Perhaps I did,' she said. 'All right, Nigel. We'll call it a no-ball.'

'You shouldn't humour him, Diana,' cried Effie. 'It'll just make him worse.'

Lady Campton heard and scowled. Nigel again took guard. Diana bowled, intending to give him an easy one so that he could score a run. He managed to hit the ball but Jeanie running forward took an easy catch.

'You're out this time,'cried Effie. 'Out for nothing.'

Nigel swithered whether or not to stage another tantrum. Deciding against, he took off the pads and ran up the pitch.

'Give me the ball. I'll bowl. Edwin, you bat.'

'What about us?' cried Effie. 'We're in the game too, you know.'

Edwin hesitated. He was afraid that if one of the girls batted, Nigel, seeking revenge, would try to hit her with the ball. Sighing, he put on the pads and prepared to bat. He loved cricket but knew he was a duffer. Never before had he wanted so much to bat brilliantly.

Nigel bowled. It was really a throw and was yards wide.

'You threw it,' cried Effie.

'And you ran over the line,' cried Jeanie.

'If you don't all shut up,' he screamed, 'I'll get my mother to send you home.' Liking the idea, he rushed over to his mother and shouted that the Sempili girls were cheats and he wanted them to be sent home.

Scorning the puerile accusation that they were cheats, the girls waited to see if his mother would cuff his ear and order him not to be a spoiled brat or would do what he wanted and send them home.

'Sorry about this,' muttered Edwin.

He looked miserable, and, as Effie was to say afterwards, no one in the world was better at looking miserable than poor Edwin, with his big, skinned nose.

Whatever his mother whispered to him, probably she promised him some treat, Nigel consented to come back. He did not however join in the game, but stood aside with his arms folded, as if, said Effie, he had just scored a century. He jeered at every bad shot and refrained from cheering at the good ones. In spite of him the others enjoyed themselves. Diana was top scorer with twenty-two runs.

Meanwhile two maids had been carrying out things for tea.

Rebecca needed to go to the bathroom.

'We would like to wash our hands, please,' said Diana.

'Is it necessary?' asked Lady Campton.

'Yes, it is.'

'Oh, very well. Simpson, show them where they can wash their hands.'

The maid did not take them into the house by the front door but led them round to the side to the servants' or tradesmen's entrance. They went through the big kitchen. They were shown into a bathroom too small for the five of them. It was one used by servants. Rebecca was horrified at having so little room in which to piddle, but her need was urgent. The others said they would wait till they got home.

They held a meeting.

'We're being patronised,' said Effie.

'They think we're beneath them,' said Jeanie.

'This isn't the bathroom they use themselves,' said Rowena.

'Perhaps Lady Campton thought it was the most convenient one,' said Diana.

'Don't make excuses for them, ' said Effie. 'What time is it?'

'A quarter past four,' replied Diana.

'I vote we don't wait for Papa. Let's go home now. We can walk.'

'That wouldn't be polite,' said Diana.

'Polite!' cried Jeanie. 'Is it polite to make us use this smelly bathroom?'

'We shouldn't give them the satisfaction of knowing they've humiliated us,'said Diana.

'Well, I'm not going to eat anything,' said Effie.

Suddenly Rebecca started to cry. She didn't often cry. Her feelings must be hurt. They comforted her.

'All right,' said Diana. 'We'll tell them Rebecca wants to go home. Does everyone agree?'

Everyone did.

As they went through the kitchen they remembered to thank Simpson. It wasn't her fault.

They waited at the side of the house while Diana went to tell Lady Campton they were leaving.

'Ask Edwin to come and play badminton with us,' said Effie.

Diana did not falter as she addressed her hostess. 'We're sorry, Lady Campton, but Rebecca wants to go home. We've decided not to wait for Papa. We'll walk. It's not very far.'

Lady Campton frowned. She did not give a damn whether they went or stayed but objected to their making the decision themselves. 'Don't you want any tea?'

'No, thank you.' Diana looked at Edwin, who blushed. 'If you'd like to come and play badminton with us at Bell Heather Cottage you'd be very welcome.'

'What about me?' demanded Nigel. 'Have I to come too? I'm better at badminton than he is.'

'Neither of you is going,' said their mother. 'Have you forgotten that we're expecting friends?'

'That's not till next week,' mumbled Edwin.

'Goodbye.' As Diana walked away she heard Lady Campton say: 'Impudent little bitch! Who the hell does she think she is?'

'A descendant of the Johnny that helped to do Rizzio in,' said Sir Edwin, with a chuckle.

'I think she's super,' said Edwin, defiantly.

She imagined herself turning and shouting: 'I'll tell you who I am, Lady Campton. I'm one of the Sempill girls. We're going to live in Poverty Castle whether you like it or not.'

She was more pleased with Edwin's compliment than she should have been. It wasn't likely she would ever meet him again.

'What did they say?' asked Effie.

'Lady Campton said I was an impudent little bitch.'

They gasped with indignation.

'Did you invite Edwin?' asked Jeanie.

'Yes, but his mother said he couldn't come.'

'Poor Edwin. How does he manage to be so nice living with that family.'

'Isn't Nigel awful?' said Rowena.

She then began to give imitations of Nigel's awfulness. They were so funny that her sisters couldn't talk for laughing.

When they got home and told what had happened Papa was for rushing off to Kilcalmonell House to horsewhip the insolent baronet. He was disconcerted when his daughters pointed out that he didn't have a horse, never mind a horsewhip. Besides, they'd liked Sir Edwin, though he didn't know anything about cricket. He was afraid of Lady Campton. So was Edwin. Awful Nigel was her favourite.

They asked Rowena to give her imitations of Nigel.

'Poor boy,' gasped Mama, with tears of laughter in her eyes.

9

For years there had been agitation in the village to get rid of tinkers whose encampments on the foreshore were insanitary eyesores. They defecated behind rocks. They spent most of their money on drink. They assaulted one another. They indulged in drunken sex in front of their children. Those children never went to school; this was deplored in theory but welcomed in practice, for God knew what diseases they would have transmitted, in addition to nits, lice, and fleas. If a respectable and law abiding houseowner wanted to install a caravan in his own garden he had to have permission from the planning authorities. Yet the tinkers who paid no rates or taxes and lived on Welfare could clutter up every space on the shore with battered caravans, decrepit cars and vans, and tents made out of potato sacks, and authority said nothing. The police kept clear, owing to some absurd policy of non-harassment. A letter of protest had been sent to the Secretary of State. One of his minions had replied with insulting vagueness.

There was to be still another meeting in the village hall to discuss the problem. Papa thought it was his duty to attend but first he had to hear the tinkers' side of the argument. So he took time off from supervising the work being done on Poverty Castle to pay them a visit.

He was pleased when the girls asked to be allowed to go with him. Children, he said, were more logical than adults and had a fresher sense of fairness. Mama was doubtful. She was afraid they might see and hear things that would distress them. They were only little girls, after all.

They had debated the matter among themselves and were inclined to sympathise with the tinkers but had agreed not to make up their minds until they had seen how the tinkers really lived. That they used the shore for their lavatory was not disgusting, as people seemed to think. If you didn't have a bathroom it was as good a place as any. As Effie said everybody's found its way to the sea in the end.

They went in the Daimler. It was another sunny afternoon.

'They may think we are invading their privacy and be resentful,' said Mama, as they approached the first group of caravans.

As if to prove her right an old man, his hair as white as a seagull's breast, rose up from behind a rock on the shore. No one needed to ask what he had been doing. He shook his fist. At the same time an oyster-catcher piped shrilly. It was easy to imagine the sound as coming from the old man's mouth.

'You see,' murmured Papa, 'they have feelings to be hurt, like the rest of us.'

He stopped the car.

Immediately there rushed at it three mongrel dogs, ill- nourished and bad-tempered, barking and snarling. They were followed by some children, boys and girls, three of them red-haired.

Two women were seated on stools outside a caravan, peeling potatoes. One was big and red-haired, the other white-haired and old. The children came closer to the car and stared up at its occupants. Two held out their hands, as if begging. They all jabbered. It sounded like a foreign language.

'It's like being in Africa,' said Mama, 'except that the natives are white.'

'Brown,' said Effie.

Her sisters put their fingers to their lips. The agreement was to take note but say nothing.

'They are as Scottish as we are,' said Papa. 'They have names like Williamson, McPhie, and Mac-Donald. It is said that a long time ago their ancestors were cast out by their clans. No one knows why.'

Two men almost fell out of a caravan. One had a shotgun over his shoulder, the other an almost empty bottle of whisky in his hand.

'Let's go, Edward,' said Mama. 'That gun could be loaded and they are both quite drunk.'

Drunk but respectful. They approached the car, kicking the dogs out of their way. Shotgun touched his cap, Whisky-bottle his brow.

'Was there something you wanted, sir, or are you chust looking?' asked Shotgun.

'Are you aware,' said Papa solemnly,'that there is to be a meeting in the village hall tomorrow evening to discuss ways of forcing you to leave the district?'

'They're always haeing meetings,' said Whisky-bottle.

'It's nane o' oor business,' said Shotgun.

'I'm afraid it's very much your business. What the village people object to is the mess you make on the foreshore. Just look at it.'

'Whit mess, sir?'

Both of them peered about them. They saw heaps of miscellaneous rubbish but no mess. They saw their homes.

An infant of about two, a little boy, naked from the waist down, toddled towards the car. In his tiny fist he clutched a stone. With it he began to batter the side of the car. Feeble though his strength was in a few seconds he had done pounds-worth of damage.

The girls gasped, regretting their vow of silence. They looked at Papa. The car was his pride and joy. Most men would have jumped out and restrained the infant, not too gently either. Papa sat still, not because he was afraid but because he thought a small tinker child was more important than his expensive car.

They felt very proud of him.

A girl picked up the infant.

'Are you the gentleman that belongs to the Big House, sir?' asked Shotgun. 'If you are I want to ask you if you minded me shooting a rabbit or two, for the pot.'

'I am not the gentleman that owns the Big House,

but I should think he would mind very much.'

The big red-haired woman sauntered over. She was buxom and coarsely handsome. She wore a thin blue blouse with nothing under it and a pair of men's trousers that were not meant to house so ample and provocative a behind.

'Whit is it you want, sir?' she asked. 'You'll get nae sense oot o' this pair.'

'Is there anyone, a chief or elder, who speaks for you all?'

'If you mean a boss, we've got nane here. We please oorselves. That's the kind of life we hae, free as birds.'

'You look a sensible woman. What's your name?'

'I'm mair than sensible.' She grinned and lifted up her heavy breasts. 'Bella Williamson's my name.'

'If you and your companions, Mrs Williamson, were promised a properly designed camp-site, with sanitary arrangements, would you live in it and undertake to keep it clean and tidy?'

Shotgun and Whisky-bottle slunk off. They seemed scared of the woman.

'Would we hae to pay a rent?' she asked.

'I expect so, but surely it would be worth it, to have decent toilet facilities?'

'We don't mind sharing the shore wi' the seagulls. It's mair natural. This site, whaur would it be? Here? We think this is a grand spot.'

'Its situation would have to be decided.'

She grinned. 'I can see you're as simple as you look, mister, but there's naething wrang wi' that. Simple folk are the nicest folk. Naebody wants us on their land. We've been chased awa' a dozen times. In the auld days when we worked for fermers it was different. We were welcome then.'

'You should think of your children, Mrs Williamson. Doesn't it worry you that they get no schooling?'

'I got nane myself and I've done all right.'

'But times change. It is too great a handicap nowadays not to able at least to read and write.'

'My weans are no' ignorant, if that's what you think. They ken things your lassies don't and never will.' She winked, lewdly. She was to tell a friend later that she wouldn't have minded carrying into her caravan the braw gentleman with the blue eyes and the milk-white body.

'Please, Edward, let's go,' whispered Mama, aware of the trollop's enticement of Edward and afraid that the girls might be aware of it too.

He kept trying. 'You must find it most inconvenient having no reliable water supply.'

'Still, we manage to keep oorselves clean. Look.' She opened her blouse and showed one of her big white breasts. 'My trouble, mister, is that I feel lonely at night. Could you dae onything aboot that? My man's left me for a wee whure half his age.'

'Good afternoon.' Papa drove off.

They heard her laughing raucously.

'What a dreadful creature,' said Mama.

'Be fair, Meg. Not many women in her position would show such spirit.'

Mama lowered her voice. 'She was deliberately enticing you.'

10

When Rebecca became four she had taken her place in the girls' councils, as Rowena had done before her. Their contributions were often unexpected but useful. However, it was felt by Diana and the twins that it might be wiser to leave their little sisters out of their conference that followed their reconnoitring of the tinkers' camp. They feared Rebecca's inqusitiveness. Not about the old man doing Number Two behind a rock: the girls themselves on picnics had used rocks for the same purpose. Nor about the little boy with his boy-thing exposed. In Edinburgh one of their mother's friends had had a baby boy whom they had seen being bathed. It was the woman with red hair and big bosoms they were afraid Rebecca would ask questions about. She might want to know why the woman had kept grinning at Papa in yon funny way, and why Papa had smiled so peculiarly back. Those were mysteries that vexed Diana and the twins themselves.

The twins had looked for the word 'hoor' in Papa's huge dictionary but could not find it. Probably it wasn't spelled the way the woman had said it.

Unfortunately Rebecca, though always sweet, could be very stubborn. She insisted on taking part.

Since it was her democratic right her sisters had to give in.

Therefore all five of them met in the garden shed at Bell Heather Cottage, with upturned flower pots as seats. They were really seven, for a blackbird outside kept having his say too, and Squeaky the field mouse that lived in the shed crept out now and then and squeaked.

'Think before you speak,' said Diana.

They sat thinking.

Rowena spoke first. 'I think they should all be made to go away.'

'You have to give your reasons,' said Effie.

'They're dirty.'

'If you didn't have a bathroom with warm water and soap you'd be dirty too, Rowena Sempill.'

'The lady with the red hair said they were clean,' said Rebecca. 'She showed us,'

'Why don't they live in houses with bathrooms?' said Jeanie, hurriedly.

'They don't like living in houses,' said Effie. 'That's why they call themselves travelling people.'

'Why do we call them tinkers then?' asked Rowena.

'They used to mend pots and pans,' said Diana.

'Nobody wants them as neighbours,' said Jeanie.

'Would *we* want them as neighbours?' asked Diana.

None of them would, except possibly the blackbird, which sang passionately, perhaps to that effect.

'Their dogs are skinny,' said Rebecca. 'They had scabs.'

'They shouldn't be allowed to keep dogs,' said

Jeanie.

Rebecca was becoming dangerously talkative. 'I think the tinker children should go to school. If we have to go why shouldn't they?'

'Would you like to sit beside one of them?' asked Rowena, and twisted her face into a resemblance of a tinker child's. Even her hair seemed to turn shaggy.

'I don't see why children should have to go to school,' said Effie, 'if they don't want to. Papa says it's a free country. Being made to go and sit in a school for hours every day listening to a boring teacher, that's not being free, is it?'

'It's for our own good,' said Diana.

'They're always saying things are for our own good. They don't ask us, do they?'

'That's not fair, Effie,' said her twin. 'Papa and Mama often ask us. Granny Ruthven says they ask us too much.'

'We're wandering off the subject,' said Diana. 'What do you think of Papa's idea, that there should be camps for tinkers, with toilets, all over the country, so that they could travel about and mind their own business?'

'On whose land would it be built?' asked Effie. 'Nobody wants them.'

'Who would pay for the camps?' asked Jeanie. 'The tinkers haven't any money.'

'They've got money to buy whisky with,' said Rebecca.

'The taxpayers would have to pay for them,' said Diana.

'They would grumble,' said Rowena. 'Papa's

always saying that taxpayers grumble.'

'The lady with the red hair said they wouldn't pay rent,' said Rebecca.

'They would jolly well have to,' said Effie.

'What did she mean,' went on Rebecca, 'when she said her children knew things we didn't? What things?'

'How to skin rabbits,' said Diana. 'Things like that.'

'I don't want to know how to do that.'

There was a pause then, during which they listened to the blackbird and watched Squeaky.

'It's the grown-ups' fault' said Jeanie.

'They're always getting things in a mess,' said Effie.

'We'll all be grown-ups ourselves one day,' said Rowena.

Each of them contemplated that prospect. Rowena found it exciting: she wanted to be an actress. Rebecca thought it would be so much nicer having a real baby to nurse instead of a doll. Effie saw herself as a doctor, looking after lepers in Africa. Jeanie's vision was of herself as a vet, curing sheep with sore feet. Diana imagined herself married to Edwin Campton. She remembered him saying, 'She's super.'

At the meeting in the village hall tempers were lost. The local councillor was abused to his face, for not having got rid of the pests on the shore. The M.P. for the district had been invited but had not attended: his letter of apology was dismissed as craven drivel. It was not in the least helpful of him to remind them that he represented other communities besides Kilcalmonell, none of which would welcome the travelling people (in mealy-mouthed fashion he avoided using the honest term tinkers). It was unanimously agreed to send him a letter pointing out that Kilcalmonell had suffered far worse than those other countries and hinting that at the next General Election he need not count on their votes. Since he knew that they would have endured the Plagues of Egypt rather than vote Labour the threat was not likely to perturb him.

Papa had put forward his suggestion of a permanent camp, with sanitary facilities. Everybody had approved, on condition that it was built far from Kilcalmonell and paid for by somebody else.

'You should have heard the hypocrites, Meg,' he said sadly, to his assembled family. 'Full of goodwill towards the unfortunate creatures, provided they cleared out and never came back.'

'I am afraid, Edward, that if I had been present I might have adopted the same attitude.'

The girls looked at one another guiltily.

'Wherever I find hypocrisy, Meg, I must speak against it. I did so, in the strongest terms.'

'I hope you didn't offend them, darling. They are our neighbours now.'

'So are the travelling people our neighbours. I intend to do what I can to alleviate their conditions.'

'No, Edward, you must not go near them again. Please. I beg you. Did not that dreadful woman say that all they wanted was to mind their own business? Leave them alone, my love.'

'Perhaps we could have some of their children to pay us a visit. When we have moved into Poverty Castle, I mean. I'm sure the girls would co-operate.'

They looked aghast.

Later Effie was to hiss : 'Isn't it strange how Papa doesn't seem to understand?'

All the same, if he did invite some tinker children, though they hoped he wouldn't, they would do their best to make him feel welcome.

'We wouldn't patronise them,' said Jeanie.

A week after the start of the grouse-shooting the schools reopened after the summer holidays. It was an event the Sempill girls had been dreading. Not because it would be a pity to have to sit captive indoors after so much freedom in the sun, nor because Miss McGill, the schoolmistress, was reputed to be a 'Tartar', but because it would mean separation. Diana being almost twelve would have to attend the secondary school in Tarbeg. A bus would take her, and other pupils of secondary age, in the morning and bring them back after four. For nearly nine hours a day she would be parted from her sisters, and in the bus and at school she would meet other girls who would become her friends. She would start thinking of herself as a grown-up. The distance between her and her sisters would grow. So Rebecca, Rowena, and the twins cast up, mournfully.

She tried to comfort them, though she felt disconsolate herself. She would be home every evening and all week-end. It was true she might make friends but they would never take her sisters' place.

They remained doleful. The twins said they should have stayed in Edinburgh where they could all have gone to the same school. In two years they themselves would have moved on to secondary school, which would mean Rowena and Rebecca being left alone in Kilcalmonell. By the time *they* were ready for secondary school, Diana would have gone to University. It was no good Diana or Mama or Papa pretending otherwise, this was the beginning of the break-up of the family. Papa tried to cheer them up by saying how happy they would all be when they moved into Poverty Castle in a few weeks' time.

Mama was saddest. She had an additional anxiety, which she kept private. It concerned her son still to be born, indeed still to be conceived. If he came too late he would find the nest empty. Poor wee soul, he would be the loneliest of them all. He would never know the joy of having his sisters round him. We must hurry, Edward, she whispered at night. In a magazine she had read that a certain brew, concocted from herbs and plants, including ragwort, increased fertility. For some time she had been taking it, though it smelled like urine. Now she urged Edward to take it too. He sipped once and was sick.

Three days before the primary school reopened, in accordance with a summons from Miss McGill, the headmistress, Papa and Mama with the twins, Rowena, and Rebecca presented themselves at the school, for purposes of enrolment and instruction in the rules. Diana went with them but waited on the shore among the dippers and sandpipers.

Miss McGill, a grey-haired spinster of fifty-nine, stared at her new recruits and said, with a sternness she did not feel: 'The wearing of jewellery and make-up is not allowed.'

She herself wore none, not so much as a ring.

Their mother, dozy creature, was red in the mouth, white in the cheeks and neck, and blue above the eyes, with make-up. As for jewellery she dripped, glittered, and tinkled with it. Miss McGill used only soap and water and sensible clothes, on the present occasion a navy-blue costume, with the skirt below her knees, a white blouse with a high collar, and low-heeled black shoes, in great contrast to Mrs Sempill's long loose yellow skirt, pink blouse and high-heeled sandals. That she was tall and slender did not in the schoolmistress's opinion justify her wearing clothes more suitable for a girl of eighteen with hippy notions. Miss McGill herself was small and stout. Being honest she admitted that there might be in her disapproval of Mrs Sempill's flamboyancy a trace of jealousy; no, a great deal more than a trace, for Mrs Sempill possessed what Miss McGill would have given her soul for: four beautiful well-mannered little girls. Miss McGill's objecton to their jewellery, which amounted only to beads on their ear-lobes and a ring or two, had been her arcane way of saying how delightful she found them. Often she praised by finding fault. This wasn't because she was a sour-faced curmudgeon (though this was her reputation) but for the opposite reason, because, like her friend Peggy McGibbon, she was at heart a sentimentalist. Such a person if not restrained would never have made an effective teacher. Therefore Miss McGill had restrained herself relentlessly for over forty years.

Rebecca, she said curtly, was too young to be enrolled that term.

'Oh, I hope not,' said Mrs Sempill. 'It would break her heart to be separated from her sisters.'

'In my experience children's hearts don't break all that easily.'

It was the kind of perverse remark with which she disguised her true feelings. Better than most she knew how deeply children could suffer.

'Head Office decides,' she said. 'Usually they stick by the regulations.'

'Even if she cannot be admitted officially,' said Mr Sempill, with one of his gay-cavalier smiles, 'can it not be done unofficially?'

He was as fond of peacockery as his wife. His trousers were pale blue, his shirt red, and his jacket white. He was too fragrant.

'I'm afraid that is out of the question, Mr Sempill.'

It wasn't of course. In her school Miss McGill was queen. It would not be the first time that, in professional language, she had told Head Office to go to Hell.

'I can always recommend her admission. That is the most I can do.'

First the parents thanked her, and then, without

bidding, the girls. They were greatly relieved that they weren't going to be separated.

'The twins are very alike,' said Miss McGill, gruffly. 'I would appreciate it if they wore ribbons of different colours: until I know them better.'

'I'll wear yellow,' said one twin. 'Jeanie can wear pink.'

'As long as you tell me which is which.'

Miss McGill never had favourites. Seldom indeed had she been tempted. Most children were lovable. Now she saw temptation in front of her. Rowena Sempill was the most fascinating child she had ever seen.

It wasn't just the long fair hair bleached by the sun, the eyes of milkwort blue, the tanned skin smooth as silk, and the perfectly shaped mouth. It was something else, rarer than physical beauty, which Miss McGill, expert in the physiognomy of children, could not name for she had never seen it before. She had had children in her classes who had afterwards gained first-class honours degrees at University, but that had been intellectual capacity, not all that uncommon. What Rowena Sempill had was much rarer. She might not be particularly smart at lessons though she would be no dunce, but she had a distinction that would make her famous one day.

Miss McGill had heard that the Sempills were well-off. According to report they were making a palace out of Poverty Castle. But it was in themselves that their greatest riches lay.

She found herself doing what she had never done before. She babbled to strangers what ought to have been kept confidential.

'You know about the tinkers,' she said. She had seen and heard Mr Sempill at the meeting. 'About an hour ago I had a visit from one of them, a woman, who wanted to enrol her child, a girl of eight.'

'Not a big red-haired woman?' cried Mrs Sempill.

'No. A small black-haired one. Her child can hardly read or write. She wishes to remedy that.'

'How very commendable,' cried Mr Sempill.

'Yes, but there are difficulties.' Miss McGill looked at the girls. 'I think you should go and join your sister.'

It was evident, from their surprise, that they were not often excluded, but they did not whine or whimper. Excusing themselves, they left at once.

Their names kept bothering Miss McGill. There was something odd about them. Rebecca and Rowena, so pretentious. Effie and Jeannie, so plebian. Diana, so upper-class.

'What difficulties?' asked Mr Sempill.

'Parents of other children have warned me that if any tinker child is allowed into the school they will immediately withdraw theirs.'

'How mean-spirited!' he cried.

'But, Edward,' said his wife, 'they have a right to be concerned. Those children we saw at the caravans, they looked so rough and alien. Surely they would be a disruptive element.'

'The girl in question would not be disruptive,' replied the schoolmistress. 'Not in herself. Her presence might be, however. She is small and shy. She could suffer.'

'What of cleanliness?' whispered Mrs Sempill.

'Is that important?' cried her husband.

'It is very important,' said Miss McGill,' but as far as cleanliness is concerned this child could take her place in any school in the country. She is very much a credit to her mother.'

'I hope, Miss McGill,' said Mr Sempill, earnestly, 'that you are not going to succumb to this blackmail. Is it not an empty threat? This is the only primary school in the district.'

'They say they will drive their children into Tarbeg.'

'How many are involved?'

'At least a dozen. We would lose Miss McKay, our second teacher.'

'Could you not find replacements among the tinkers? We saw lots of children of school age.'

'An influx of children unable to read or write would ruin the school.'

'Why should it? Would it not be a magnificent challenge?'

At the meeting about the tinkers someone had said his name should have been Simple, not Sempill. He was a gomeril who, if not discouraged, would do more harm with his well-meaning but stupid interference than the laird did with his lack of interest. That, though, had been a male opinion. His simple-ness, if that was what it was, had made the women want to protect as well as cherish him. Miss McGill herself had not been immune.

Now she merely smiled at his fatuous optimism. 'I could cope with one little girl, but only if I could depend on help from other parents and other children.'

'You will certainly have our help,' said Mr Sempill,' and our girls will give you theirs. Won't they, Meg?'

She seemed doubtful. 'They didn't say much after we took them to see the camp.'

'Are you saying, Meg, that in a matter of humanity our girls will be found wanting?'

'They won't have Diana to advise them.'

It was then that it occurred to the schoolmistress where the names had come from. Well, if they were named after heroines let them be heroic. 'I shall be glad of their co-operation, but it must of course be voluntary.'

Going back in the car Papa explained, enthusiastically. The girls listened in silence. They were not as spontaneously magnanimous has he had hoped. He felt depressed. Meg, he thought, knows them better than I do. Is it because like them she is female? Do they share secrets from which I am forever shut out? Young though they were, the world had already corrupted them. Here they were having to ponder the consequences before agreeing to a kindness. He had failed them.

'She's not going to take Diana's place,' said Effie, dourly.

'Of course she isn't. Nobody could. She's only eight, remember.' He looked to Diana, pleading with her to persuade them; but she tightened her lips and said nothing.

'There could be girls we like better than her,' said Jeanie.

'She could be sneaky,' said Rebecca.

'She could smell,' said Rowena.

'Miss McGill assured us she is very clean.'

'What's her name?' asked Jeanie.

'Miss McGill didn't say.'

'I think we should meet her first before we promise,' said Effie.

'You disappoint me, girls. Even if she did smell and was sneaky surely you could still be kind to her, especially if others were being unkind?'

'Was she the girl that picked up the wee boy who was banging the car with the stone?' asked Rebecca.

'No. That girl had red hair. I think this one has black, like Diana.'

That was another appeal. Again Diana refused to respond. They were more resolute realists than he. They knew the difficulties and their own limitations. He felt desolate.

'What do you think, Mama?' asked Jeanie.

'Of course you must be kind to her.'

'What if she doesn't want us to be kind to her?' asked Effie. 'Some children are like that.'

'Nigel would hate you to be kind to him,' said Rowena.

'You can't compare her with Nigel,' said Papa. '*He* has every advantage, and she has none.'

'It's all right, Papa,' said Effie, a little impatiently, 'we'll help her, if we can; but it will be easier if we like her, that's all.'

He had to be content with that. The wisest of philosophers could not have summed it up more cogently.

12

Diana did not want her parents to take her to the secondary school either before the opening day or on that day itself. She knew who she was, she said: she could answer any questions about herself. If she was treated with courtesy she would be courteous. If she was treated rudely she would still be courteous. They wouldn't dare treat her rudely, cried her sisters. They would soon see how unafraid she was, amidst those hundreds of strangers. Hadn't she told them, lots of times, to do and say what you thought right, no matter what other people said?

Papa listened and felt relieved. His young daughters were not corrupted. He had been pessimistic. Here they were challenging the world. They would not be defeated, as he himself had been so often. At the same time he felt sad. They would have to pay for their victories. Already he saw in Diana the woman she would become: formidable, like her grandmother Ruthven. Even little Rebecca, sweetest-natured of children, not yet five, was capable of remarks that abashed him with their uncompromising honesty.

On that first morning of separation Diana calmly kissed her parents and then, escorted by her sisters, went out to the road to wait for the school bus, under the big lime tree. Her sisters recognised and respected her mood. They had seen before that severe smile that softened when she looked at them, and that head held high, all the more impressive now because of the silly school hat. She was their Diana whom they knew so well and loved dearly, and on whom they depended so much. She was setting off for an alien country, and though she would come back to them in the evening a part of her would be lost to them forever. They felt forlorn therefore, particularly Rebecca who cried a little though she had promised the twins she wouldn't.

It was a sunny morning with blue skies and birds singing. But for stupid school they would have gone swimming or climbing trees or gathering mushrooms or exploring the grounds of the Big House. Whatever it was they would have done it together. Again and again the pain of separation struck them: it was worse than toothache. They dreaded the coming of the bus that would take Diana away. What if she never came back? They stared at one another in terror.

Diana read their faces. 'Things have to change, you know.'

'We don't want them to change,' said Jeanie.

'Of course you do. You don't want to remain little girls all your lives, do you?'

'We're not little girls,' said Effie.

Just then the bus roared round the corner. Effie and Jeanie made sure it stopped by standing out on the road and holding up their arms. Diana climbed aboard. Boys and girls grinned down. They were friendly, but it was to them and others like them that a part of Diana had to be surrendered.

After the bus was gone they were silent. Rebecca sobbed.

'Do you remember,' said Effie, 'Sir Bedivere, after the barge took Arthur away?'

Papa had read the poem to them not long ago.

They remembered.

'Well, that's how I feel.'

It was how they all felt.

An hour later it was their turn to go to school. In the back seat of the Daimler they were quiet, with resigned but martyred faces. Their parents glanced at each other and sighed. Evidently a conference had taken place and it had been decided that, though it was a terrible injustice to send them to one school and Diana to another, they would endure it without complaint but would speak only if spoken to and even then as little as possible.

Miss McGill might or might not welcome untalkative pupils, but if she suspected that their taciturnity was deliberate, a protest against the school, she would be cross.

There was too the tinker girl. Probably she would not show up but if she did and was hostilely received this Trappist quartet would be no help.

Not for the first time Papa found himself wishing they were boys. He would not have loved them more but he might have understood them better.

Several cars were parked outside the school. Almost at once the Daimler was approached by a group of young women, their faces bitter with grievance and their voices harsh with it. One of them carried a baby.

'Good morning, Mr Sempill,' they said.

'Good morning, ladies.'

Mrs Sempill said good-morning too.

The four Misses Sempill pretended they weren't there.

'Have you heard?' asked the woman with the baby.

He smiled. 'Heard what?'

'A child from the tinker's camp is being admitted to the school this morning.'

'Miss McGill did mention it. I thought it was splendid news. What's the trouble?'

'That's the trouble.'

'We're amazed to hear you call it splendid news.'

'We think it's abominable news.'

'Would you like your girls to sit beside her and catch some awful disease.'

'We're getting up a petition. Miss McGill says she's obliged by law to take this child. Well, if she does we're taking ours out.'

He gave them his most winning smile. 'Have you seen the little girl in question?'

'No we haven't and we don't want to.'

'They're all the same. They live like animals, so they've got habits like animals.'

Still he smiled. 'According to Miss McGill this particular child from the point of view of cleanliness could take her place in any school in the country.'

'How could she be clean, living in those conditions?'

'It must be difficult but it seems this little girl's mother has achieved it. Surely she is to be commended. She wishes her daughter to receive an education. Is that not commendable too?'

Like most women they found it hard to be angry with him. Like most women too they blamed his foolishness on his wife. They were not deceived by her false smiles. It must be because she domineered him in private that he uttered such nonsense in public. Look how her girls were afraid to open their mouths!

In the playground children screamed, and on the shore seagulls. A battered blue van drove up and stopped behind the Daimler. If it had contained the devil, horns and all, the village women couldn't have stared at it with greater revulsion. It contained a loutish young man with a freckled face, a small thin-faced black-haired woman, and between them a small dark-skinned girl in a white dress with a white ribbon in her hair.

The Sempill girls refused to turn and look out of the rear window.

The woman and the girl got out. The woman smiled at the village women who scowled back. The girl glanced up at the Sempills. They went through the gate into the playground, behind the high stone wall.

'Does she look such an ogress?' asked Sempill

'You don't understand, Mr Sempill. If we let one in they'll all want in.'

'I doubt that, but even if it was true we could not deny children, any children, the right to an education.'

'They pay no rates, so why should they get an education?'

'Everything for nothing, that's their way of life.'

'Let them live like pigs if they want but we shouldn't be made to associate with them.'

'Just look at that clown, he's fairly enjoying this.'

It seemed to Sempill that the tinker fellow's grin was one of great unease.

'Here she comes, bold as brass.'

Though she did not cringe the tinker woman looked anxious, having left her lamb among wolves. Sempill gave her a friendly wave.

Suddenly his daughters scrambled out of the car and out into the playground.

A chant arose. 'Tinker trash, tinker trash.'

'Good God,' muttered Sempill.

His wife held on to his jacket. 'Don't interfere, Edward.'

'What are our girls doing, Meg?'

'Minding their own business, I hope.'

Suddenly they heard a furious scream: 'Shut up, you stupid bullies!' It was Effie's voice, followed by Jeanie's equally impassioned: 'You shoud be ashamed of yourselves.'

Sempill's heart rose. 'Thank God.'

'Rebecca might get hurt. You'd better go and stop it.'

Before he could get out of the car a whistle blew. Silence fell in the playground. Miss McGill had arrived. Her voice was scornful. 'There will be no bullying in my school.'

'The village women were indignant. 'She's got no right to speak to them like that.'

They blamed Mrs Sempill. 'We knew your girls ran

wild, Mrs Sempill. Now we learn they've never been taught manners.'

'They have been taught to abhor injustice,' said Mr Sempill grandly.

Still they could not bring themselves to blame the big handsome simple soul. He had been trained to say what his wife was too shy to say herself.

Sempill walked along to the tinker's van. He stood by the window on the woman's side.

'Good morning,' he said. 'My name's Sempill. My girls too started school this morning.'

The man grinned servilely but the woman was wary. 'Oor name's McPhee, Mr and Mrs.'

'What is your little girl's name?'

'Annie.'

'She's a very pretty and very brave little girl. You should be proud of her.'

'She's mabye no' as braw as some but there's no many wi' mair hert.'

'I'm sorry some of the children were rude to her. They didn't really mean it, you know. Left to themselves children have no prejudices.'

'I don't ken aboot that, they mean it a' right. There was hate in their voices. Was it your lassies took her part?'

'Yes.'

'Annie's like me, no' easily feart. I warned her there micht be trouble but she still wanted to come.'

'Good for her.'

'She'll stick it as long as she can.'

'It will be all right, Mrs McPhee. The children will soon come round. Besides, Miss McGill is a fair-minded woman.'

'It's not just here, it's back at the camp as weel.'

He should have realised that there would be jealousy and resentment among her own kind. Mrs McPhee and Annie were even braver than he had thought. McPhee too, to be fair. He did not look too bright. Education meant nothing to him. He would want to be at accord with his boozing companions. Yet he was standing by his wife and child.

'We could be forced to leave,' said Mrs McPhee, 'though we like it here weel enough.'

For a few mad moments he was the point of offering them space for their caravan at Poverty Castle, though it wasn't really his to offer.

The children had all gone into school.

No rejected little girl crept through the gate.

'We can go noo, Jimmy,' said Mrs McPhee. 'Thanks, Mister.'

The van drove off.

Sempill went back to the Daimler. The village women had gone.

'They think I put you up to it, Edward,' said his wife.

'Put me up to what, Meg?'

'Taking the side of the tinkers. Encouraging our girls. They like you, Edward, but they do not approve of me.'

'They're jealous, my love. You are so much more beautiful.'

'Didn't you find that girl with the baby attractive?'

'In an immature kind of way. There are no depths in her or in any of them.'

'The baby's a boy. She wouldn't let me hold it. I was on the point of telling her I would have my own one day.'

She had read recently that conception could be helped if some unusual place was chosen for love-making. Such places were not plentiful in Bell Heather Cottage. Edward took cramp so easily and was quick to grumble about discomfort. There was that patch of grass in the garden that the girls called the bower, a sun-trap, surrounded by rhododendrons and overlooked only by crows. Was it not likely that if they made love there like Adam and Eve, sung to by birds, Edward's sperm count would even be increased sufficiently for her to conceive again?

Conception was a mystery wrapped in other mysteries.

She put her hand on his knee and squeezed.

Gallantly he smiled. He knew what was on her mind. Seeing a baby boy always had this effect. She never gave up hope.

13

The girls had lunch at school with the other children. They had said they would walk home unless it was raining heavily. So it was half-past four before their parents saw them again.

To Mama and Papa's many questions they were not forthcoming. Their taciturnity this time was noticeably different from that of the morning. It had deeper reasons not so easily diagnosed. Even Rebecca was affected. Exhausted by the day's events she consented to lie down for a little while before Diana's bus was due. When Mama at her bedside asked how she had got on at school she pretended to be sleepier than she really was. Mama was upset. She knew that Rebecca loved and needed her, and yet here she was, not yet five, keeping secrets from her: not secrets really, but discoveries that she and her sisters had made that day, about themselves and other people, which they would want to examine closely before revealing, if they ever did reveal them. Mama's own mother had warned her: 'They'll form a society of which you'll never be a member, Margaret. Weans instinctively gang up against adults as soon as they're old enough to know that adults are not always to be trusted.'

Meanwhile in the living-room Papa questioned the twins and Rowena, 'What happened after Miss McGill got you all into the school?'

'Nothing,' said Effie.

'Surely she said something to the children who chanted Tinker trash?'

'She said they weren't to do it again,' said Jeanie.

'Did they do it again?'

'Yes, but she didn't notice.'

'She didn't notice lots of things,' said Rowena.

'What about the other teacher; Miss McKay?'

'She didn't notice lots of things either,' said Jeanie.

'Are you telling me that this campaign of hostility towards that little girl continued, behind the teachers' backs?'

'Not just behind their backs,' said Effie.

'In front of them sometimes,' said Jeanie.

'I am astonised. I would have thought Miss McGill would miss very little that went on in her schoolroom.'

'Well, she missed a lot.' said Effie.

'Miss McKay was always looking at herself in the mirror,' said Jeanie. 'She thinks she's good-looking.'

'Is she good-looking?'

'She's got big bosoms,' said Effie.

'What about the village children? Surely some of them are nice.'

'John McLeish is a beast,' said Rowena. 'He's worse than Nigel.' Her face changed, became fat and ugly, as she muttered, 'Tinker trash.'

'Is he the ringleader?'

'His father's got a farm,' said Effie. 'He boasted that he wasn't afraid of bulls.'

'And what of little Annie McPhee, at the centre of it all, tell me about her.'

Their faces went blank.

'I had a chat with her mother. She's a very brave little girl, you know. It's not just children at the school who are unkind to her. So are the children at the camp, and the grown-ups too.'

'She didn't cry,' said Rowena.

'She didn't say anything,' said Jeanie.

'That's why she's at school, to learn to read and write. Everyone should help her.'

'We helped her,' said Rowena.

'She doesn't like to be pitied,' said Jeanie.

'Poor child, did she appear very unhappy?'

They looked at one another and shrugged their shoulders.

'Did the van come for her at four o'clock?'

'The man said he'd give us a lift if we wanted but we said we'd walk.' That was Effie, speaking dourly.

'Do you think she'll go to school again tomorrow?'

Jeanie looked at the clock on the mantlepiece. 'It's time for us to go and wait for Diana's bus.'

'It's not due till five. Will she come back tomorrow, or has she been frightened away?'

'What she's not going to do,' said Effie 'is take Diana's place.'

So that was it.

'I don't think you need to worry about that. In any case her mother thinks they may have to leave Kilcalmonell.'

'Why?' asked Jeanie.

'Because too many people are unkind. That's why I want you to be her friends.'

'She doesn't want anybody to be her friend,' said Effie.

'She spoke to no-body,' said Rowena. 'Except Rebecca. She spoke to Rebecca.'

'Rebecca asked her if she knew how to skin rabbits,' said Effie. 'She said she didn't.'

'I think we should go and wait for the bus,' said Jeanie.

'What about Rebecca?' asked Rowena.

Mama came in then. 'She's asleep, the little darling.'

'She wanted to be with us when we went to meet Diana's bus,' said Effie.

'She'll be awfully disappointed,' said Jeanie. 'She kept saying all day how she was looking forward to seeing Diana again.'

'She'll see her when she wakes up,' said Papa.

'She wanted to see her coming off the bus.'

He understood. It would be one of the happiest and most memorable moments of their lives. Rebecca would never forgive herself for being asleep or for them letting her sleep.

The problem was solved by Rebecca appearing at the door, sleepy-eyed but eager.

They all hurried out to wait under the lime tree.

'If we have a little boy, Edward,' said Mama, 'how fortunate he will be, with such loving sisters to look after him.'

There still clung to him the remnants of the foolishness he had felt when making love in the bower that morning. The pain of ant bites lingered too. He had had to wait, with cramp in his legs and ants biting and a wasp buzzing dangerously near his exposed rump until Meg was satisfied that she had received the last precious magical drip. Earlier she had let fall a remark that had chilled him from heart to scrotum. Wine, she had read, could have deleterious effect on spermatazoa, making them lazy and unventuresome. Perhaps, if the present love-making failed, he might abstain from wine for a few weeks. Consider, she had said, what compensation and reward a beautiful little boy would be.

Though Tarbeg was less than twenty miles away the school bus took over an hour to reach Kilcalmonell, because of the many stops it had to make to put down pupils who lived along the way. Several times the Sempill girls' hearts almost stopped with joy, but it was a private car that came rushing round the corner. At last though it was the bus, red and yellow, more glorious than any other bus in the world. They stood back in the shadow of the tree. Effie held Rebecca's hand. The bus halted. A girl climbed down wearing a black blazer, grey skirt, and silly hat. She was the same size and age as Diana. She waved to other girls on the bus. Then she turned and said, coolly: 'How long have you foolish creatures been waiting?'

She was Diana, their sister, and yet somehow she wasn't. One day in the alien country had changed her. This Diana did not seem to be aware as the old Diana certainly would have been, that their waiting for her return had been a joy as hard to bear as pain and their meeting of her again should have been joyful too, with happy cries and kisses and even tears. Instead on her part it was affectionate but cool, in the way that grown-ups were cool. She did crouch down and hug Rebecca, who clung to her. She did, in her old way, pinch Effie's nose, tweak Jeanie's ear, and stroke Rowena's hair, but she seemed to be doing it because she had done it before and knew that they would be expecting her to do it, and not because there was nothing else she would rather have done.

Without saying anything they made excuses for her. She was tired after her long day among

114

strangers. She would have had new experiences and met new people. It would take her a little while to re-adjust. By teatime she would be their own dear Diana again. She would have forgotten everybody else except them and Mama and Papa.

They did not really believe it. Even Rebecca was aware that there had been a change which would be followed by other changes, not only in Diana but in them all. Effie and Jeanie, being older, knew that not all of those changes would be for the worse, some indeed would be welcome, but that was not much consolation then as, taking turns to carry Diana's case, heavy with books, they went up the avenue to the house.

'Who were you waving at on the bus?' asked Rowena.

'Some girls. No-one in particular.'

'Did you meet anyone in particular at school?' asked Jeanie.

'Yes, I did.'

They were shocked.

'It wouldn't be a boy, anyway,' said Effie, dourly.

Diana laughed. 'Why wouldn't it be a boy?'

'Because you've already got one.'

Yesterday she would have pulled their hair or tickled their ribs playfully at this reference to Edwin Campton. He had been seen lurking outside the gate of Bell Heather Cottage and had fled when they had called to him. He had passed them twice in his father's car and had waved, to them all Diana had said but they had known better. The big wistful nose had been pointed in her direction.

Today she just laughed, in a superior kind of way.

'You really are a bunch of silly little kids.'

They were mortified. She couldn't have said a crueller thing. It increased the distance between them.

In the house they listened in silence to her off-hand replies to Mama's and Papa's questions about her new school.

'What class did they put you in ?' asked Papa.

'1B.'

'That's not the top class is it ?'

'There's no top class in First Year. Selection starts in Second Year.'

'Still, they should have put you in 1A.'

'They said they didn't have any information from my primary school.'

'But just looking at you, by listening to you, they must have seen you were well above average in intelligence. Isn't that so, Meg ?'

'Indeed it is, darling.'

'Next year I'll be in 2A.'

'Won't 1A get the best teachers.'

'Teachers don't matter, Papa. It's up to the pupils themselves.'

'But, my dear,' said Mama, 'any girl you would wish to make your friend is most likely to be in 1A.'

'I've already got a friend. Yes, she's in 1A. Her name's Fiona McTaggart. Her father's a dentist.'

Effie could not resist asking: 'Has she got good teeth ?'

Diana showed hers, in an amused grimace: they were white, even and strong.

Mama was worried. 'I think your father should go

and see the headmaster. We've got your reports from St. Mabels. They're all excellent.'

'I can manage on my own, Mama.'

'But as your parents it's our responsibility to give you all the assistance we can.'

'I know that, Mama, and I am grateful, but I don't need assistance.' Diana then turned to her sisters.

'How did you lot get on? Do you like Miss McGill? Did she object to your earrings? Was the tinker girl there?'

They found themselves answering her politely but cautiously, as if she was a stranger.

'We got on all right.'

'We don't know yet if we like Miss McGill.'

'She didn't say anything about our earrings.'

'Yes, the tinker girl was there. Her name is Annie McPhee.'

'Was everybody nice to her.'

'A lot of them weren't.'

'Especially John McLeish. His father's got a farm.'

'He says he's not afraid of bulls.'

'He's afraid of Effie, though.'

'You seem to have had quite an exciting time, though I must say you don't look it. What solemn faces!'

'Be proud of them, Diana,' said Papa. 'Some of the village children were quite beastly to the little girl. Your sisters took her part.'

'I hope they did it sensibly. Fiona McTaggart's got a collie called Faithful. When are we going to get a dog, Papa?'

'When we move into Poverty Castle you can have

all the pets you want.'

'But when will that be?'

'I hereby announce that Poverty Castle will be opened on Saturday, 3rd September, in less than three weeks' time.'

'That's marvellous!' Diana looked at her sisters, expecting them all to be as pleased as herself. She knew she might have hurt their feelings by using the word 'sensibly' but they ought not to be so sensitive.

Their faces remained solemn.

'There will be a celebration,' said Papa. 'An At Home. Everyone in the village will be invited.'

'Can Fiona come ?' asked Diana.

'She's not from the village,' said Effie coldly.

'Of course she can come. Invite all your friends.'

'Can Annie come ?' asked Rebecca.

'She would be an honoured guest, my sweet. Her mother too.'

Afterwards in the room they shared Effie and Jeanie discussed the situation and came to philosopical conclusions. The change in Diana was not something she had brought on deliberatley: it had just happened to her, like having bosoms. It would happen to them too, whether they wanted it or not. They were lucky; for being twins they would always be close to each other. Rebecca was the one of the family most to be pitied. Being the youngest she would be left behind, except if Mama had the baby boy she was always talking about. In that case he and Rebecca could be companions for years. That was to say, if nothing bad happened to Mama. They had heard Granny Ruthven telling Mama not to be foolish, five children were enough for any woman,

118

and besides, wasn't Edward always moaning about the over-population of the earth? Diana had told them having a baby could be dangerous for a woman if she was over thirty. Mama had been quite ill after having Rebecca. So it might be just as well if she didn't have another. Did it happen by accident or had something to be done to make it happen ? When Diana was asked she had been confused and evasive. It seemed to be a secret that she hadn't yet been let into.

They forgave her for calling them a bunch of silly little kids. They were sorry they had teased her about Edwin.

14

A notice, designed by Papa, with a sketch of the house, was put up in the village shop: 'Mr and Mrs Sempill, and the five Misses Sempill, late of Edinburgh, cordially invite their neighbours to an At Home on Saturday, 11th September, from 3pm to

6pm, to celebrate the re-opening, after years of dereliction, of Poverty Castle, formerly known as Ardmore.'

The girls were sure that nobody in Kilcalmonell except Miss McGill would know what dereliction meant, but it wasn't the use of the big show-off word that provoked criticism from Mr Campbell's customers, it was the cheek of the new-comers in calling their house Poverty Castle.

'Surely they know that it was just a nickname!'

'Some poverty! They're spending thousands on it.'

'Is it legal to call your house a castle? Doesn't it have to be registered at the court of Heraldry or something like that?'

'The Big House has never called itself a castle.'

'It's her doing, if you ask me. She fancies herself as lady of the manor. All that jewellery! All that waving of her arms!'

'And she's got those five girls as bad as herself. They think they own the earth, that lot.'

'Semple himself seems a nice person.'

'He's too soft for her. You can see she's been spoiled.'

'Not to mention the girls.'

'You wait and see, they'll want to keep Ardmore beach for themselves.'

'They can't do that. It belongs to the estate. It's the estate that puts up those Private notices.'

'All the same, my mother, who's over eighty as you know, was born in the village, says that folk at Ardmore always had use of the beach. It must be in their title deeds.'

'Well, I don't think you'll see me at their At Home.'

'Why not? It might be interesting to see inside. I hear only the best materials have been used, expense no object.'

'They've painted it white. It looks like a lighthouse, seen from the sea.'

'Four men have been working on the garden for weeks.'

'They've put in central heating.'

'They've made use of land that doesn't belong to them. The laird won't be pleased.'

'He thinks he's the laird.'

'She'll have put the idea in his head.'

'I wonder where they got all their money. He's an architect, they say, but he seems to be retired.'

'Is it true, Dugald, that there's to be champagne ?'

Mr Campbell confirmed that there was to be champagne, as well as coca-cola for the children and beer for the men that wouldn't thank you for champagne. Dougary's, the biggest and best bakers in Tarbeg, were to do the catering. There would be strawberry tarts.

'Well, upstarts they may be, but we've got to admit they're taking more interest in the village than the new laird's ever done. I might take a look-in, just for curiosity's sake.'

That summed up a general attitude. Mr Campbell warned Mr Sempill to expect an invasion of nosy-parkers who wouldn't say no to a glass or two of champagne and a strawberry tart.

Special invitations were sent to Mr Patterson the

lawyer and his wife; Miss McGibbon, his clerkess; Mr McDermott the builder and his wife; Miss McGill and Miss McKay; and the Rev. Mr Angus Buchanan, of the Church of Scotland, and Mrs Buchanan. All accepted except the minister who not too truthfully pleaded other business. He had once called at Bell Heather Cottage to welcome his new parishioners and had discovered a nest of incorrigible pagans.

Annie McPhee and her mother would not be present. There had been trouble at the camp. The police had had to be summoned. It seemed that Annie's father had got into a fight with two other men who had insulted his wife and daughter. He had gone to Knapdale, with a black eye and teeth missing. Annie had not yet enrolled in school there: this Miss McGill had learned from a telephone conversation with her colleague.

Rebecca was sad because she would never see Annie again. The twins urged Diana to telephone the Big House and invite Edwin. She declined, so they did it themselves, to be told by the caretaker that the family had returned to their home in England and would not be back in Scotland until next summer. Diana pretended not to care but her sisters noticed how she went off to be by herself for a while. When she came back she was in a peculiarly cheerful mood, but they weren't deceived: they knew her heart was breaking.

Fiona McTaggart was being brought in Mr Patterson's car.

The Sempills themselves flitted into Poverty Castle on the Wednesday. The girls took the day off school. They had seen the reconstructions and renovations in all their various stages but they were still astonished and enchanted when Papa took them on a tour of their new home. Proudly he pointed out how the ceilings had been replaced with real plaster and not shoddy plasterboard. The elaborate cornices were of a kind popular at the time when the house was built, in 1812, before the Battle of Waterloo. He had assured them many times that the exterior of the house, with its unadorned four-foot thick walls and rather small windows was not as bleak as many people might think (including his wife, it so happened) but solid and dignified. Those were the qualities he had been after: solidity and dignity. Examples were the mahogany doors and foot-high skirting boards, not to mention the lavatory pans, of white porcelain decorated with flowers, in one case roses, in another forget-me-nots and primroses, and in the third, in his own private closet, thistles. They had not been easy or cheap to obtain but they were well worth it. Effie whispered to Jeanie that it didn't matter, did it, where you piddled? But they didn't giggle, for Papa had worked very hard and they had never seen him so happy and self-confident. In this house, in its every aspect, from the door handles to its coal scuttles, he had expressed not only his artistic temperament but also his secret longings. It might be, to begin with, an awkward place to live in for it was like a kind of museum where nothing was to be displaced. When Effie picked up a wooden carving of Don Quixote on his horse Rosinante and put it down again two inches from where it had been Papa without a word replaced it. They loved him for his enthusiasm and were glad that he was so happy, but they were afraid that he would not be able to keep it up and would lose heart, as he always did.

In all the rooms and on every landing were vases,

of crystal, china, pewter, and silver, full of flowers culled from the garden or bought from a florist in Tarbeg.

In spite of the garden's many flowers, shrubs, trees, statues, and urns, in Papa's eyes its glory was the big rowan, at that season of the year resplendent with crimson berries. He had carved all their names on the trunk, as in the song. He would stand beside it, looking lonely and vulnerable, so that the girls wanted to protect him, though from what they could not have said: himself, they vaguely felt. On the evening before the At Home they saw him from the window tying something to the tree. They ran out and found it was a flag, the Lion Rampant. With a faraway look in his eyes he explained that in Borneo there were sacred trees in which the natives believed ancestral spirits dwelled. In honour of these they festooned the branches with coloured rags. The girls knew him so well that they could tell he wasn't joking. They had heard Granny Ruthven say to Mama, 'I declare, Margaret, there are times when I'm convinced Edward is simply not all there,' and they had come to realise what she must have meant. Part of Papa was hidden away where even they could not get in. It was true that sometimes all of Mama was missing, but it was never for long and when she came back she was always her old familiar self, frequently inattentive, but wholly knowable. There was really no mystery about her, as there was about Papa and never more so than when he worshipped at his rowan tree.

15

Accustomed to suiting themselves as to what they wore the girls were indignant when Diana forbade them to put flowers in their hair instead of ribbons: it would make them look ridiculous. Rowena paid no heed and went on arranging the blue lobelia. The twins, who hadn't been sure it was a good idea, were now determined to go ahead with it. They chose red roses and helped Rebecca to choose pansies.

Diana no longer conferred with them: she just ordered them about like a grown-up or rather like all grown-ups except Mama and Papa. If the girls had worn nothing but bikini bottoms Mama would merely have murmured that it might not be wise with so many clegs and wasps about, and Papa would probably have said that when the missionaries in Africa made the natives put on clothes they hadn't given them innocence but had taken it from them.

Papa himself wore a kilt, for the first time in his life. After much self-examination he had bought one, with accessories. Belonging to no particular clan the Sempills, it seemed, had no tartan of their own. He had chosen one called the Jacobite, because he had liked its colours yellow, red and green, and also because it had been sported in 1707 by Lowlanders protesting against the infamous Act of Union.

The girls thought he looked magnificent in it, even if his legs, to use Granny Ruthven's word, were like spurtles.

Mama wore a dress with lots of yellow in it, and green combs in her hair. Either she forgot to put on a brassiere or more likely decided one wasn't necessary, her bosoms being able to support themselves.

They knew about her bosoms because they sometimes went in and chatted with her while she was having a bath. She had told them they were still beautiful, especially since she had had five children. They had pretended to believe her, though they had really thought that having big shoogly lumps on your chest must be an inconvenience. They had been fascinated by the hair on her body but were too polite to enquire about it. It must be one of the more gruesome consequences of growing up.

Diana wore the same white dress in which she had played cricket at the Big House. Rebecca guilelessly asked if it was because it reminded her of Edwin. Diana rather grimly kissed her but didn't answer.

The visitors would come by the resurfaced splendid new road. Cars would be parked in the enlarged courtyard that had been cleared of brambles and briers and paved with flagstones.

More cars could be accommodated in the wood, in grassy spaces between trees. Guests would walk past the gable to the front of the house where they could go in either by the main door or stay out in the garden sipping cold champagne. A barman had been borrowed from the hotel to dispense the drink and the woman who cooked the school lunches was put in charge of the eatables. Against the girls' advice a piper had been hired, to play patriotic and nostalgic tunes.

The first car to arrive was Mr Patterson's. Diana raced to welcome it, pursued by her sisters who were as eager as she was to greet Fiona, though for different reasons. They hadn't made up their minds yet how they should treat her. She had stolen some of Diana's affection but perhaps that wasn't her fault, and wasn't Papa always saying that love had no limits? If he was right there was room in Diana's heart for them and Fiona too, not to mention Edwin Campton. It would depend on whether or not they took to Fiona. Diana's description of her had been very brief and rather snappish: so much so they wondered if Fiona was fat or cross-eyed.

What she was was shy, more so even than Annie McPhee, who had so much better cause. Fiona hung her head, peeped at her toes, blushed, and spoke in babyish whispers. In appearance she was passable though she wore spectacles, and her skirt and blouse were all right if a bit old-fashioned, but it remained a puzzle as to why Diana, fierce as a lioness, should have made this timid doe her friend. Could it be because she knew that Fiona would be easy to boss? Granny Ruthven often referred to her as 'Miss Bossy-boots.'

Meanwhile Mr Patterson was introducing his small stout wife to their tall slender hostess. He had instantly fallen in love again with the delightful lady in the dress with the huge yellow spangles. At some

time that afternoon, he vowed, he must touch that soft delectable body, not in lust but in homage. After a few glasses of this excellent champagne he might well have had the temerity to attempt it, but alas, Bessie who might not have noticed a furtive momentary lovelorn graze of knuckle against thigh or buttock, for she was of the mistaken opinion that erotic passion had long since deserted him, would certainly have noticed any glass he drank beyond the two that she had reluctantly agreed it would be safe for him to drink. Neither she nor Peggy McGibbon could drive. That they would be able because of that deficiency to drink as much as they liked was, she would have said, being a keen bowler, the rub of the green. Indeed she had already finished her first, supplied by Mr Sempill himself, whom, like every other woman present that afternoon, she would have liked to tie a ribbon on and take home with her: a confession she was to make that night while getting ready for bed.

Mrs Patterson, however, like Miss McGibbon and Miss McGill, was not one of those ladies whom their host invited to stroll round the garden with him. This could have been because they were not young and comely enough, but a more honourable reason was that, being disillusioned by age and varicose veins and collapsed stomach muscles, they might have dismissed as nonsense his metaphysical musings on the beauty and magic of the rowan tree.

Unfortunatley the young and comely ladies, including the narcissistic Miss McKay, turned out to be consumed by mundanities, such as what the tartan was in his kilt, how much the restoration of the house cost, and were his wife's pearls genuine.

16

At half-past four Papa addressed his assembled guests. Mama had suggested, backed up by the girls, that he should say something very short like 'Thank you for coming. Enjoy yourselves.' They were afraid that he might give a lecture on what was wrong with the world and how it could be put right. Therefore when, standing on a beer crate, he rang the small bronze bell that one of Granny Ruthven's uncles had brought from a temple in Lhasa, and the guests gathered round him expectantly, Effie, Jeanie, Rowena, and Rebecca rushed upstairs to watch from their playroom window, with their fingers crossed.

They saw Diana lurking behind some rhododendrons with Fiona. She had shocked her sisters by muttering that she hoped Papa didn't make a fool of himself. That was something not even to be thought far less spoken, particularly in the presence of an outsider.

Mama stood beside Papa. The girls never loved her more than when she was giving him support, even though she was wishing he wasn't doing what he was doing.

He raised his hand. The piper, somewhere on the machair, just at the right distance, began playing The Rowan Tree. In spite of seagulls screaming jealously everybody recognised the tune.

'I hope he's not going to ask Mama to sing,' said Effie.

'Maybe he's going to read them a story,' said Rebecca.

Papa often read the girls stories, usually from one of Sir Walter Scott's books.

He rang the bell again and then spoke. 'I asked Mr McLeod to play that tune because, as you all know, it represents for us Scots the sanctities of home or should I say hame? Let me most cordially welcome you to mine and my family's: Poverty Castle. I have been asked several times this afternoon if that is what the house is now to be called. Yes, it is. I have also been asked why. Well, in the first place, that is the name by which it has been known locally for the past thirty years, when it lay in a state of dilapidation. Happily, as you see, it has been restored.'

He turned and looked at the tall white house which gleamed in the sunshine like a lighthouse. His audience looked at it too, to the embarrassment of the girls who hid behind the curtains.

'Some of you have told me it no longer deserves the name Poverty Castle and should revert to its original name Ardmore, which as you know means in Gaelic 'the big field', but such a name though a fine one in itself has merely local connotations,

whereas it seems to me Poverty Castle is a name with national significance. Does it not sum up the situation of Scotland itself, a country in some ways grand and noble but in other ways small-minded and poverty-stricken ?'

The girls saw Mama giving his kilt a tug.

Effie groaned. 'He's giving a speech.'

On the beach John McLeish and some of his friends were skiffing stones along the surface of the water. They had no right to be there for the beach was private but the girls almost wished they were with them. They hated the way some of the men were laughing at Papa.

'In one thing it will always be rich,' cried Papa, 'and that is hospitality. Do not, I beg you, make this your one and only visit. I hope to see you all here many times.'

The girls groaned. Yet, though appalled by the prospect of all those people dropping in whenever they liked, they could not help feeling proud of Papa. No one tried harder than he to like people, whether they deserved to be liked or not.

He continued. 'Some of you have been asking about Ardmore beach, surely the most idyllic and safest on the whole coast. What glorious views of Jura! Look how those white sands shine.'

Everybody turned and looked. The sands indeed were shining, as if Papa's command. The sun at that moment had just come out from behind a cloud. All the same, if anybody deserved to perform a miracle it was Papa.

'According to the title deeds, as Mr Patterson will confirm, the owners or occupiers of Ardmore, now

Poverty Castle, are guaranteed unrestricted use of the beach, though it lies within the grounds of the estate. Are you not all my friends? From today upon every one of you is conferred the freedom of Ardmore beach.'

The girls groaned again. In theory they thought it right and proper that the villagers should be allowed to use the beach, but they were dismayed that a place which they had come to regard as their very own might be frequented by hordes of outsiders. Luckily, something would prevent such an infestation: difficulty of access.

Papa was not finished. 'I know, from painful experience, that it is far from easy to reach the beach, coming through the fields. But have you not come here, along the new road, with ease?'

His audience were very much interested now. Ardmore was a beach that they would certainly wish to visit often, not just because it was idyllic and safe, with glorious views of Jura, but also because from time immemorial it had been forbidden. The question was, did Sempill, the simpleton, have the authority to make the offer?

'That's very kind of you, Mr Sempill,' cried one, 'but what about the estate? What about those notices?'

'Wouldn't Sir Edwin object? cried another.

'Not to mention Lady Campton?' cried a third.

'They might well object,' replied Papa, 'but their objections would go unheeded. If anyone was impertinent enough to try and stop you all you would have to say was that you were visiting your friends, the Sempills of Poverty Castle. I shall myself make the position clear to Sir Edwin. Mr Patterson, would we have the law on our side?'

Nudged by his wife, who was on her fifth glass of champagne, Mr Patterson said that in his opinion Mr Sempill's friends would be legally entitled to use the beach.

'But wouldn't that mean close friends or relatives?' cried a women this time.

'It is for me to say who are my friends,' cried Papa, 'not Sir Edwin Campton and his lawyers.'

They were convinced. They applauded sincerely. Some went forward to shake his hand.

Never had the girls felt fonder and prouder of him, and more exasperated.

The last of the guests did not leave till after seven, when the champagne, coca-cola, beer, and strawberry tarts were finished. There had been damage. Flower beds had been trampled on, flowers wantonly plucked, bunches of berries pulled off the rowan tree. The chains of the swing had been tied in knots. Some child had been sick on the bathroom carpet. Moustaches had been pencilled on many of Rebecca's dolls. Don Quixote's lance had been snapped off. Such mishaps were to be expected, said Papa staunchly: children were by nature boisterous and rough-handed. The girls suffered that insult in silence. Mama, laughing, pulled up her skirt and showed on her left buttock a yellow and purple bruise, the result of a particularly adoring pinch. Would anyone, she cried, like to kiss it better? To the girl's open consternation and secret delight Papa did, kneeling like a knight of old.

It was then that Effie brought up the subject of the

stolen paperweight.

'Oh no !' cried Mama. She had bought it in Venice as a present for Papa, before they were married.

She rushed off to the study and came back with a tragic face.

'It's gone, right enough,' she cried.

'We said it was, Mama,' said Effie.

'It is only a paperweight, darling,' said Papa, 'worth only a few pounds.'

'It is worth a lot more than that. It is a symbol of our love.'

'Here are more precious symbols,' he said, looking at the girls.

'We'll have to get it back,' said Effie, grimly. 'It should be easy because we know who took it.'

'Are you sure it was this boy McLeish?'

'We saw him, Papa. Didn't we, Jeanie ?'

'With our own eyes,' said Jeanie.

'Why didn't you stop him?' asked Rowena.

'We couldn't. He didn't know we were watching.'

'Were you spying on him?' asked Rebecca.

'We were keeping an eye on him, because we didn't trust him.'

'If you don't trust people you help to make them dishonest,' said Diana.

'That's rubbish,' screamed Effie. 'Isn't that rubbish, Papa?'

'It is, Effie my dear, and yet it isn't. Some people will abuse trust, but there are others whom it will redeem.'

'It would be stupid trusting John McLeish. He stole

the paperweight. He whispered 'Tinker trash' to Annie McPhee though he promised Miss McGill he wouldn't.'

'He is evidently a misguided child.'

'He's not a child. He's older than us.'

'He is to be pitied. His parents have not brought him up properly.'

The twins made grimaces of impatience. Papa was always talking about people who, should be pitied. He never talked about people who should be punished.

'I want you to promise,' he said, solemnly, 'never to mention the paperweight to him.'

They were horrified. 'But, Papa, if he gets away with it he'll just steal again. Isn't that right, Mama?'

'I'm afraid it is,' said Mama. 'He seems to be that kind of boy. Perhaps we should ask Miss McGill to deal with it, darling.'

'It did not happen in the school, Meg. It happened here, in our house. We must deal with it ourselves. I say we should simply forget it.'

'That's hardly dealing with it, darling.'

'You're always saying we should tell the truth, Papa,' said Effie.

'So you are, Papa,' said Jeanie. Rowena and Rebecca nodded.

'Sometimes it is wiser to say nothing.'

'Papa is right,' said Mama, with a sigh. 'We are new here. We wish to be on good terms with our neighbours. I believe the McLeish family is well thought of.'

'John isn't,' said Jeanie. 'Nobody likes him.'

'I must say I did not take to him myself,' said Mama. 'But perhaps it is not worth antagonising our neighbours for the sake of a paperweight, even one with sentimental value. I shall buy one to replace it.'

'Blessed are those that forgive,' said Papa.

'If we see him with it,' yelled Effie, indignantly, 'because he's sure to show it off to his friends, are we just to say nothing?'

'Are we to pretend it's not ours, that we've never seen it before?' cried Jeanie.

'Yes, you are to say nothing. Yes, you are to pretend that you never saw it before. The way of the virtuous is never easy.'

Diana then threw a bombshell. 'We shouldn't forget that Rowena took that glass cat from the shop. We wouldn't have liked it if the shopkeeper had come running after us, shouting that she was a thief.'

The twins were outraged by this treachery. 'That was different,' they cried.

Mama turned pale. 'How dare you, Diana?'

Rowena smiled.

'Rowena just pretended to take it,' said Rebecca. 'It was a game.'

'Perhaps John McLeish was playing a game too. Perhaps he intends to give it back. Perhaps he's already given it back.'

'That's rubbish,' cried Effie, in tears of anger.

'He could have left it somewhere in the garden. We haven't looked.'

'We jolly soon will,' yelled Effie.

She and Jeanie rushed off to begin the search. Rowena and Rebecca followed them.

'You should not have said that, about Rowena,' said Mama to Diana. 'You hurt her feelings.'

Diana kept quiet. It amazed her that Mama who loved them and had seen them every day of their lives still did not know them all that well. No doubt it was possible to hurt Rowena's feelings, but Diana had never seen it done.

Scattered about the garden were several naked stone nymphs. In the mossy lap of one of these Jeanie found the paperweight.

17

The distance from Poverty Castle to the primary school was over a mile. The twins would have preferred to cycle but since this was as yet beyond Rebecca's strength they were all taken and brought back by Papa in the car. After losing Diana it was very important for them to keep together.

By November there had been a number of additions to the family: two Labrador puppies,

Wallace and Bruce, five cats, a white rabbit, and a dozen or so tropical fish.

The dogs always went with Papa to fetch the girls. After a day of disconsolate moping, relieved now and then by chasing the kittens and each other, they were into the car before Papa himself, whining with anticipation and barking at him to drive faster. When the girls got in their faces, hands, and knees were immediately beslobbered. Wallace kept up a shrill undulating whine which was his song of welcome, while Bruce, less musical, produced a series of ecstatic yelps.

One dull wet afternoon, when it was already dark by four, Papa said, with a chuckle, above the noises of the dogs: 'Why the gloomy faces?'

'It's always raining,' said Effie. 'It was raining yesterday and the day before.'

'We think we should have gone to Spain to live,' said Rebecca.

'You wouldn't have met Wallace and Bruce then.'

'There are dogs in Spain, aren't there?' said Jeanie.

'But they wouldn't understand English,' said Rowena.

'We would have spoken to them in Spanish,' said Effie.

'Uno, dos, tres.'

'I've forgotten mine,' said Rebecca.

'Cheer up,' said Papa. 'There's a letter for you.'

'For who?' asked Effie.

'For all of you. Addressed to Diana, Effie, Jeanie, Rowena, and Rebecca Sempill.'

'There wouldn't be much room on the envelope,'

said Jeanie.

'It can't be from Granny Ruthven,' said Rowena, 'because she writes to Mama.'

'It's not from Granny,' said Papa, 'unless she's become a pupil at Eton College.'

Even the dogs, it seemed, were surprised. 'We don't know anybody at Eton College,' said Effie.

'Are you sure?'

'How do you know it's from Eton College, Papa?' asked Jeanie. 'Did you open it?'

'Where's Eton College?' asked Rebecca.

'I am not in the habit of opening other people's correspondence. Eton College, my dear, is in Windsor, England.'

'There's a castle at Windsor,' said Rowena. 'A *real* castle.'

'Eton College is the school where the sons of the English aristocracy and renegade Scottish aristocracy too are educated.'

'How do you know it's from Eton College if you didn't open it?' asked Jeanie.

'Because it has the name embossed on the envelope. Are you sure you don't know anybody there?'

They asked Wallace and Bruce to be quiet to let them think. 'You've got short memories,' said Papa. 'What about Edwin, the long-nosed cricketer?'

They did not approve of his joke.

'It's not his fault if his nose is long,' said Rebecca.

'Didn't he tell you he was going to Eton?' They remembered.

'If it's from Edwin,' said Effie, 'it's not for us, it's

for Diana.'

'Why for Diana in particular? It's addressed to you all.'

'He would be too shy to address it just to her,' said Jeanie.

'He's in love with Diana,' said Rowena.

'And Diana's in love with him,' said Rebecca, so seriously that they all, including the dogs, laughed.

'I wasn't aware of this great romance,' said Papa. 'I don't think Mama is either.'

'I suppose it's a secret,' said Effie.

'We shouldn't have told you, Papa,' said Jeanie.

'Don't worry. I can keep a secret. Am I to let Mama know?'

'Yes, but she's not to tease Diana,' said Effie.

'Edwin didn't want to go to Eton,' said Rebecca.

The envelope was on the silver salver in the hall, with petals from a bowl of chrysanthemums fallen on it. Still with their raincoats and Wellingtons on they took it into the living-room to examine it. The words Eton College were embossed in white letters.

'Do you think he's sent his photograph?' asked Effie, feeling for it.

'No.' Jeanie was positive. 'If he was good-looking he would have sent it, but he isn't.'

'He's got nice eyes,' said Rebecca.

'You can't see a person's eyes in a photograph.'

'I think we should open it,' said Effie. 'We've got a right. It's addressed to us.'

'It's addressed to us all,' said Jeanie. 'We should wait till we're all here.'

'There are four of us. Diana's only one. I vote we

open it.'

'I vote we don't,' said Jeanie.

Both Rowena and Rebecca sided with her.

'I don't want to read it anyway,' said Effie. 'He's just written because he's sorry for himself.'

'Poor Edwin,' said Rebecca.

'I couldn't fall in love with somebody who was sorry for himself,' said Effie, disdainfully.

She had often told them about the kind of man she was going to marry. He would be as daring as young Lochinvar, as fierce as Rob Roy, and as handsome as Bonnie Dundee.

Though it was still raining and pitch dark at ten to five the twins, in spite of their parents' demurs, set off on foot for Poverty gate, carrying torches, to meet Diana and escort her home. Wallace and Bruce wanted to go with them but weren't allowed: if they were put on leads they pulled the girls off their feet and if they weren't put on leads they wandered into the woods and got lost.

Diana had firmly requested Papa never to come for her in the car. 'Never?' her sisters had teased. 'Not even if there's snow up to your knees? Not even if there's a storm?' But they had known why she wanted to walk. She was always putting herself to tests. She was really scared of the sea, so she swam out furthest. She didn't like heights, so she climbed the highest. In her sisters' eyes she was a heroine. Like Diana Vernon, after whom she was named. Or Kate Barlass. As long as it wasn't Proud Maisie. That was her favourite poem and she could recite it in such a way as to make them all shiver, especially the lines:

"When six braw gentlemen
kirkward shall carry you."

The bus was late. The twins waited at the gate,
listening to the rain pattering on their hats and on
the trees. It was a point of honour to shine their
torches as seldom as possible and then only for
seconds. This wasn't to save the batteries but to test
their own nerves. They pretended that they were the
only persons left alive in the whole world; no, the
only living creatures, for all birds and animals had
perished too. There had been an atomic war. Their
plight was infinitely more sad than Sir Bedivere's, for
though King Arthur and all the knights had been
slain there must have been peasants working in the
fields to whom he could have spoken; whereas they,
if they walked all the way to John O'Groats, would
meet no one at all, at any rate no one alive.

Therefore an immense load of sadness and terror
was lifted off their minds when they heard the bus
in the distance and then saw its lights. It stopped at
the gate. They could not see who were in it for the
windows were misted. Since the door was at the
other side they did not see Diana coming off. Then
the bus moved on and there she was, crossing the
road.

She flashed her torch and greeted them coolly:
'What are you two drookit creatures doing here? Do
your parents know you're out?'

They tried to be cool too. 'We just thought we'd
take a walk before tea.'

None of them was deceived. They knew that they
were experiencing a happiness in one another's
company that words could not describe.

144

Effie insisted on carrying Diana's case, though 'it weighed a ton.' Jeanie said she'd take it at the dead tree.

This was a very high ash like a gigantic skeleton, with its branches white as bones. Sometimes one would fall off.

'Well, what is it?' asked Diana.

'What do you mean?' asked Jeanie.

'Something's happened.'

'We've said nothing,' panted Effie.

'I can tell by the way you're breathing. Has Annie the tinker girl come back?'

'No.'

'Did one of the cats catch a bird?'

'No.'

'Were deer in the garden again?'

'No.'

'Have we got a visitor?'

'No.'

'All right. I give up. What is it?'

'We haven't said it's anything,' said Jeanie.

'But it is. So you might as well tell me.'

'Should we, Effie?'

'We'd better, for she'd never guess in a hundred years.'

'We'll give her a hint first. It's a letter.'

'Addressed to Diana, Effie, Jeanie, Rowena, and Rebecca Sempill.'

'Good heavens. It would have been simpler just to say The Misses Sempill.'

'Never mind that,' said Effie, impatiently. 'Guess

who from?'

'Some girl we knew in Edinburgh?'

'No.' Effie couldn't help giggling.

'It's from Edwin,' cried Jeanie.

'Edwin? Who's Edwin?'

They had known she wouldn't show astonishment or joy, though she would feel them, but they hadn't expected her to be quite so calm and casual.

'You know fine who he is,' said Effie. 'Edwin Campton. He's at Eton College.'

'Is he? Imagine that. What's he writing to us for? What does he want?'

'We don't know that yet,' said Jeanie. 'We haven't opened it. We voted to wait till you came.'

'That was very noble, considering how you must have been bursting with impatience.'

'We think it's really for you though it's addressed to us all.'

They had come to the dead tree. Usually ghosts and bogles haunted it, even in sunlight, but not on this dark wet night: the girls were too absorbed in their own affairs. Jeanie took the case and groaned at its weight.

'Why should you think it's for me?' asked Diana.

'You know why,' said Effie.

'I do not.'

'Because he's in love with you, that's why, and he's not in love with us.'

'And you're in love with him,' added Jeanie.

'What a pair of romantic little idiots you are.'

'She's just pretending,' said Effie. 'That's what people in love do in stories. Isn't it Jeanie?'

'Yes, they're in love but they pretend they're not.'

'When did you two start reading love stories?' said Diana.

'Years ago.'

'Well, you're forgetting something.'

'What's that?'

'I'm not in a story. I'm real.'

Keeping up her pretence of indifference Diana merely glanced at the envelope when it was handed to her by Rebecca. If they didn't mind, she said, with a little yawn, she would read it after tea: *they* were at liberty to read it anytime they liked. Dourly they contained themselves till the meal was over. Then, adding to their exasperation, she said that she had a lot of homework to do and ought to do it first, since it was more important. In any case she shouldn't be wasting time over a letter from a boy she hardly knew.

That settled it as far as her sisters were concerned. They rushed to the playroom where without any more palaver Effie tore open the envelope and took out two sheets of notepaper. She looked again to make sure there was no photograph.

'It's an awful scribble,' she said, 'and he can't spell.'

They knew she was making poor Edwin suffer for Diana's perverseness.

'Read it to us,' said Rebecca, 'and don't make it sound silly.'

'If it is silly I'll have to make it sound silly, won't I?'

'Let me read it,' said Rowena.

They were against that. She would imitate Edwin's

voice and make them all laugh, which wouldn't be fair.

Effie began, in a flat voice: 'Dear Girls –'

'You're going to make it sound silly,' objected Rebecca.

Effie's voice became much livelier. 'Dear Girls, I am sorry we did not meet again after the cricket match. That was the best day of my hols in Scotland. I did not enjoy the grouse shooting because you told me it was cruel to kill birds for sport.'

'I told him that,' said Jeanie.

'When I saw them dead and their feathers covered with blood I made a vow never to go shooting again. I didn't shoot but being there was just as bad.'

'I don't think being there was just as bad,' said Rowena. 'Anyway, birds kill other birds, don't they. Hawks kill sparrows.'

'They don't know any better,' said Jeanie.

Effie continued. 'The boys here call me Snozzle because of my big nose. Maybe it's a punishment that I deserve. I don't like it here. If I was good at some game like football or cricket it would be different but I'm not. As you know I can't play for toffee.'

'It was me said that,' said Effie.

'I wish we lived in Scotland all the time and I went to school there. Have you got all the pets you said you were going to have when you moved into Poverty Castle? One of the boys asked me who I was writing to. I said friends. He asked where they lived. I said in the Highlands of Scotland in a house called Poverty Castle. He was impressed. It is a smashing name for a house. I didn't tell him you were girls. I've got a pet mouse. Sorry I can't tell you what I call her. Give my regards to your Mama and Papa. My mouse sends hers too.'

'It's a very nice letter,' said Rebecca, after a pause.

'It's not bad,' said Jeanie, 'but he's nearly thirteen.'·

'His writing's a scribble,' said Effie. 'Miss McGill would have made him do it over again.'

'I wonder what he calls his mouse?' asked Rowena.

'That's easy,' said Effie. 'It's a she. So he calls her Diana or maybe just Di. If it had been some other name he wouldn't have been too shy to tell us what it is, would he?'

'It's not fair them calling him Snozzle,' said Rebecca. 'He can't help it if his nose is big.'

'Well, are we going to answer it?' asked Effie.

'I can't,' said Rebecca, 'because I can't write yet.'

'You could tell us what to say and we could write it down for you,' asked Jeanie.

'It wouldn't be private then.'

They laughed. 'What would you want to say to him that has to be private?' asked Jeanie.

'That's private too.'

They laughed again and hugged her. They felt sorry for Edwin for not having a wee sister like her, and having instead a brother like awful Nigel.

'He's not happy,' said Jeanie, 'so maybe we should write and cheer him up.'

'Let's go and see what Diana thinks,' said Effie.

After what they considered a reasonable interval — it was about twenty minutes — they went to Diana's room. Effie put her head in. 'Finished your home-work yet?'

'I've hardly started.'

'Oh. Well, we've read the letter and we want you to read it and tell us what you think.'

'Good heavens, what's the hurry?'

'You're being very aggravating, Diana Sempill.'

Behind her the others made noises of agreement. 'We think he wants us to write to him. We don't know if we should.'

'There's no law against it.'

'We know that. We want your advice. He's got a pet white mouse. We think he calls it Diana or Di, after you.'

'Thanks very much. I've always wanted to have a white mouse called after me.'

'He doesn't say what its name is. We think he was too shy.'

'Oh, come in, all of you. I can see I'll get no peace until I've read this wretched letter.'

They hurried in and sat on chair or bed or floor. They hadn't expected her to shed tears of joy but her impassiveness vexed and disappointed them.

'Well?' asked Jeanie.

'Well what?'

'What do you think? Should we write and cheer him up?'

'It's considered impolite not to answer a letter.'

'What will we say?' asked Effie.

'I'm sure you'll think of something.'

'I'll tell him about Dominie Sampson,' said Rebecca. That was her white rabbit. She herself had given him the name. Her sisters didn't think it suited him at all.

'Should we write one letter, signed by us all?'

asked Jeanie. 'Or should each of us write one of our own?'

'Please yourselves,' said Diana.

'I think each of us should write one of our own,' said Effie.

Her three sisters agreed. Diana was pretending to be back at her homework.

'Will we let each other see what we've written?' asked Jeanie.

'I don't mind anybody seeing mine,' said Effie.

'Letters are supposed to be private,' remarked Diana.

'I vote we show what we've written,' said Effie. She put up her hand. Jeanie and Rowena put up theirs.

'You can't take a vote on a thing like that,' said Diana.

'Why not?' said Effie. 'That's democracy, isn't it?'

'If one of us wants her letter to be private she's got a right.'

'She wants to write a love letter,' said Effie.

'As a matter of fact I might not bother to write at all. But you'll have to get it into your heads that you can't take a vote on everything.'

'We've always done it before,' said Jeanie.

'We were all children then.'

It was another indication that Diana had left them and gone over to the grown-ups.

18

Rebecca's letter, with Diana her patient amanuensis, took a long time.

Dear Edwin,

I am glad you have a pet mouse. I would like to tell you about my pet rabbit. His name is Dominie Sampson.

Dominie Sampson is a schoolmaster in one of Sir Walter Scott's books which Papa read to us once. Dominie Sampson in the story is skinny but my rabbit is fat. He is poor looking but my rabbit has got a rich white fur. He is always saying 'Prodigious', but my rabbit never says a word. So my sisters say it is not a suitable name. But when Papa was reading about Dominie Sampson I had a picture of him as very sad, Dominie Sampson I mean not Papa, and my rabbit has very sad eyes. That's all.
Goodbye,

She signed it herself, a large painstaking scrawl: *Rebecca Sempill.*

Rowena wrote hers herself and refused to let anyone correct the spelling or punctuation, as it would be cheating.

Dear Edwin

I am sorry you do not like school I like mine all right except that Miss McGill is always saying Im daydreaming. Papa says I can have a peacock next summer Jeanie wants to be a vegytarian She says its crool to look after animals and then eat them Effie thinks Diana has become too grown-up. I wish I was grown-up being a childs not fair.

Yours truely
Rowena Sempill, aged 7 ³/₄

After much chewing of her pen Effie decided to concentrate on giving advice on how to succeed at cricket.

Dear Edwin,

Do you remember me telling you when we played cricket to keep your eye on the ball, you never did and so you always missed or nearly always. Maybe you need spectacles. Are you frightened that the boys at your school would call you Specky but they couldn't for they already call you Snozzle. Thats why Diana is good at cricket, she always keeps her eye on the ball. Shes good also at croquet, tennis, rounders, and badminton because she keeps her eye on the ball except that at badminton its the shuttle she keeps her eye on.

Trying to help
yours faithfully
Effie Sempill

Jeanie was a great reader of school stories. This had an effect on her letter.

Dear Edwin,

Papa says that at your school you are made to wear an old-fashioned uniform with a funny collar that must hurt your neck Well at St Asaph's, a girls school I was reading about they had an old-fashioned uniform too with skirts down to their ankles nearly Well Hilary and her chums led a strike until the headmistress gave in and changed their uniform to a more sensible modern one. You could start a strike at Eton It would help to take your mind off all your other troubles like you being called Snozzle and not being able to play cricket for toffee. It was me said that and I'm sorry even if it is true. If you come to Scotland next summer we'll be glad to see you. Nigel too, I expect. Give your mouse a pat on the head for me. Effie thinks its name is Diana.

Best wishes

Jeanie Sempill

Diana's was brisk and informative.

Dear Edwin,

Thank you for your letter. It was kind of you to send it. We have now moved into Poverty Castle and are very comfortable. We have two Labrador puppies, called Wallace and Bruce, one black and the other golden. Rebecca has a white rabbit. Effie and Jeanie would like hamsters but Mama says they make her shiver. Rowena wants a peacock. Papa says she can have one next summer. Wild rabbits come out of the wood and play on our lawn.

I am at Tarbeg High School, in class 1B. My subjects are English, History, Maths, Science, and French. Spanish is not taught in the school. When I have finished school I am going to University. I go by bus and come back by bus.

Sometimes when we are out walking we see your house in the distance. It looks very lonely.

The tinkers are still camped by the roadside. Shona Campbell of the shop is at Glasgow University.

Yours sincerely   Diana Sempill

In the end they realised that they would rather not read one another's letters. This wasn't just for Diana's sake but for all their sakes. They had not realised how revealing it was to put yourself on paper. Even sisters who loved you could not be trusted to understand exactly what you meant. They might think you were showing off.

The letters were put into one envelope, which was posted by Diana in Tarbeg.

Six days later came a reply, addressed to Diana only. They were all mentioned in it, she said, and offered to read it to them. They declined, with dignity. Speaking for them all, Effie said that they had known from the beginning that he hadn't really wanted to write to them but felt he had to, out of politeness. Well, he needn't have bothered. If he thought they liked writing letters to him he was mistaken. They had lots of more interesting things to do.

So Diana was the only one who wrote to him from then on.

19

There came a time when Mama's prolonged disappointment at not having conceived a male child began to effect her health and her mind. She grew quite gaunt and her dwams lasted for hours instead of minutes. She became bad-tempered, even with Rebecca, then 11, but especially with Papa, at whom, suddenly, for no reason, she would shout incoherent accusations.

At first it seemed to the girls that the death of Granny Ruthven a few months previously might be the cause, but they could not see why she should blame poor Papa for that. He had taken them all to Edinburgh for the funeral.

One evening he stealthily invited Diana, then 17, and the twins who were 15 , to his study. Rowena and Rebecca, he muttered, were too young to hear what he had to say.

As usual he had drunk more wine than he should. Now that they were no longer children the evening meal was dinner instead of high tea. This suited Papa's wine-drinking. Potato scones and wine had never gone well together.

'I want to talk to you about your mother,' he said, hoarsely, as if he'd been crying. 'She has been acting very strangely of late.'

'We've noticed, Papa,' said Effie.

'She's not got cancer, has she?' asked Jeanie, in a terrified whisper.

'It's nothing like that, thank God.'

'Do you know the reason, Papa?' asked Diana, sternly. She did not have as much patience as her sisters with his vinous ramblings.

He stared at the paperweight made famous by John McLeish. 'You've heard your mother express a wish for a baby boy?'

'Hundreds of times,' said Effie.

'It has become an obsession that could, I'm afraid, destroy her reason. She has got it into her head that she has let me down. I have assured her that it is not so. How could I, with five beautiful and talented daughters, feel ill-done by? Few fathers are as fortunate as I. Alas, she has continued to have this delusion that my life has been blighted.'

Something had, if not blighted his life, at any rate kept it from blooming. They did not think that it was the want of a son.

He had tears in his eyes. Excessive wine did that to him but to be fair so did affection. 'I love you all,' he said.

'She's not too old to have a child, is she?' asked Effie. 'She's only forty-four. Lots of women have children at that age, don't they?'

Papa moaned, as if in pain.

'Aren't there fertility pills she could take?' asked Jeanie.

'Don't be ridiculous, Jeanie,' said Diana. 'If Mama took those she could have five at a time, like a cat.'

'And we couldn't give four away and just keep one,' said Effie.

'It's not a joke, Effie,' said Diana.

'I'm not laughing, am I?'

'According to three doctors who have been consulted,' said Papa, 'having only one child could kill your mother. She had a difficult time with Rebecca.'

They remembered.

'If she wants a boy so much why doesn't she

adopt one?' asked Jeanie.

'The child has to be mine.' Papa closed his eyes. 'You're not children any longer, you are young women. You know what causes pregnancy and what can prevent it. Your mother would never allow it to be prevented. So, in the light of the doctors' advice I had no alternative but to, in a sense, live apart from her. She has never forgiven me.'

'Oh!' That was Effie's exclamation but it also expressed her sisters' reaction. They wondered, six years ago, why, on moving into Poverty Castle, Papa had insisted on having a bedroom of his own.

Papa opened his eyes and looked at them. 'I need your help in getting your mother to accept the situation. It has not been your fault, as you've inevitably looked outwards more and more, but your mother feels you have neglected her, all of you but Rebecca.'

They nodded. Comparing their own attitude to Mama with their youngest sister's they had to admit that they had neglected her or at least had let their love for her to be taken for granted.

'It has been our fault,' said Effie. 'We've been selfish.'

'Is it really out of the question her having a baby?' asked Jeanie. 'The doctors could be wrong. She'd be so happy. I mean. wouldn't it be worth the risk?'

'No, it wouldn't,' said Diana, sharply. 'Papa's right. We must help Mama get over this crisis. She'll become reconciled once she's past child-bearing age.'

'That's what Dr Grant thinks,' said Papa.

During the weeks that followed, though they all lavished their love on Mama she got worse. She took to carrying about one of Rebecca's dolls and calling it Roderick. They wondered if she was aware that it was a doll and was being provocative, in a not very sane way; or if she really believed it was a live baby, in which case she was dangerously deranged. Then one day the doll disappeared. It was not returned to Rebecca's collection but at any rate Mama no longer nursed it. They were all relieved. Until one evening she rushed into the living-room, screaming that they had killed her baby.

Papa tried to comfort her and got his face pummelled.

Rebecca ran upstairs for Diana.

Diana quickly came, taller than her mother, and put her arms round her tenderly but firmly. Her voice that could be so sharp was soft and persuasive. Mama soon grew quiet and let Diana take her up to her room.

None of them said anything till Diana returned half an hour later. Mama had taken a pill and was asleep.

Late that night Diana went to the twins' room. They were in bed. Effie switched on a bed-lamp. 'What's wrong,' she asked. 'Is it Mama?'

Diana sat on Effie's bed. 'Not so loud. We don't want to waken the others. Yes, it's Mama. I know what's the matter with her. She told me.'

'But I thought we knew what was the matter with her?' said Jeanie.

'Yes, but there's something else. She thinks Papa has been unfaithful to her for years.'

'You mean, has had other women?' asked Effie, incredulously.

'Yes, though that's rather a crude way of putting it. She says that when he goes into Tarbeg for his Arts Club meetings and stays so late he's seeing another woman.'

What had worried them about Papa's belated returns from Tarbeg was the likelihood of his being stopped by the police and breathalysed or his landing upside down in the loch. They had certainly never suspected illicit amours.

'I don't believe it,' said Effie.

'I don't believe it either,' said Jeanie, 'but if it was true could the other woman be Mrs Grierson? She's got a reputation, hasn't she?'

Mrs Grierson owned a small art gallery in Tarbeg. She was a painter whose pictures were bold and gaudy like herself. Papa had bought two. They were hanging in his study.

'What could Papa see in her?' asked Effie.

Mrs Grierson was small and squat, so unlike their tall and graceful mother.

'Do *you* believe it, Diana?' asked Effie.

'Mama believes it, that's what matters,' replied Diana.

'What are we going to do?' asked Jeanie. 'We can't very well tell Papa.'

'We'll have to,' said Diana, grimly.

Effie groaned. 'Yes, we'll have to.'

'What if it's true?' asked Jeanie. 'He might say it's none of our business.'

'Mama's health *is* our business,' said Diana. She stood up. 'He's in his study. Let's go and talk to him.'

'Shouldn't we wait till tomorrow?' asked Jeanie.

'The sooner the better.'

'Yes, but at this time of night, it must be nearly mid-night, everything always seems worse than it is.'

'Are you coming?'

Sighing, they got out of their beds and put on dressing-gowns and slippers.

Wallace, the golden-haired Labrador, came yawning out of the living-room when he heard them coming down the stairs. He had never recovered from Bruce's death, from poisoning, two years ago. They patted his head and he went back to the living-room carpet where he had chosen to sleep. He no longer sought company.

Papa was seated at his desk. In front of him was one of his aborted manuscripts.

The girls realised then as never before how lonely he looked and must feel. Yet for them the house had always been crowded and busy, with footsteps and shouts and laughter and banging doors and loud music and barking dogs and mewing cats.

He looked up and smiled. 'Another meeting of the conspirators?'

They sat down. Books and prints had to be lifted off chairs. Two of the paintings on the walls were by Mrs Grierson. They were of fishing boats in Tarbeg harbour.

The twins were glad to leave the talking to Diana. She would shirk nothing. It was no wonder that Edwin's parents were inclined to look on her as a suitable wife for him. He was too shy, too timid, and too nice for the position he would have to occupy one day. He would need someone like Diana to make him live up to his responsibilities.

'Last night, Papa, when I took her up to her room Mama said something that we think you should be told.'

He looked anxious, but, thought the twins, in the way a husband should whose wife was ill.

'She thinks you are having an affair with another woman.' How like Diana, they thought. No easing off the elastoplast bit by bit, but altogether, in one quick cruel-to-be-kind movement.

Papa frowned, not taking it in.

'She thinks that when you return home late from Tarbeg you have been with this woman.'

'Poor Meg. Is that what she told you?'

'Yes.'

'What woman?'

'She doesn't know.'

'That's not surprising, considering that she doesn't exist. I may have been unfaithful, to your mother, to you and to myself many times, but never in that way.'

The twins looked at each other. Here was a hint of a life that had gone on in his mind, in their midst, and yet remote from them.

He misread their dismay. 'You don't believe me?'

'Yes, Papa, of course we believe you,' said Diana.

'She never will. Even if I went down on my knees and swore it. If we were believers I could swear it on the Bible. Not that everything sworn on the Bible is necessarily true.'

'There's something you could do, Papa, that might convince her.'

The twins stared at Diana in astonishment. They had no idea what she was going to say.

'Share the same room with her again. Sleep with her.'

Here, thought the twins, is the future lady of the manor in action. They had heard that patrician note in her voice before. They had been its victims then, now it was Papa's turn.

'But, Diana,' he said, with remarkable meekness, 'I have explained why I cannot do that.'

The twins held their breath. What in heaven's name would Diana say next?

They could never in a lifetime have guessed. Indeed, many times afterwards they were to talk about it, with awe.

'Isn't there an operation you could have, Papa, which would prevent pregnancy, without Mama knowing?'

Papa was not as shocked as the twins. 'I've thought of that, but would it not be the most despicable of deceptions?'

'What would that matter, if Mama was happy again?'

Papa covered his face with his hands. Was it to hide tears or a smile or both?

'I think you should go to bed now, girls. Good-night.'

Effie and Jeanie grabbed hold of Diana and took her with them. 'Good-night, Papa.'

Outside the room Diana was angry with them. 'Do you think I don't love him too? And honour him? I had to say what I did.'

'All right,' said Effie. 'You had to say it and you said it. Let's go to bed.'

When they were back in their room the twins were silent until they were in their beds and the light was out.

'What's going to happen now, do you think?' asked Jeanie.

'He'll have the operation but he won't tell us. He'll tell nobody. To save us from being part of the 'despicable deception.''

'Yes, I think you're right. Poor Papa. Good-night.'

'Good-night.'

A minute later Effie said: 'You know, if Diana wasn't my sister I could hate her.'

'That's a terrible thing to say.'

'So it is. I'm sorry.'

The novelist's wife writing to her daughter: 'Your father still goes for his daily walk, or stagger I should say, rain or shine. Yesterday young Willie McDonald, the son of the farmer who's our nearest neighbour, brought him home in his trailer, on top of empty fertiliser bags. He'd found him collapsed on a bank. 'Among foxgloves and campion' your father had the nerve to say when he had got his breath back. Talking of flowers, his face was as white as daises and his lips blue as scabious. What amazes me is where he finds the mental energy to keep working at his novel and put life into his characters, most of whom are lively young girls. It's mean of me but I refuse to praise it. In fact I tell lies and say that it's not very interesting and the characters aren't convincing. I do it for his sake. If he keeps on the way he's doing, hours and hours on end, sometimes till well after midnight, he'll kill himself, nothing's surer. He's desperate to get it finished. He doesn't want to leave his characters lost in limbo, he says. As if they existed! I have to admit though that I sometimes find myself wondering what's going to happen to them, because to tell the truth I seem to know them, better than I do Mrs McDonald for instance, the farmer's wife, though her house is only three minutes' walk from mine. The annoying thing is that if I ask what's going to happen to them he still insists that he doesn't know.

Behind his back I telephoned the doctor who said that I shouldn't worry about him working so hard, it was probably that which was giving him the will to live. The dangerous time would be when the book was finished. That would be all right, I thought with a bitterness I was ashamed of afterwards, he wouldn't mind dying then, even if it meant leaving me in limbo.

He wants to pay a visit to Kilmory, the village where he was born. In his book he calls it Kilcalmonell. I suppose I would enjoy a short break, though for him it would be work, connected with his book. God forgive me, Jessie, I have this grievance against him and yet what existence could be more harmless than his, sitting at a desk for hours and then going for a walk among cows and sheep and then back to the desk again?'

Part Two

PART TWO

One evening in May, in Mrs Brownlee's boarding-house for women students, not far from Glasgow University, word spread that room-mates Diana and Peggy were having another of their disagreements. It was worth leaving off washing one's hair or telephoning one's boyfriend to go and listen, not so much because of what they would say but because of who they were.

Diana Sempill, aged twenty, came from Kilcalmonell in the West Highlands, where she lived in a fourteen-roomed house quaintly called Poverty Castle, with her father, a well-to-do retired architect, her mother, and her four younger sisters, two of whom were twins. Judging by the photographs in her room they were all, like Diana herself, not only good-looking but superior-looking too. She was tall, with a fine figure, held herself straight, and had dark hair, though all the others in her family were blond. She had recently become engaged to the son and heir of a wealthy English baronet. Her accent was a marvel, in that it would not be out of place among her fiancé's relatives and friends and yet in a Glasgow bus, where affectation was instantly detected and abhorred, it would draw smiles of appreciation and goodwill. Everyone, including herself, expected her to take a first-class honours degree in political economy, which was the rather surprising subject she had chosen to specialise in. No one could have been less of a socialist, and yet, on behalf of the poor, she was more passionate than Peggy, who always stayed cool. Some of the girls in the boarding-house had at first resented her coming among them. Unlike them she could easily have afforded more comfortable and commodious lodgings. But she seemed content to live as frugally as they, except that her clothes, though never showy, were always of the best quality: no bargain basement acrylics for her, but lambswool and cashmere.

Peggy Gilchrist, also twenty, came from Carron where she lived in a council flat with her father, an unemployed labourer, and her mother, who worked in a supermarket. She had a married brother who drove a coal lorry. She was small, thin, and flat-chested, and walked with a swagger, caused, she said, not by gallousness but loose bones. Her hair was the colour and texture of mouldy hay; her own description. She had dingy teeth and wore spectacles. She had no boyfriend, which surprised no one. She wore cheap clothes, from necessity, but did not make a virtue of it: she would have preferred better ones. In any case she would rather spend what money she had on books. As befitted an honours student she spoke articulately and grammatically but made no attempt to modify her working-class accent. It disconcerted many that so common-looking and common-sounding a girl should have such a quick sharp clear mind. Her specialist subject, history, was as unexpected as Diana's. Her interest, however, was not in the achievements of kings and queens but of the working-class. She would say, with an irony so subtle that most people were deceived by it, that Sir Christopher Wren did not build St Paul's Cathedral single-handed, he had needed the help of hundreds of unknown masons, joiners and plasterers. Nor had the Duke of Marlborough won his famous battles by himself: many thousands of nameless, ill-recompensed, and frequently maimed soldiers had assisted. Would she, her fellow students wondered, with some malice, remain faithful to her class and marry some plumber or mechanic when she had got her degree, or would she marry some other brainy deserter from the working-class, with a doctorate perhaps, and have children who would attend private schools and be ashamed of their check-out grannie?

It was not an accident that she and Diana were room-mates.

When she had first appeared at the boarding-house, Diana — though she was never to know this — had almost been turned away by Mrs Brownlee, who had seen from one glance at the expensive leather suitcase and another at the similarly up-market face, that Miss Sempill was quite unlike Mrs Brownlee's usual boarders, the impecunious daughters of teachers and shopkeepers, and therefore might not fit in. On the other hand she would show an example to those of the girls who got up to lower-class tricks like smuggling young men into their rooms or wandering about with next to nothing on. So Mrs Brownlee, crushing her qualms, had said all right, expecting her new boarder to ask for a room of her own, which she could certainly afford; but no, Miss Sempill had wanted to share, and when she had heard about Peggy Gilchrist, whom none of the other girls were keen to have as a room-mate, not because she smelled or anything like that but because she was always studying and needed silence, she had at once said she would be pleased to share a room with her. Whatever her motives were Mrs Brownlee had no idea, but it made no difference, for one thing was certain, Miss Sempill would never be able to patronise Peggy.

It had not been necessary to consult Peggy, who after all was not paying the rate for a room of her own.

At first the two girls had been polite but cautious, Diana because this rather uncouth but very clever girl was the first member of the industrial poor that she had ever been close to, and Peggy because it would have been foolish and unfair to blame this beautiful, well-off, fortunate girl for all the injustices heaped on the poor throughout the centuries.

They soon came to respect each other. Peggy had no difficulty in establishing herself as Diana's equal, in spite of the manifest inferiority of all her possessions, from underclothes to rings, while Diana admired her room-mate's determination not to be looked down upon simply because she had had the misfortune to have been born into a class lacking culture, education, and money.

Sometimes, though, in public they disagreed, to the amusement of the other girls.

What sparked off the latest encounter was an item on the Scottish television news. It showed a princess opening the wing of a hospital in Glasgow. A number of girls were watching them, among them Peggy and Diana. Peggy's anti-royalist views were known. It was inevitable that she would be baited.

'Isn't she beautiful, Peggy?'

'Her clothes are anyway.'

'We're lucky to have such a hard-working royal family.'

'I doubt if she would change places with a miner, who works a lot harder for a lot less money.'

'My father says they're worth every penny. A president would cost a great deal more.'

'We wouldn't have to pay his aunties and uncles too.'

Nun-like in her dark-blue dress Diana winced at these heresies, but she kept quiet.

'The royal family unites the country, Peggy. You can't deny that.'

'They symbolise class. What's more divisive than class?'

'It's just communists and people like that who want to fight the class war.'

'The upper-classes occupy all the citadels of power and wealth. The walls are centuries thick. A few revolutionaries beat their fists against them. That's the class war.'

'You're a little commie youself, Peggy.'

'I'm a republican, like William Hazlitt.'

They had never heard of William Hazlitt, but, since after all they were University students, they did not want to betray their ignorance. They looked to Diana to rescue them. 'What do you think, Diana?'

She smiled, 'Society is unjust in many ways. We all know that.'

'We do little about it,' said Peggy.

'Be fair, Peggy. Surely as a student of history you must agree that there has been a great improvement in the way that society treats its less fortunate members.'

'I was reading in the *Guardian* the other day that the gap between rich and poor in Britain is growing greater, not less.'

'Oh, the *Guardian* .' That was a general groan. Peggy was too fond of quoting that newspaper, which most of them found boring, with its long paragraphs.

Diana then expounded her creed. They had heard it before but were still fascinated.

In spite of their shortcomings it had been the nobility of Scotland who had given the country whatever distinction it had. What were the most famous names in Scottish history? Robert the Bruce. The Marquis of Montrose. Mary Queen of Scots. Prince Charles Edward Stuart. All aristocrats. People from overseas came to visit the castles and palaces. They thought of Scotland as a land of romantic and splendid causes. It was the nobility of the past who deserved most of the credit.

Some of the girls, though on Diana's side, were vaguely aware that hers was a somewhat naive view, which anyone with a knowledge of Scottish history could easily make fun of. They waited anxiously for Peggy to do it.

Just then a girl looked in and said that Diana was wanted on the telephone. 'Your sister Effie. Said it was urgent.'

'Excuse me, please.' Diana rose, gave them all but particularly Peggy a regal smile, and left. Even when she hurried she had elegance.

'She's like a princess herself,' said one of the girls.

'One day we'll all be proud to have known her,' said another. 'You too, Peggy.'

Peggy said nothing. By saying nothing she often said a great deal.

'Effie's one of the twins, isn't she?'

Peggy nodded.

'I hope it's not bad news. I don't think her mother keeps well. Isn't that so, Peggy?'

That was a curious and provoking thing. Peggy knew more than any of them about the Sempills. It was true that she was Diana's room-mate, but it was strange that Diana should have confided in someone who opposed most of which she and her family represented.

As they stared at scruffy wee Peggy and compared her with tall genteel Diana they felt sure that even if she got the better of the historical argument most people, including the working-class themselves, would side with Diana.

2

As she ran downstairs to the telephone in the hall Diana recalled the twins urging of her to invite Peggy Gilchrist to Poverty Castle. They had been intrigued by what she had told them of her proletarian room-mate. Diana herself was doubtful, not because she did not want Peggy to come but because it might look like an attempt to win her over, corrupt her, Peggy might say, with one of her ironical smiles.

She picked up the telephone. 'Hello. Diana here.'

It was Effie. 'Oh, thank goodness, Di.'

Diana smiled. Trust Effie to be dramatic. Rowena wasn't the only actress in the family.

'The world's fallen in on top of us, Di. The luck of the Sempills has ended. Isn't that so, Jeanie?'

Jeanie's voice was calmer, but did it tremble a little? 'It's not as bad as that. Not yet anyway.'

'What's the matter?'

It was Effie again. 'You've got to come home this weekend, Di. You must.'

'But the exams are next week.'

'Bugger the exams. We need you here. Don't we, Jeanie?'

'Yes, Di, we do,' said Jeanie. 'Please come if you

can possibly manage it.'

'You haven't told me yet what's wrong?'

'Mama's pregnant.'

Diana's own breathing stopped. 'She can't be,' she said at last.

'She oughtn't to be, you mean, but she is. Nearly three months.'

But, thought Diana, hadn't Papa taken her advice and had that operation, three years ago? He had slept with Mama ever since. Mama had been happy and hopeful again.

'I know what you're thinking,' said Effie. 'That operation should have prevented it. But, according to Dr Grant, there's a million to one chance that the bits that were cut can come together again of their own accord. Nature striking back, you might say. Mama's kept it a secret until now. I don't think she could believe it herself.'

'How is she?'

'Overjoyed. Transfigured. Exalted. The happiest woman in the world. It would make you weep to see her. It would also make you laugh, because she is so outrageously happy.'

'But how is she physically?'

'That's the big question, Di. Dr Grant was blunt with Papa. He said that having the child could kill her.'

'Was he as definite as that?'

'Yes, but he's bringing a specialist from Glasgow to see her next Wednesday. She says herself she feels great, and Di, she looks it. Colour in her cheeks again. Sparkle in her eye. When we got home from school today do you know where she was? Running on the sands.'

Yes, but Mama, if there was any danger of the child being taken from her, would dissemble to prevent it. Even if she was in severe pain she would say she felt fine.

'How's Papa taking it?'

'Absolutely stricken. Blames himself. It would make you weep, Di, Mama thinks he's the most wonderful husband in the world, he sees himself as her murderer. He's actually used the word.'

'Papa's too pessimistic. I suppose Rowena and Rebecca know?'

'Di, the moles under the ground know, the birds in the air. Mama's been shouting it to the skies. Literally. She even went out and kissed the rowan tree.'

'What are Rowena and Rebecca saying?'

'Rowena? Nothing, as you'd expect. Rebecca's delighted because Mama's delighted. But she's just a kid.'

Rebecca was thirteen.

'All right,' said Diana. 'I'll take the bus on Saturday morning. You can meet me in Tarbeg.'

'No, Di. Come on Friday. A ferry leaves Gourock for Dunoon at five past five. We'll be waiting on the pier.'

'But that would mean a long drive for you.'

'Just ninety beautiful miles.'

The road ran past mountains and alongside three lochs.

'Will Papa agree to that?'

'Like the rest of us he sees you as our rescuing

angel. The sooner you get here the better.'

'That's nonsense, Effie. What can I do?'

'Stiffen our sinews. Help us persuade Mama to abide by the specialist's verdict. We hate the word, Di, but she may have to have an abortion.'

Diana hated it too, 'All right. I'll see you on Friday evening on Dunoon pier. Look, I'll have to go now. This is a busy telephone. There's someone waiting to use it. Look after Mama. Goodbye for now.'

'Hasta la vista,' said Effie.

'Ciao,' said Jeanie.

Diana smiled at the girl who was waiting. 'Sorry, Cathie.'

'That's all right, Diana. He won't be there anyway. They're all the same, aren't they?'

Diana returned her smile but not conspiratorially. Her Edwin was not like other young men. He could be relied on. Cleverness wasn't everything. In any case, as his father had said, she was clever enough for the two of them. He had not achieved the necessary scholastic standard to enter Oxford or Cambridge, and of course no other University would have done. A position had been found for him with a firm of stockbrokers in London. Effie made silly jokes about a financial collapse being imminent. The joke would be on her and all his detractors when Edwin came into his inheritance. When he and Diana were married they would live in Kilcalmonell House. A great deal of renovation would have to be done.

She did not go back into the lounge but went straight up to her room.

Peggy was there, at her desk, reading and taking notes. The book was a history of the Crusades. Peggy was a very unusual kind of student in that she read widely beyond the prescribed books.

She could read for hours at a time in silent concentration, with no annoying habits like shuffling her feet or picking her nose. The other girls said, spitefully, it was because success was so much more important to her than to the rest of them. Unless she got a brilliant degree it would be the check-out counter for her, beside her mother. Diana knew differently. Peggy's absorption was that of a scholar.

She asked, quietly: 'Everything all right at home?'

To any other girl in the house Diana would have replied briefly: 'Yes, thank you,' but she always felt that Peggy, truthful herself, deserved to be told the truth.

'Not really,' she said. 'I'm afraid I have to go home this weekend.'

'You didn't intend to.'

'No. It's my mother.'

'I'm sorry. Is she ill?'

Diana hesitated. The secret was not only hers, it was her family's. She would not have told it to Lady Campton. Surely then not to this small nobody with holes in her slippers?

'Not really ill. She's going to have a baby.'

She restrained herself from asking Peggy to keep it to herself. There was no need. No one was less likely to treat it as a piece of gossip.

Peggy smiled. It was exactly the right kind of smile: intelligent, sympathetic, concerned and sincere. Diana loved her for it.

'Naturally we're worried. Mama's forty-eight,

which is rather old to be having a baby.'

'She'll be all right. It's not as if it was her first.'

'Rebecca's thirteen. It's rather a big gap.'

'Is your mother pleased?'

'Very pleased.'

'That's good.'

Peggy then, seeing that Diana didn't want to speak any more about it, in the meantime anyway, went back to the events in the Holy Land ten centuries ago.

Diana herself could not settle to study or even to read Edwin's last letter. Was Effie right? Had the luck of the Sempills come to an end? It had, if anything happened to Mama.

'Do you mind if I talk, Peggy?' she asked.

Peggy put down her pen and pushed the hair back from her eyes. 'Not a bit.'

'Your own mother must be very proud of you.'

An ironical smile. 'I suppose she is, in her own way. But she thinks I'm wasting my time at the University. She didn't want me to come. My dad's the one that values education.'

'But you've done so well, won prizes. Surely everyone's proud of that?'

'Dad is.'

There was a pause.

Peggy glanced at the photograph by Diana's bed. It was of all the Sempills, plus a peacock. In the background was the big white house they called Poverty Castle. Mrs Sempill was a tall fair-haired woman with, Peggy thought, a thin medieval face. She had wondered if Mrs Sempill might have some wasting disease. Perhaps she would not be strong enough to have a safe and successful delivery.

'You once asked me to visit your parents, Peggy.'

Peggy grinned. 'Yes, I think I wanted to let you see how the other half live. Very childish of me. I didn't know you so well then. To be honest I thought too it would be a treat for my mother. She's a great fan of royalty and aristocracy. Reads Mills and Boon romances. Never misses an episode of Dallas. A visit from someone like you would have been the highlight of her life.'

That was said ironically but affectionately.

'I would like to visit them, Peggy.'

'Why?'

Yes, why. Diana had to think. It had to do with her own mother's present predicament. It had also to do with a desire for Peggy's approval. She who was so proud that she did not care if she had Lady Campton's somehow seemed to need this working-class girl's.

'Sorry,' said Peggy. 'I come from a tribe that sometimes confuses frankness with rudeness. Some Sunday afternoon then, after the exams?'

'Yes, thank you. In return you must come and visit my family. They're eager to meet you.'

'Me?' Peggy's incredulity was genuine.

'I often tell them about you. Some weekend in June, perhaps. Or longer if you liked. There's plenty of room and it's a beautiful place.'

Peggy again looked at the photograph. She had never seen a happier or more fortunate family. Would the baby, before its birth and after, add to their happiness or threaten it?

'Edwin will be in Kilcalmonell then. I'd like you to meet him.'

Peggy thought: how naive Diana is, for all her apparent self-assurance. But then she's not yet twenty-one. Neither am I, but twenty in her tribe is like forty in mine. As Dad says there's nothing like a struggle with poverty for putting years on people.

'I'd like to meet him,' she said, and meant it. She wanted to meet all kinds of people. Otherwise her opinions about society would be merely theoretical. The heir to a baronetcy would be for her like a penny black for a philatelist. 'But I'll probably be working in June. Mum's trying to fix up a job for me in the supermarket.'

'Before you start work, perhaps?'

'Sure. Thanks. I'd like very much to meet your family. I feel I already know them.'

She had looked at their photograph often enough and had imagined herself as one of them. Was that her, to the right of the peacock?

3

A seagull was standing on top of Highland Mary's head, but it wasn't this that was causing the crick in her neck. She was said to be gazing sideways across the firth towards Ayrshire, home of her lover Robert Burns. Behind her rose the grassy rock on which Dunoon Castle had stood centuries ago. Robert the Bruce had stayed there once, and Mary Queen of Scots. Now only a few stones were left. This sunny May evening a flag was flying: the blue and white St Andrew Cross of Scotland. The twins would be pleased. Like Papa they were staunch nationalists, foolishly, in Diana's opinion. But what, she thought, as the car ferry Juno approached the pier, would it matter who governed Scotland, what would anything matter, if Mama died?

She was instantly cheered by the sight of her sisters among the people on the pier. As always they were attracting looks of admiration. As tall as Diana herself they were alert, healthy, full of vigour, and interested in everything. They had their hair arranged in ponytail fashion, tied with red ribbons. Their jeans were blue, their jackets red, and their sports shoes red and white. They were not only splendid, they were also very clever. In October Effie was to become a medical student at Edinburgh University and Jeanie in the same city was to attend the Veterinary College.

They greeted Diana with kisses and led her to the Daimler parked on the pier. It was ten years old but still opulent.

They could have come in the new white Escort but, said Jeanie, they had wanted to show off.

Effie was to drive as far as Lochgilphead and Jeanie the rest of the way to Kilcalmonell.

Diana sat in front.

They sped along the promenade towards the Holy Loch.

'Any developments?' asked Diana.

Effie shook her head. 'Mama's still in a state of rapture.'

'Rapture's the word,' said Jeanie, from behind.

'We've decided,' said Effie, 'that it's going to turn out all right. Without bringing in God or anything like that, surely happiness like Mama's, because she's going to have a baby, deserves to be rewarded?'

'What could be more deserving of good luck,' said Jeanie, 'than a woman who's deliriously happy because she's going to have a baby?'

'A baby boy, after five daughters,' said Effie.

'Is she so sure then?' asked Diana.

'Utterly.'

'You're both speaking as if you think she's going to go through with it.'

'Oh, she's going to go through with it,' said Effie.

'But what about the specialist?'

'If there were ten specialists telling her it would be fatal, never mind dangerous, she'd still go through with it. Wouldn't she, Jeanie?'

'Yes, she would. We're hoping the specialist will be able to advise us how to take care of her, so that everything will be all right in the end.'

'When would it be?'

'October. We won't be at home then. It'll all be left to Rowena and Rebecca.'

'And Papa.'

'Yes, but we're afraid, Di, that if things went wrong poor Papa would go to pieces. He's going to hire a nurse of course.'

It so happened that they were then driving through the village of Sandbank. On their right, in the Holy Loch, was the American depot ship *Hunley*. Two nuclear submarines nestled close to it.

Here were monstrosities that could kill a million women and their babies. Effie and Jeanie hated them and wanted to be rid of them, Diana hated them but thought that they prevented war. This evening they did not quarrel about it.

'How's University?' asked Effie.

'Busy. The exams are next week. How's school?'

'The Drama Club's doing 'Julius Caesar'. Jeanie and I are hoping to produce. Rowena's Portia, Brutus' wife. It isn't a big part as you know but she makes all the rest look amateurish. Everybody says so. She's astonishingly good.'

'And so beautiful,' said Jeanie. 'Everybody just gasps when she comes on to the stage.'

'And Rebecca?'

The three of them smiled happily. Their youngest sister always had this effect on them, and on others too. Her sweetness of temper captivated everyone.

'They were now driving by the side of dark deep Loch Eck.

'She says she'd love a little baby brother,' said Effie.

'She makes us feel ashamed,' said Jeanie. 'We never thought about congratulating Mama till she did.'

'To tell the truth, Di,' said Effie, 'Jeanie and I like our family as it is. We don't want any changes. This baby, boy or girl, will change everything.'

'Rebecca says it will bring us all closer together,' said Jeanie.

'Anyway, it's marvellous to see Mama so happy again,' said Effie. 'Even if she does say and do peculiar things. Like kissing the rowan tree.'

'Like asking us to feel her tummy,' said Jeanie.

'Like starting to knit bootees,' said Effie.

Mama was a notoriously bad knitter.

'Like telling us the baby's not just hers or Papa's but all humanity's,' said Jeanie.

'She's just the vessel through which he will come into the world,' said Effie.

'Lots of things like that,' said Jeanie, fondly.

That ended the conversation about Mama in the meantime, though each of them kept thinking about her.

They passed the end of the road that led to the village of Cairndow on the shore of Loch Fyne. The poet John Keats had stayed at the inn there during a walking tour more than a hundred years ago. The Sempills had once made a detour to see 'Keat's room.' Every time they came this way they quoted some of his poetry. They were young and he had died young.

Effie spoke the opening lines of *La Belle Dame Sans Merci* :

"Oh what can ail thee, knight-at-arms,

Alone and palely loitering?"

Jeanie finished the verse:

"The sedge is withered from the lake

And no birds sing."

They fell silent then. They realised it was a picture of how the world would be if Mama died.

They crossed the bridge at the head of the loch and turned westwards towards Inverary.

'I've invited Peggy Gilchrist for a weekend,' said Diana.

'Peggy Gilchrist?' said Jeanie.

'The girl I share a room with. I've mentioned her often. You've said you'd like to meet her.'

'The labourer's daughter that studies history?' asked Effie.

'Yes.'

'Is she coming?' asked Jeanie.

'I think so.'

'When? I hope not soon. We've got this matter of Mama to settle first, haven't we? We don't want strangers about.'

'Sometime next month I suggested, if she can get off work.'

'What work?' asked Effie.

'In a supermarket.'

Diana felt disappointed and annoyed too. The twins, especially Effie, called themselves radicals. They should have been enthusiastic about Peggy's visit.

Have we, she thought, become so selfish, so satisfied with ourselves, that we resent intruders, no matter who they are?

'I would like her to meet Edwin,' she said.

'That should be interesting,' said Jeanie.

'If she meets Nigel that would be more interesting still,' said Effie.

'I don't think it would be necessary for her to meet Nigel,' said Diana, rather peevishly.

'I'm a bit surprised she's agreed to come,' said Effie.

'I'd have thought, from what you've told us about her, that she'd have refused. Doesn't she regard us as the sort to be abolished come the revolution?'

'If I was in her place I'd want to abolish people like us,' said Jeanie, 'living on the fat of the land on unearned income.'

'Peggy's not like that.'

'Then she ought to be,' said Effie, 'if she's as poor as you've said she is.'

'If this is your attitude I had better cancel the invitation.'

'Perhaps you should,' said Jeanie.

They were then passing Inverary Castle, built in the eighteenth century in the style of a French chateau. The original castle had been sacked by Montrose and his Irish caterans in 1644. The then Marquis, chieftain of the Campbells, had fled in a boat to Greenock, leaving his clansmen to be harried and slaughtered, and earning himself the name of coward.

4

Though she would marry and have children and live in a grander house Diana knew that she would never experience a greater joy than returning home to Poverty Castle, even after a short absence. No one was particularly demonstrative, not even the dogs or cats or peacock. They were all deeply and quietly glad to see her and she to see them. The twins rushed in, shouting that they were home and very hungry. Rowena came down the stairs, with one of the cats in her arms. Rebecca appeared wearing an apron, for she had been helping in the preparations for dinner. Papa in his shabby kilt made for the sherry bottle and glasses. Mama rushed in with floury hands, took her glass of sherry, kissed Diana, and asked how the journey had been. Diana herself, at the centre of all this affectionate attention, felt grateful and humble.

Later, alone in her room for a few minutes before dinner, she found herself in tears. It could hardly be because of anxiety about Mama, because Mama had seemed the most carefree of them all. Nor could it be because of Papa's melancholy eyes, which were familiar. It couldn't be either because the twins, whom she loved, disapproved of her marrying into a titled family. Had they not 'forgiven' her for that? It must be the sadness at the heart of things, 'lacrimae rerum', which made the poetry of Keats so moving, memorable and truthful.

There was a knock on the door. Quickly she wiped away the tears.

It was Rebecca. There was no one Diana would have been more pleased to see.

She had changed into a pretty pink dress. 'Dinner will be ready in five minutes,' she said. 'I wanted to talk to you first. I thought you looked so worried.'

'Did I? I thought I was hiding it. I am worried of course, about Mama. Though I must say it's a long time since I saw her look so well.'

'She's often in pain.'

Diana was taken aback. 'How do you know? Did she tell you?'

'Yes, but she made me promise not to tell anyone. I haven't told Papa yet or the twins or Rowena. I had to tell you, Diana. I need your advice.'

'Does the doctor know?'

'He didn't, until I told him.'

'Some doctor!'

'Be fair, Diana. How was he to know? Mama keeps telling him she feels fine.'

'Why doesn't she tell him about the pain?'

'She's afraid she won't be allowed to have the baby. She agreed to let the specialist examine her as long as it was understood that he was going to advise how she could have the baby safely, and not that she should get rid of it. We've all had to agree with that, Diana. You'll have to agree to it too, so please don't try to make her change her mind.'

If none of them dared to say it Diana saw that she must. 'But if the specialist says that it would be too dangerous for her to have the baby, are we to say nothing? Are we to let Mama die in front of our eyes?'

'It's her decision, Diana. She's thought about it a long time. She's got a right to take the risk, if that's what she wants to do.'

Diana hardly recognised her sweet-natured thirteen year-old sister in this resolute realist in the pink dress, who had made a heart-rending decision and was going to keep to it.

Something else had to be said. Diana kept bitterness out of her voice, though she felt some. 'Is this baby more important than the rest of us?'

'I knew you would say that, Diana. It's not fair and it doesn't help.'

'I have to say what I think, Rebecca.'

'As long as you don't say it to Mama.'

'What if it isn't a boy? Would Mama think the risk worth taking if she thought it would be another girl?'

'Yes, she would. If it's a girl she'll love it just as much.'

'She'd be terribly disappointed.'

'We would all be, wouldn't we, for her sake? But if we helped her she'd soon get over it. Do you know what I think, Diana? I think this baby, whether it's a boy or girl, will bring us together again.'

'Aren't we together now?'

'You know what I mean. We're not nearly as close to one another as we used to be.'

'That's inevitable. We're all getting older.'

'Well, I think this baby could bring us all close together again.'

Yes, if all goes well, thought Diana.

Rebecca changed the subject. 'The twins said you've invited Peggy Gilchrist for a weekend.'

'I've changed my mind.'

'Why? We would all like to meet her.'

'When I mentioned it to the twins they were far from enthusiastic.'

'They're not very enthusiastic about anything just now. Because of Mama. Don't change your mind, Diana. Invite her. I mean, urge her to come. From what you've told us about her I think she could be good for us.'

'In what way?'

'Well, she's always been poor and we've always been well-off. It's not been our fault, it's just been our good luck, but maybe it's made us selfish in some way we can't see ourselves. She might help us to see it.'

They heard then the bell being rung for dinner. They wondered who could be ringing it so merrily.

'It must be Mama,' said Rebecca.

When they went downstairs they found that it had been Mama.

Except when they had guests they ate in the big whitewashed kitchen. It made things easier for the cook, who was Mama, her assistant Rebecca, and the waitresses, who were in turn Effie, Jeanie, and Rowena. Papa was in charge of the wine. On most occasions it was only his own glass he kept refilling, not because he was too greedy to share but because Mama put a limit on what the girls were allowed to drink. This evening she did not. Four bottles were consumed, and everybody, including Mama herself, ended up tipsy. She kept saying that this over-indulgence on her part was unpardonable, however she was sure little Roderick would forgive her, since this was no ordinary dinner but a celebration: it was the first time the whole family, all eight of them, were together. She could feel Roderick stirring and growing inside her. She laughed at that and at many other things. It was, Diana thought, to defy the pain.

'I keep calling your little brother Roderick, though we haven't yet discussed his name. What do you think? Is there a Roderick in Sir Walter, my love?'

Papa gravely replied there was.

'Didn't you once say, Mama, that if you have a boy you would call him Nigel?' asked Effie.

'Nigel is no longer popular among the Sempills,' said Jeanie.

'What do you think, Papa?' asked Rebecca. What name would you like?'

'Nigel. Guy. Quentin. Roderick. Peveril. Any one of those would suit.'

'Not Peveril, my dear,' cried Mama.

'Lets try them out,' said Effie. 'Nigel Sempill.'

'Guy Sempill,' said Jeanie.

'Quentin Sempill,' said Rebecca.

'Peveril Sempill,' said Diana.

'Roderick Sempill,' said Papa.

They were all agreed that Roderick Sempill sounded best.

'Of course his middle name must be Edward,' cried Mama.

After dinner Papa proposed that they should have one of their old Sir Walter Scott nights. The girls would rather have listened to some new Bob Dylan records but agreed that they ought to give Papa his wish. So, after clearing away and washing up, they went to the living-room where they found that Papa had brought the white plaster bust of Sir Walter from his study and placed it in the middle of the room on a pedestal, where it was in danger of being knocked over by Rab, the collie who had taken Bruce's place. He was always pretending that he was chasing sheep, and Sir Walter's white head did have a sheep-like look about it, said Effie, who then had to kiss Papa to atone for the blasphemy. Rab was ordered to lie in a corner. Wallace was stretched out in front of the fire, and Macho the big orange tom-cat, dozed on a window ledge, paying as little attention to the hubbub within as to the splendid view outside, of the sea and the bens of Jura, tinted with evening sunshine.

Mama was first. With Jeanie accompanying her on the piano she sang the ballad *Jock o' Hazeldean* , with spirit and enjoyment, especially the last two triumphant lines:

"She's o'er the border and awa'
wi Jock o' Hazeldean."

At one point Diana noticed her mother clutch her side but it was so momentary that she would have missed it if she hadn't been watching intently.

The twins then recited *Lochinvar* , verse about, and the last verse together. Now and then they consulted the book, but this had always been permissible. Rowena though, when she began to enact the dramatic poem *Roseabelle* did it all from memory, and did it so well that the others were enthralled. When they were younger and living in Edinburgh Papa had taken them to Roslin Chapel, where they had seen:

" .... that chapel proud

Where Roslin's chieftains uncoffined lie,

Each Baron, for a sable shroud,

Sheathed in his iron panoply,"

though there had not been then any 'wondrous blaze.'

Diana had always known that much of Scott's poetry was sad, indeed that was one of its attractions for Papa, but never before had she realised the tragic quality of that sadness so keenly as she did then listening to Rowena: "But the sea caves rung, And the wild winds sung" and watching Mama who, like the Maid of Neidpath, sometimes "grew an ashy pale."

Rebecca sang *Bonnie Dundee* with everybody, including Wallace, joining in the chorus. They were all defying not the "Lords of Convention" or the "sour-featured Whigs" or the "cowls of Kilmarnock" but Fate that had had the impertinance to threaten the happiness and security of the Sempills.

Diana herself kept up that defiance. The twins asked for *Proud Maisie* but she read instead the *Pibroch of Donuil Dhu* , with its rousing summon to war:

'Come as the winds come when

Forests are rended

Come as the waves come when
Navies are stranded.'

It was not Clan Donuil but the Sempill family that she was exhorting. If they kept faith with one another they would prevail. Though she read it quietly her family recognised her purpose and when she finished were silent, until Mama cried, 'Do you know, Diana, when I was a little girl of ten I knew that poem by heart?'

Papa's contribution was always kept to the last, because it was always much the longest, being a reading from one of the novels. This evening it was from the *Legend of Montrose* and described Sir Dugald Dalgetty's adventures in Inverary Castle. He read it well, with the red rays of sunset, another 'wondrous blaze', shining on him through the window.

As she listened Diana, who such a short time ago had been rallying them all to be hopeful, confident, and brave, suddenly was overwhelmed by a surge of foreboding. Mama was going to die. Diana felt like a character in a Scott poem, smitten by a tragic prophecy. Like proud Maisie indeed, except that it had been her own death that Maisie foresaw. Outwardly calm, with her hands still in her lap, Diana rebuked herself for being so foolish, she was Diana Sempill who had always been contemptuous of superstition, and yet that black knowledge covered her mind. Was it the effect of the wine? Or was it because she had been told about Mama's secret pain? Or was it a feeling that it had been decided, somewhere, that the Sempills had been lucky long enough? Whatever the reasons she sat in the room reddened by sunset, close to the others and yet remote from them. They were looking not only hopeful, confident, and brave, but happy too.

When they were all in bed except Papa, Diana went downstairs to his study. She had not yet had a private conversation with Mama, and now shrank from it.

Papa was drinking brandy, though he had promised Mama not to drink any more that night.

'Well, have you come to castigate me?' he asked, gloomily.

She felt ashamed. He would not have said that to any of her sisters. She had always been the one who castigated. Bossy-boots had wanted to set them right.

'No, Papa. I just wanted to talk to you about Mama.'

'What can a man do if his own body betrays him? Your mother calls it a miracle, not knowing just how miraculous. Look how grateful she is and yet I've as good as murdered her.'

Did he, wondered Diana, have the same premonition as herself?

'Looked at objectively,' he said, 'it could be seen as a comedy, an ironical comedy, with myself fate's buffoon. Like Sir Dugald. Though his role, as a soldier of fortune, was so much more straightforward. What did you want to say to me about your mother?'

'The twins told me a specialist is coming on Wednesday to see her.'

'A quack, like the rest of them, in spite of the letters after his name. Doctors today laugh at the ignorance of their colleagues a hundred years ago. Cannot you hear the doctors of a hundred years from now laughing at the ignorance of doctors today? One would not hold it against them if it wasn't for their arrogant assumption that they know it all when the truth is that they know damned little.'

It was not like him to be so captious.

'If this was America I could sue for ten million dollars. Except that I daren't say a word because it would let your mother know that I have been deceiving her for years. Be sure your sins will find you out. Not that she would reproach me. Has she not got at long last what she has always wanted?'

He's not talking to me, thought Diana, he's talking to himself, he's got into a habit of talking to himself, because we've all got out of the habit of listening to him. We've lavished our love on Mama because we've felt that she needed it and he didn't. We've known about his unhappiness and loneliness and sense of failure but we've not tried very hard to console him. That's why he's drunk so much wine. We've been wrong and now it's too late to remedy it. He's out of our reach.

'We're going into Tarbeg tomorrow morning to do some shopping, Papa.'

Those Saturday morning shopping trips to Tarbeg had always been great fun, for the girls and Mama at any rate. They had not realised that Papa might have felt left out. They had gone merrily in and out of shops, leaving him half the time on the pavement outside. Latterly, when the twins and Diana had learned to drive he had made excuses not to accompany them.

'We'd like you to come, Papa. Mama's coming.'

'Shouldn't she be staying at home and resting?'

The girls had discussed it. They had decided that the outing would do Mama good. They would see to it that she didn't over-exert herself. They hadn't bothered to consult Papa. That was another habit they had got out of.

'We'll all crowd into the Daimler. Good-night, Papa.'

'Good-night, Diana.'

She almost asked him to drink no more but managed to restrain herself. From now on she must be more humble.

5

Though somewhat red-eyed, Papa not only accompanied the expedition to Tarbeg but rather fussily took charge of it. Eating next to nothing himself he urged them to hurry with their breakfast. If they dilly-dallied all the strawberry tarts, doughnuts, fresh bread, and avocados would be sold out. He handed out money liberally. What they didn't spend they could give to Oxfam. He was the only one of the family who frequented that shop, where he liked to browse among the miscellany of curios and books (he had once come upon a Bible in Latin) while all round him the poor of the district, including tinkers, bought second-hand clothes and shoes for very low prices. Sometimes the girls sneaked in with contributions. The volunteer ladies, who knew who they were — everybody in Tarbeg did — always assured them that their father was a gentleman, as well-mannered towards the smelliest old tinker wife as he would have been to the Queen.

They all crowded into the Daimler as they had done when younger and smaller, though Papa was concerned lest Mama be crushed and jostled. She cried happily that a woman in her condition was under many protections.

Rowena sat in front with Papa and Mama. The other four sat behind, with Rebecca on Effie's knees. She was to change to Jeanie's at Seal Rock.

Papa said he would take it easy, particularly where the road was bumpy. After all, on a bright May morning like this, with the hills and loch at their most splendid, who wanted to dash? When they did get going he drove so slowly that there was soon a honking procession behind, on the single-track road. Mama had to ask him to drive a bit faster.

'What did Mama mean by saying she was under many protections?' whispered Rebecca, into Effie's ear.

Effie, the prospective doctor, whispered her reply: 'Well, you see, Rebecca, nature's chief concern is the continuation of the species. Therefore she makes sure foetuses are not easy to get rid of.'

Diana shook her head, deploring this conversation.

'Women who wish they weren't pregnant,' went

201

on Effie, 'jump up and down, fall off ladders, take all sorts of things, make themselves as sick as dogs, all in vain. Babies have been born alive though their mothers were dead.'

'For heaven's sake, Effie,' murmured Diana.

'Yes, talk about something more cheerful,' said Jeanie.

'Shall we stop at Old Kirstie's?' cried Papa.

'Yes, Papa,' said Effie. 'Did you know she's ninety-three next week?'

The Daimler stopped outside the small white cottage. Papa was a favourite of Old Kirstie's. When they were younger the girls had often been impatient with him for spending so much time talking to the half-blind, half-deaf old woman. Five minutes would have been long enough, they had thought. Sometimes he had stayed for half an hour. Since then, they had learned better the nature of kindness.

The girls last night had held a quick conference to decide whether or not Mama's pregnancy should be kept a family secret for a little while longer, at least until after the specialist's visit. They decided it should. Papa, they were sure, would talk about it to no one. Mama, though, might tell everyone she met in Tarbeg, whether she knew them well or not. So she had to be told about their decision and begged to agree with it. None of them however had volunteered. The twins had said Diana should do it because she was the oldest, but when they had seen how unhappy she was about it they had not pressed her. Rowena suggested they should all go together and speak to Mama, but this was rejected since it would look too much like a deputation. In the end

Mama had not been told.

So, as they trooped into Old Kirstie's cottage the girls waited, with trepidation, for Mama to shriek the announcement. She would have to shriek it, at least twice, if Kirstie was to hear it.

The old woman was seated on a chair in front of the fire, with a tartan hap over her knees and a black shawl across her shoulders. With her hairy shrivelled face and hands spotted like toadstools she had once reminded the girls of a witch in a picture-book they had, although they had never really been afraid that she would turn them into puddocks. They had been more afraid of her big black cat with its yellow eyes.

Her daughter, red-cheeked and white-haired, was pleased at the fuss these gentry made of her mother, even though they did drop in at inconvenient times.

They stayed for ten minutes, which was quite a long time really, for Old Kirstie's deafness was very bad and everything had to be shouted, to the annoyance of her cat.

When they were on their way again Papa proposed that they buy the old woman a birthday present. He asked for suggestions.

'Tobacco,' said Rowena, for they had once surprised Kirstie smoking a pipe.

'Slippers,' said Effie, for she had noticed that Kirstie had been wearing what Granny Ruthven would have called 'bauchles', meaning decrepit and shapeless footwear.

'Sweets,' said Jeanie, for she had seen sweetie-papers at Kirstie's feet.

'A plant,' said Rebecca, for the cottage had been like a garden with flowering plants.

'A shawl,' said Diana, for she had noticed that the one Kirstie was wearing had a hole in it, 'a really good shawl.'

'A shawl is a very good idea,' said Papa.

'What do you think yourself, Papa?' asked Effie.

'Earrings.'

They were all taken aback. 'Earrings?' They could not remember seeing Old Kirstie wear any jewellery, except a cameo brooch which had once belonged to her mother she had said, which was easy enough to believe, and showed the face of Burn's Highland Mary, which wasn't.

'She has a photograph of herself when she was young,' said Papa. 'In it she's wearing earrings, rings, and bangles. She often admires your mother's jewellery. Doesn't she, darling?'

'I don't know about admiring it,' said Mama. 'She certainly likes to finger it.'

'She's got fingers like hens' claws,' said Rowena.

At Seal Rock the road came close to the loch. A seal was basking on the rock. They were delighted to see it. It was often there. They regarded it as a friend. It stood for all that was normal and sane and decent. When they were old women, wherever they were, they would remember it.

But they were young this morning, savouring the experiences that would be remembered in old age. Every fresh green leaf, every bird on the shore, and every sparkle on the loch, like the seal called on them to enjoy the present and leave the future to trust.

6

Most of the streets in Tarbeg ran steeply downhill to Harbour Street, which had shops on one side and fishing-boats on the other. Especially when the sun shone, there was an invigorating smell of fish, seaweed, and gulls' droppings. These last were everywhere. There was a saying that just as there were more deer than sheep on Jura so there were more gulls than folk in Tarbeg.

It was never easy to find a parking space. This morning the Sempills were lucky in that there was a space in front of the Royal Hotel. According to a notice it was reserved for hotel guests but Papa said that since they would be having coffee in the hotel later they were really guests. In any case, as Rowena said, anybody seeing the Daimler would think that its owners were staying at the hotel.

It was always hard for the Sempills, when they were all together, to stroll along the Harbour Street, recipients of many glances of respect and admiration, to pretend that these were not deserved. Seven of them, six fair-haired, all tall, for Rebecca too was going to be above average height, good-looking, healthy, casually but expensively dressed, affable, ready to exchange greetings even with people who did not know them well, they were a credit and an adornment to the town. Tarbeg knew it. They knew it themselves, they could not help knowing it as they looked at one another. They were properly modest but forgivably pleased.

The townspeople had seen Rowena in school plays and had gasped at her talent and beauty. It was known that Effie was to be a doctor, Jeanie a vet. As for Diana, she was famous: she had been dux girl of her year and captain of the hockey team. She was now at Glasgow University where she was doing very well, but her greatest triumph was in becoming engaged to the son of Sir Edwin Campton, present laird of Kilcalmonell.

Whatever shop the Sempills went into they would be welcomed, for they were not only prodigal but cheerful spenders. Other customers listening to them were encouraged themselves to go for the best and dearest.

Diana saw she was the only one showing anxiety. All the others, including Papa, seemed to have convinced themselves that Mama's pregnancy would turn out all right, she would have the boy that she had wanted so long, and the family would be knit closer together. As a consequence they were happy and jolly. Seeing them and listening to them, in the busy street, with friends greeting one another all around her, and on one of the boats a fisherman singing as he mended his net, she tried to banish last night's premonition, but could not. Whenever she looked at Mama she saw, on that dear face, in between the bright smiles, visitations of pain and fear.

Suddenly too Diana had a feeling that there were not seven of them but eight. The additional one was not remote little Roderick, but Peggy Gilchrist, in their midst, saying nothing but noticing everything.

'What's the matter, Di?' asked Effie.

'Nothing.'

First they shopped for things to eat, in the baker's, the greengrocer's, the butcher's, and the delicatessen, all of them together except in the butcher's, which Jeanie, the vegetarian, refused to enter. They carried the packages to the car and stowed them in the boot.

The twins had bought some rolls for the swans, but when they threw the pieces the expert Tarbeg gulls swooped and caught them in their beaks in mid-air. The swans looked cross. 'We feed wild swans while millions of human beings are hungry,' said Diana, ostensibly to Rowena but really to Peggy Gilchrist.

'Don't be silly, Di,' said Rowena

Peggy wore one of her baffling smiles.

They went off then to buy things for themselves. They were to meet outside the hotel in forty minutes.

In the luxurious lounge the waitress who attended them was a girl who had been at school with Diana though never in the same class. Cissie had not been a successful scholar. As she put their coffee and cream cakes in front of them she chatted with Diana about some of their contemporaries.

'Do you ever hear from Fiona?' she asked.

Fiona McTaggart had gone to Aberdeen where her father had bought a lucrative practice.

'Not very often.'

Cissie giggled. 'She'll think your're too high above her in the world now. She was always shy, wasn't she? Not like me. Did you hear about Mary Buchanan? You mind Mary? Daft about dancing. Would you believe it, she's married a shepherd up Knapdale way, at the back of beyond. Lives in a cottage with outside toilet. Nice speaking to you, Diana. Have to go. Old Sourpuss is watching.'

The manageress was certainly frowning, for she did not approve of her underlings being familiar with guests, but the Sempills were regular freely-spending customers whose peculiarities had to be humoured. Well-to-do themselves, living in a house called a castle, they talked, as if to equals, to people like Cissie McLean whose father was a dustman and who lived in a council house. It cost them nothing, gave them the name of being friendly, and emphasised their superiority.

There were two shops in Tarbeg that sold best-quality highly-priced Scottish woollens. In choosing a shawl for Old Kirstie, Papa said, expense was to be no object. He took part himself in the quest. The one finally chosen was of soft Shetland wool, hand-knitted in a Fair Isle pattern. Since its price was thirty-two pounds the shopkeeper was more than willing to wrap it in gift paper and put it in a box. A card was slipped in, inscribed: 'From the Sempills of Poverty Castle, to a grand old lady on her ninety-third birthday.'

'Now for the earrings,' said Papa.

'Isn't the shawl enough?' said Effie.

'We promised earrings, so earrings it must be.'

'We didn't really promise Kirstie anything,' said Jeanie.

No one else said anything.

Papa led the way to the jeweller's.

Only Rowena helped him and Mama to choose the earrings. The others stood by, refusing to give their opinion. Papa and Mama didn't notice. Rowena did, but just shrugged her shoulders. The pair selected, out of dozens looked at, had cairngorms set in silver. They were made in Scotland and cost eight pounds more than the shawl.

Rowena was aware that seventy-two pounds was too much to spend on birthday presents for an old woman who after all was just an acquaintance, but it didn't bother her. It did her sisters, especially Effie.

'What's the matter ?' asked Rowena, as they walked to the car.

'It's far too much,' said Effie.

'We can afford it.'

'That's not the point.'

'Yes it is. If we couldn't afford it it would be far too much.'

'They'll give Kirstie a lot of pleasure,' said Jeanie, doubtfully.

'They'll embarrass her daughter,' said Effie, 'or even humiliate her.'

'Can you humiliate people by giving them expensive presents?' asked Rowena, laughing.

'Yes, you can. It's not like Papa to make a mistake like that.'

'You're talking rot, Effie. Isn't she, Diana?'

Diana smiled. She thought Effie was right but for

the wrong reason. What would Peggy Gilchrist's judgement have been?

At the car Papa proposed that for a treat they should go and have lunch at Heatherfield Castle, once a nobleman's home and now a very exclusive hotel, about two miles out of town.

Mama was keen but Effie said dourly that they could go if they liked, she would have sausages and chips in Mac's. Her sisters knew what was the matter with her. She was ashamed of being well-off, though she enjoyed its consequences as much as any of them. Usually she could keep her shame under control but sometimes it made her sulky and rebellious. Effie's was an attitude that Jeanie sympathised with but did not feel compelled to share, that Rowena and Rebecca did not understand and in the former's case did not want to, and Diana herself had little patience with. She had often pointed out to Effie that by spending their money the Sempills gave employment to people, and she had asked did Effie want a revolution in which many people might be killed and which could well result in universal poverty and misery. Being lucky was a burden that she would just have to bear. When she became a doctor she could go and practise in Ethiopia and be as poor as she liked.

Effie had said that if Peggy Gilchrist met Nigel it would be very interesting. So it would be if she herself met Peggy. What was insincere and immature in her moral and political attitudes would be shown up. Peggy worked very hard at trying to understand the human situation. Reading books like the History of the Crusades was part of her attempt. Effie just depended on superficial feelings.

210

'Well, are we going to stand here all day?' asked Mama.

'Let's have a special lunch at home,' said Rebecca, the peace-maker. 'Papa and Mama will be our guests.'

'Good idea,' said Jeanie. 'You cook and we'll help.'

'In the dining-room,' said Rowena, 'not the kitchen.'

'What about it, darling ?' asked Mama. 'Shall we accept this invitation?'

It had occurred to Papa that a decent bottle of wine at Heatherfield Castle would be costly. He could afford it, but should he? Extravagance for other people's sakes was permissible, but not for his own. It troubled him, as a theoretical socialist, that though he had done no paid work for the past ten years he was better off now than ever, owing to the profitability of his investments. Having lunch at a five-star hotel with water instead of wine would be a penance, but only if dry bread was eaten with it and not gourmet food. But to be fair it wasn't to avoid that hardship which made him accept the girls' offer. Last night, after his conversation with Diana, he had vowed to stop being sorry for himself and to start finding his own happiness in that of his family.

'We'll let you have one of your best bottles, Papa,' said Jeanie.

He laughed. 'Thanks very much. Right. Let's go.'

'What about Oxfam ?' asked Diana. 'We were to hand in what money we had left.'

'Salves for our consciences?' sneered Effie.

Diana could not imagine Peggy Gilchrist ever sneering so cheaply.

The girls emptied their pockets and purses. It came to six pounds and sixty-five pence. Papa made it up to ten pounds. They stopped at the Oxfam shop. Rebecca ran in with the money. Then they headed for Kilcalmonell. Rebecca sat on Diana's knee.

'About the earrings, Papa,' said Effie, not heading Jeanie's dig in her ribs, 'do you think we should give them to old Kirstie?'

'If you don't I'll have them,' said Rowena.

'Why on earth should't we give them to the old woman?' asked Mama. 'They were bought for her.'

'Isn't the shawl enough?'

'Heavens, Effie, it's not like you to be so niggardly.'

'I'm not being niggardly, Mama. It's just that I think too much is as bad as too little.'

They were passing Seal Rock. The seal was missing. That was nothing remarkable, thought Diana. No doubt it was enjoying itself somewhere else. She would see it again on her way back to Dunoon pier tomorrow evening. But she could not help having that premonition again. Her family was no longer protected by benign unseen forces. They were as vulnerable as any other family.

Jeanie felt she had to give her twin some support. 'Old Kirstie might be embarrassed,' she said.

Papa chuckled. 'She's long past being embarrassed.'

'Her daughter then.'

'Why not give her the earrings for Christmas?' asked Rebecca.

'She might not be with us at Christmas.'

'Effie's being silly,' said Rowena.

'What do you think, Diana?' asked Papa.

'Perhaps the shawl would be enough.'

'So you agree with Effie?'

'Not for the same reason,' muttered Effie.

Mama laughed. 'What a to-do about a pair of earrings.'

Papa stopped the car. 'Shall we have a conference?' he asked, making fun of them.

'We've been having one,' said Rowena.

'Has everyone had her say ? Good. Shall we take a vote? Who's for giving both the shawl and the earrings?' He put up his hand.

Mama put up hers. 'I'm not sure I know what's going on.'

'It's all very silly,' said Rowena, putting up her hand.

All parts of that road were beautiful, but where they had stopped was particularly so. The loch glittered. Yonder was the lonely promontory called in Gaelic the place where herons nested. What was it like, thought Diana, to be a heron?

'We're waiting for you, Di,' said Jeanine. 'It's three against three so far.'

'You can't abstain,' said Effie, dourly.

'Why not?' asked Papa. 'Voting is not compulsory in this country or this family. We can toss a coin.'

'You said a shawl should be enough,' said Rebecca, 'so you're really on our side.'

'Perhaps she's changed her mind,' said Rowena. 'You're allowed to change your mind.'

Diana wondered what Peggy Gilchrist would have

made of this scene. 'All right,' she said. 'I vote to give only the shawl now, and keep the earrings for Christmas.'

'The shawls have it,' said Papa, and drove on.

'I don't think we should all go in and give it to her,' said Rebecca. 'You do it, Diana. Old Kirstie would like that.'

Since Diana's engagement old Kirstie and her daughter had looked on her as real gentry, not would-be gentry like the rest of the family. Kirstie's husband had been a gamekeeper.

Effie said nothing. Perhaps it was because Jeanie was gripping her hand tightly.

'I'd rather not,' said Diana. 'You do it, Mama.'

'Mama's tired,' said Papa. He stopped the car outside old Kirstie's cottage. 'Who's it to be then?'

'Rebecca,' said Jeanie.

The others agreed. Rebecca was always the happy compromise.

'All right,' she said. 'I'll just hand it in.'

They watched her go through the gate. The black cat was sitting on the wall in the sunshine. It rose, hunched its back, and showed its teeth in a miaow that those in the car could not hear.

'I hope she doesn't try to pet it,' said Mama, anxiously.

'It looks quite dangerous.'

'It's just old,' said Papa.

'It's got the reputation of being cantankerous,' said Effie.

Rebecca came back through the gate. She was about to stroke the cat but changed her mind.

'I think it's ill and in pain,' she said.

'That certainly would account for its cantankerousness,' said Mama.

7

On Wednesday evening, waiting to telephone home to learn what the specialist had said about Mama, Diana was in her room studying. She found it hard to concentrate, because of worry as to what she might be told, and also there was the problem of Peggy. Now and then she would steal a glance at her room-mate, trying to see in her the wisdom, tolerance, and understanding that her imaginary presence in Tarbeg had seemed to possess. Of course those rare qualities were not there, nor could they possibly be, in this very ordinary-looking girl in the cheap acrylic jumper and shabby jeans. What Peggy had were diligence and perseverance, and also a cunning ability to make a small store of knowledge seem great, by apt quotations and pertinent instances. Evidently she used it in her essays too with success, to account for the alphas they got. It was not dishonesty on her part: she was entitled to make full use of what few advantages she had. She had admitted that she belonged to a tribe that confused rudeness with frankness. It had many other faults. For all her cleverness she was inevitably affected by them. It was perverse of her not to improve herself wherever she could. She did not have to retain that coarse accent.

She deserved to be helped and for that reason the invitation to visit Poverty Castle must not be withdrawn. She would make sure she got full value out of it. Perhaps she ought to be introduced to Nigel. His arrogance would reinforce her prejudice against the upper-class but his wit and polish and cultured accent were bound to impress and chasten her.

For the past two hours she had not uttered so much as a sign or raised her eyes off her book, a history of Tudor England. Such absorption was admirable, but was she not being characteristically sly too. She knew why Diana had to telephone home and therefore must be thinking about Mama and the specialist as well as Mary Tudor and the burning of heretics, yet she gave no sign of it. Perhaps she just did not know what to say. Diana and her sisters knew instinctively what to say whatever the circumstances, but Peggy, afraid of confusing frankness with rudeness, had always to think before speaking and as a result often did not speak at all. All her life she would never be at ease in the company of people born into a higher and better educated class. It was not inconceivable that she might gain a brilliant degree and still end up working in a supermarket.

Diana looked at her watch. It was five to seven. She shut her book and rose.

'I hope Sadie's not telephoning,' she said.

Sadie Meiklejohn had many boyfriends. She spoke to them on the telephone for an hour at a time.

'Good luck,' said Peggy, rather oddly.

All the same it was luck that was needed.

Diana did not hurry. There were girls in the house who would have rushed downstairs, lamenting to anyone they met. They believed they would have been showing how human they were. They thought that Diana put being ladylike before being human. Effie had come to think that too.

It was so untrue as not to be worth denying. Vulgarity cheapened emotion, dignity enhanced it.

Sadie *was* telephoning, and from her animated gestures seemed to be in the throes of a conversation not likely to be cut short. Her cronies would have cried, 'Pack it in, Sadie, you've had your ten minutes,' and they would not have discreetly retreated. Diana said nothing. On her way to the breakfast room to wait there she heard Sadie say: 'For fuck's sake, Rab, you can't hold that against me.' She was not wearing a brassiere, though her breasts were large. Her boyfriends were mostly rugby-players who, according to her accounts, were boisterous lovers. She sometimes entertained the other girls with tales of her sexual adventures. Their hilarity could be heard all over the house. She always shut up whenever Diana or Ruth Brodie appeared. Ruth's father was a Baptist minister and Ruth herself a pious prude, but what in Diana caused the sudden reticence was not so obvious. Diana herself thought it was because she made Sadie realise she wasn't being just immoral, but vulgar too.

But Diana was ready to admit that vulgarity did not necessarily exclude decency. Sadie was goodhearted. In a minute she came and told Diana the telephone was free.

Diana smiled and thanked her. She had often noticed how graciousness on her part caused others, even promiscuous girls like Sadie, to be gracious too.

'It's my way of helping people,' she had once said to Effie, making fun of her. Effie was not quick at detecting irony, especially if her own principles and ideals were being mocked.

Diana asked for the charge to be reversed. It saved the bother of putting in coins. She imagined her sisters gathered round the telephone in the playroom, ready to snatch it up. She thought it would be Jeanie who would answer. Effie might be in one of her high-minded huffs.

It was Jeanie. 'Hello, Di. Well, he's been but he might as well never have come.'

'What do you mean? What did he say?'

'He said he couldn't give a definite opinion unless Mama went into his nursing-home in Glasgow for some tests.'

'That seems sensible.'

'Do you know how much it would cost? A hundred pounds a day!'

Diana frowned. Jeanie was voicing Effie's indignation, not her own. Effie was opposed to private medicine and made unfair charges against it. A hundred pounds a day was steep but it would bring not only expert and immediate medical attention but also comfort and privacy.

'Surely expense doesn't matter,' she said. 'What does Papa say?'

'Well, you know what his opinion of the medical profession is, after his botched vasectomy. I must say Effie and I didn't think much of the specialist. We stayed off school so that we could speak to him. He wouldn't tell us anything. He said we'd to ask Papa.'

'Did he say what could be causing her pain?'

'Pain? What pain? Mama's never said anything about having a pain. Not to me, anyway: or to Effie. Did she tell you?'

'No, but I've noticed her wince several times.'

'We've noticed how she sometimes turns pale.'

'It's just as well then that she's going to have these tests.'

'But she's not, Di. She absolutely refuses. She's afraid they might take the baby from her.'

'But they would only do that if her own life was in danger.'

'She doesn't care if she dies, as long as the baby lives.' Suddenly Jeanie could not speak for crying.

Effie now spoke, her voice cold. 'Hello, Di. We'd like to know more about this pain of Mama's. How do you know about it if she didn't tell you? Is it a secret that the rest of us are not allowed to share?'

Diana then heard Rebecca speaking.

Effie's voice was a little less cold. 'Rebecca's just explained. Poor Mama. She didn't say a word to the specialist about any pain. We shouldn't blame him.

How was he to know? I do blame him though for charging exorbitantly. Are you coming home this weekend?'

'Yes, of course. I'm depending on you all to take care of Mama.'

'She looks so well and happy, Di. Perhaps this pain means nothing. Perhaps it'll go away as lots of pains do. By the way, we've got a servant who lives in. Papa engaged her through Mr Patterson. A Mrs McDougall. She's a widow who lives in Tarbeg. She seems very competent. She and Mama get on well. Another thing, Di. Papa wants us to spend the summer in Spain, in that villa he nearly bought. He thinks the sunshine and warmth would do Mama good.'

Diana wondered how skilful and reliable were Spanish doctors.

'Edwin could come with us. So could your University friend Peggy what's-her-name. Jeanie and I are sorry we were so beastly when you told us you'd invited her to Poverty Castle. Please insist that she comes.'

'All right. But I can't see her coming to Spain with us. In the first place she couldn't afford the fare.'

'We'd pay it. Papa wouldn't mind.'

No, but Peggy would. 'In the second place she's going to be working in a supermarket during the summer.'

'I see. Well, invite her here anyway. See you on Dunoon pier Friday evening. Here are the others wanting to say good-night.'

First Rowena, then Rebecca, then Jeanie, and finally Effie herself said good-night.

Feeling lonely and useless, Diana went slowly upstairs; she should be at home helping to look after her mother. Compared to that her University career was unimportant.

Peggy was still poring over her book. No wonder her eyes often looked tired.

They were sharp enough to detect Diana's pessimism.

'Bad news?' she asked.

'No news at all, really. The specialist didn't commit himself. He wants my mother to go into a nursing-home for some tests. She refuses.'

'Perhaps she feels they aren't necessary. She's all right, isn't she?'

'She seems well and happy.'

'Why look for trouble then? My dad says: leave well alone.'

'My father says so too.'

Diana sat down and opened her book, but she soon found she could not face the jargon of economic theories. 'I think I'll go for a walk in the Gardens.'

'Do you mind if I go with you?'

'I'd be pleased.'

So she would, even if such an incongruous pair as she, tall and well-dressed, and Peggy, small and scruffy, drew puzzled glances among the early roses.

8

With the examinations past and also her visit to Peggy's parents Diana wrote a long letter to Edwin. She did it in the Mitchell Library Reading Room. She would not have felt comfortable in the boarding-house with Peggy present, though she had no intention of writing anything contemptuous or malicious.

She was as serious-faced as any of the students round her, who still had their examinations in front of them. She never found it easy to express affection, whether on paper or in speech. It bothered her a little that her letters must be a disappointment to Edwin, though he had never complained. His to her, brief and composed of boyish clichés, were nevertheless more affectionate. She had a feeling, foolish but persistent, that certain things had to be done, and certain positions had to be reached, before she would be able to declare her love freely.

But what she was about to write now was not a love letter, since it would be mainly about her visit to Peggy's parents.

Therefore she was able to begin without the usual hesitations.

'Dearest Edwin,

This will be the last letter I'll write to you from

Glasgow for some time, because in a day or two the long vacation begins and I shall be going home to Kilcalmonell.

The examinations are over. I think I have done well. I seem to have the knack of spotting questions. Peggy, my room-mate, never even tries to 'spot'. She studies a subject for its own sake, more widely and intensively than is required for examination purposes. Also she reads books simply because they interest her. But she seems to be very skilful at displaying her knowledge, so that examiners are impressed. It's very important for her to do well. I think of her as climbing a very steep and slippery cliff. One false step, represented by poor marks and a failure, and down she would fall, making the next ascent all the harder.'

She paused then, for it had occurred to her that what she had written might hurt Edwin who had not passed many examinations. Effie had once said, cruelly, that the Camptons had consented to Diana's engagement because 'they badly need an infusion of brains, that lot.' That was unfair to Edwin. He might not say anything original or brilliant — few people did — but he had a shy commonsense that suited his nature.

'Last Sunday afternoon I paid my visit to Peggy's parents in Carron. It's a rather run-down industrial town, about forty miles from Glasgow. We went by bus. I remember your mother saying she had never travelled in a public bus in her life. I suppose the worst inconvenience is that you have no control over who your neighbours will be. We had an old man who coughed and spluttered all the way, and a woman with a four-year-old very much spoiled child, who whined and whimpered. But I didn't mind. I've always wanted to see the working-class, the lower orders as your mother calls them, at close quarters, and I was certainly doing that.'

She paused again, thinking how enraged Effie would have been by the last sentence.

It was no good her trying to make her account humorous: she could not have done it and she would not have been true to herself. In any case if she had made jokes Edwin would not have seen them. Unlike her he was always eager and willing to laugh but was never sure when. Even Rowena was laughing when Edwin was still wondering. The twins thought he would make a very dull husband: his being so good-natured would compensate enough. What gave their sarcasm an extra edge was their knowing that years ago she had often said that the man she would marry must be very brave. Edwin was curiously timid.

'We came off the bus in the main street. Litter lay everywhere. Shops were closed, not because it was Sunday, but because they were derelict. Peggy pointed out the supermarket where her mother works and where she herself hopes to find a job this summer.

We had to walk to the council housing estate where she lives, called Netherlee Park! On our way we met two of her old school friends.

What horrors, as Effie and Jeanie would have said. Their hair was pink and arranged in spikes. Their faces were ghastly white. One had pink jeans with yellow patches, the other yellow jeans with pink patches. They chewed gum all the time. Their voices were quite hideous. At first I couldn't make out a word they were saying. They seemed pleased to see Peggy and in a peculiar way were proud of her. 'Christ kens whaur she got her brains.' 'No' jist her brains, her guts.' 'See this lassie? She's suffered a million insults and never let them get her doon.' After greeting her and asking how she was getting on at University they turned their attention on me. My height amused them, both being under five feet: working-class women are often stunted. 'Is it cauld up there?' They had tries at mimicking my accent. My name was a great joke. Did I know I was the first Diana they had ever met?

I expected Peggy to keep quiet concerning me, but no, for some reason of her own, she told them I lived in the Highlands in a house called Poverty Castle, I had four sisters, I was engaged to a baronet's son, my engagement ring had real diamonds, one day I would be Lady Campton, mistress of a house with forty rooms. What her motive was in telling them all that I couldn't tell then and I still can't. Was she making fun of all of us, me, her weird friends, and herself?

You should have seen the astonishment and incredulity on those white faces. They were at a loss what to say, which I'm sure didn't happen often. I saw no sign of animosity or jealousy. They didn't want to drag me down to their level. They would far rather have raised themselves to mine, if it had been possible. Effie would have called them traitresses to their class. She really has a lot to learn.

As we came among the blocks of flats where Peggy lives I realised something about the working-class that I had never thought of before. They live so close together, in crammed ghettos, that they are more or less obliged to take an interest in one another and also to be in a way responsible for one another. Some of the gardens or rather strips of ground that surrounded the flats were a disgrace, with hardly any grass and no flowers at all but a great deal of rubbish, including dogs' poo. Since these 'gardens' are communal the shame of their condition belongs to everyone. I thought that if I had to live there I would have tried to do something about it. I would have cleared away the milk cartons and bottles, the cigarette packets, potato crisp bags, and other miscellaneous rubbish, from my own area. I suppose the most anti-social would at first jeer and take pleasure in undoing such efforts, but if one persevered even they would come to realise that if the place was kept clean and tidy everyone would benefit. It seemed to me that that was the only way by which the conditions and standards of the poor could be raised. It is no good their thinking that politicians will do it for them. They will have to do it for themselves. We must of course encourage and help them.

I said nothing of all this to Peggy, but my sympathy for her increased. No wonder her peculiar friends had praised her courage. I don't suppose many are born here with exceptional abilities like hers but most of them, I'm afraid, will simply succumb to the overwhelming difficulties. It makes her perseverance all the more admirable.

When I began this letter I was eager to tell you about her parents, but I now find myself reluctant. It seems somehow like betraying a confidence. Still, I can tell you things that I would tell no one else.'

226

She stopped to consider that. Was it true? Would she really tell Edwin things that she would not tell her sisters or parents? Yes she would, and not only because he never criticised or questioned. She trusted him more than she did them: which was incredible, for they would have given their lives for her and she hers for them. His love for her and hers for him was different, requiring greater intimacies. Though she saw his faults clearly she felt that he was growing closer and dearer all the time, and she to him, whereas she and her sisters were inevitably growing apart. Even Rebecca was aware of it, which was why she hoped that the baby would bring them together again as they had been when children.

'Except for the daughter-in-law, ludicrously called Sonia, they are ordinary working-class people, decent, respectful, and hospitable. Peggy's mother, a small prim woman with grey hair recently permed (perhaps for my visit!) apparently patterns herself on some heroine in one of the romances she reads, a duchess perhaps! You should have seen her drinking tea. Pinkie outstretched, and immense care not to slurp. The best china was taken out of the display cabinet in my honour: the imitation silver teapot too. The house was spotless and smelled faintly of disinfectant. I gathered that Mr Gilchrist is not allowed to smoke indoors. He is a funny little man, quite a midget and very bald. I got the impression that he usually wears his cap in the house. He kept pulling at the skip that wasn't there. What I liked about him was his great pride in Peggy. It's because of him that she's been given her chance to go to University. Her mother would have put her in the supermarket as soon as she left school, which she would have done at sixteen.

Nowadays it's not uncommon in Scotland for clever working-class girls to have a University education and become school teachers, there are some in Mrs Brownlee's boarding-house, but none of them is an intellectual like Peggy. When they've got their degrees and their teaching posts they'll be perfectly satisfied and will never open another 'serious' book in their lives. Peggy may have to become a teacher for want of anything better being offered, but she'll go on reading history all her life. It's a pity about her appearance. It shouldn't count but it does. Suppose she and I applied for the same post? Who do you thing would get it? Yes, even if my qualifications were not as good as hers.

Sonia, I'm afraid, I did not take to at all. She's only nineteen but nastily fat, through eating all the wrong things. She finished a box of chocolates while I was there. She's eight months pregnant too, which doesn't help. She had the gall to ask me to put my hand on her stomach and feel 'Wee Eerchie' kicking. I declined. She was as inquisitive as a child of five: in her of course it was barefaced impudence. She wanted to know all about my family, and yours too. She grabbed my hand and inspected my ring. Anyone could see they were real diamonds, she said. She assured me at least three times that I was very lucky.

Visiting Peggy's people was a test for me. Looking over this account I see that I do not deserve high marks. Effie would fail me completely. One of the cardinal sins among the Sempills is to patronise people. I did not patronise anyone during my visit, not even Sonia, but I have patronised them in this

228

letter, haven't I? I can see what Effie finds 'insufferable' in me. I find it insufferable myself.

Accompanying me to the bus-stop Peggy was evasive when I repeated my invitation to come and spend a few days with us at Poverty Castle. When I stepped on to the bus she said, 'Thanks for coming.' I realised then how very lonely she must feel. Like someone else I know and love. No, not you, darling!

See you soon. All my love,

Diana.'

9

In the eight large blocks of council flats where she lived, with more than three hundred families all of the working-class, there was not one person with whom Peggy could have discussed, say, the economic conditions in Scotland in 1314 or 1745.

Indeed, if she had widened her scope and taken in the whole town, including the High School, the Rotary Club and the local branch of the Labour

Party, she would still have found it difficult to find anyone interested in such far-off matters. In the two small rooms smelling of old paper and cigarette smoke where the Labour Party branch met, she had once, aged eighteen and a new member, after listening to morose condemnations of Party leaders who had once again betrayed socialist principles, stood up and pointed out to those dour elderly men that this contradiction between idealistic intention and pragmatic performance was nothing new, and she had given examples ranging from Ancient Greece to the French Revolution. When she was finished they had praised her erudition, pitied her naive enthusiasm, and deplored her disillusionment. Time enough for her to be disillusioned when she was as old as they and had been let down as often. But for her then disillusionment had not come into it: she was simply fascinated by the human situation, without making judgements or taking sides. By the time she was twenty, after two years at University, she had begun, cautiously, to move towards a personal position.

She supported the CND and sometimes attended their rallies, though she did not wear their badge. She disliked wearing badges of any kind: she wasn't sure why but it had to do with her fear of being diminished as a private person. For someone like her, living in a place as public as an ant-heap, and owning none of the things that conferred and protected privacy, it had been hard to stay private and she had had to pay a bitter price. She loved her parents, was to a large extent financially dependent on them, and hated to hurt them, yet day by day, watching her father read his Daily Record and her mother her My Weekly Romances, she had grown

230

apart from them. She had sat in front of the mirror in her room and called herself an intellectual snob, guilty of ingratitude and conceit. What was there in that common-looking face to justify her conviction that she was someone special, given dispensation to go her own way no matter who was left behind? Nothing at all. She could see, only too plainly, who she was, in the world's eyes: wee Peggy Gilchrist, aged twenty, scarcely five feet in height or seven stones in weight, flat chested and skinny-legged, daughter of an unemployed labourer and a check-out assistant, a student at Glasgow University, and with luck a future teacher of history in some east-end school appropriate to her antecedents, social status, appearance, and speech.

Her way of speaking had always been a problem. As a child she had spoken like her parents and neighbours, saying 'widnae' for 'wouldn't' and 'Ah' for 'I'. At secondary school she had begun to speak carefully and grammatically. What had then remained was for her to modify or refine her broad working-class accent. This she had tried to do at University, in Mrs Brownlee's boarding-house, in shops, on buses, and occasionally at home. Sonia had noticed, 'Are you trying to speak posh, Peggy?' But Sonia had not been resentful or contemptuous. On the contrary she had understood and sympathised. 'If you're gonny be a teacher you'll hae tae learn tae speak properly.' She had invited Peggy to practise on her and had promised not to laugh, unless Peggy overdid it.

For a few days after Diana's visit Peggy gave in to the temptation to imagine that she was not Peggy Gilchrist but Peggy Sempill. There were not five sisters but six. As well as Rebecca, Rowena, Effie,

231

Jeanie and Diana there was also Peggy. She remembered the photograph by Diana's bed and saw herself in it. The big white house behind was her home. The tall bewildered-looking man with the moustache was her father, and the woman with the thin medieval face and mass of fair hair was her mother. She did not have to mind how she spoke: it came instinctively. If she wanted to stay in her room and read a book like the CONQUEST OF MEXICO, no one would think it odd.

When it was being decided whether or not she should go to University, as her headmaster advocated and her father wished, her mother had said: 'It's no' that Ah grudge ye it, Peggy. It's juist that Ah'm feart you'll never be happy amang folk no' your ain kind.'

Peggy had not said a word on her own behalf. She had known what sacrifices they would have to make. If her father hadn't been uncharacteristically resolute she would have gone into the supermarket, where, as her mother had said, hoping to entice her, she could have risen to be a charge-hand, with all those certificates she had.

They had made the sacrifices, they were still making them, and she was repaying them by depriving them of their existence so that she could see herself as one of the Sempills.

Yet, when during her visit Diana had urged her to come to Kilcalmonell, Peggy had not given a straight answer. Likely therefore the invitation no longer stood. The Sempills were too well-bred to persist.

Diana had remarked that they were all going to Spain for most of the summer. They would not give Peggy a thought. They themselves were all the company they needed. They had Mama to look after.

It was probable that the Sempills had gone out of Peggy's life for good, even Diana, who had dropped a hint that next session she might move into more commodious digs.

10

The small grey-haired manager of the supermarket had been good at history himself when a schoolboy. He could still recite the dates of all the battles fought on Scottish soil. He demonstrated: 'Battle of Largs 1215; Battle of Bannockburn 1314; Battle of Culloden 1746.' He challenged Peggy to give the date of the Battle of Pinkie. She said she had no idea. '1547!' he cried, in triumph. He couldn't remember why it was fought, it was only the date that had stuck in his mind: no wonder, seeing that it had been belted into him. He was delighted that he had shown himself better at history than this University honours under-graduate. All the same he wouldn't have studied history himself if he'd been lucky enough to get to University: he'd have gone in for science.

'I was hopeless at science,' said Peggy.

It was the right reply. 'If she's one of those stuck-up know-alls,' he'd said to his wife, 'I'll tell her nothing doing.'

'It's usually during July and August when girls go off on holiday that we need replacements. It's mostly putting things on shelves and sticking price-tabs on.' He grinned. 'Not what you would call suitable work for a University student who's won prizes.'

Her father who was proud of her achievements never boasted about them, her mother who didn't value them much frequently did.

'I'd be very grateful, Mr Stevenson,' she said.

He saw she meant it. There were at least half a dozen girls working for him who had more sex appeal, and she didn't look all that stuffy — it was tiring work keeping shelves filled — and probably her mother had exaggerated about those prizes, but there was something genuine about Miss Gilchrist that he liked. She could have waffled when he had asked her the date of the Battle of Pinkie but she had honestly said that she didn't know. She could be trusted. She would work hard. She would get on well with the other girls.

'Right then, Miss Gilchrist. I'll let your mother know when we want you. It should be at the beginning of the month.'

The Sempills would be setting off for Spain then. But she had promised herself not to think of them.

'Thanks very much, Mr Stevenson,' she said, as she

rose.

He was left with the warm exalted feeling that comes from helping someone who deserves it.

As she went through the big shop some of the girls in the blue uniforms smiled at her. One, who had been at school with her, came over and spoke. 'Glad you're going to be with us for the summer, Peggy.' She was glad, too.

Her mother, at one of the check-out counters, waved. Other check-out assistants also waved. Peggy waved back.

These are my people, she thought. Why then did she suddenly feel desolate?

Out on the street there were more of her people, housewives carrying heavy shopping bags and young mothers pushing prams. Old men looked wandered, old women purposeful. Was it because the former were lost with no jobs to go to, while the latter still had homes to run?

Peggy knew that she could never deceive herself. There was always, behind the lies and pretence, the small voice of truth which might not be heeded but could not be silenced. Therefore when she came to the post office in the main street and went in, it was no use her telling herself that a minute ago she hadn't known that she was going in. The intention had been lurking in her mind all morning.

There were queues of people waiting to be served. Most had pension books in their hands. She went past them to the far end of the counter where there was a pile of telephone directories. She picked out the one for Lomond and Argyll and looked through it until she came to the name Sempill. There was more than half a column of Semples but only one Sempill. That was the posh way of spelling it. Sempill E.I. it said. Poverty Castle. Kilcalmonell 288. She looked up the Code No. but did not bother to write it down. There was no need, not because she would remember it but because she was not going to make use of it. Did she really mean that? Yes, she did. She was not going to telephone the Sempills.

She had meant to visit the public library and then go for a walk through the public park, but she changed her mind and set off for Sonia's. Instead of talking to the Sempills in their castle she would talk to Sonia in her room-and-kitchen.

Sonia and Bobby lived in a run-down part of the town, in a flat above a derelict shop, reached by an outside stair. It did not have that ultimate degradation, an outside lavatory shared by other families, but it did not have a proper bathroom either. What it had was a tiny toilet contained in a ramshackle wooden porch. Even Peggy with her short legs found her knees scraping the wall as she sat on the lavatory seat. Sonia's latest complaint was that if her belly got any bigger she'd get stuck. She hated that toilet. It affronted her dignity as a mother-to-be. She waited till she was in agony before she would go and use it; especially when icy winds blew through cracks in the wooden walls.

Sonia and Bobby had their name down on the council housing list. There were more than a thousand names in front of theirs. The birth of little Archibald would not advance them much. It took six weans to make any difference, Sonia had said. She was quite prepared to have them, for other reasons besides that, but it would take too long.

She was surprised but pleased to see Peggy. Her flat was clean and comfortably furnished on credit. The wallpaper and carpets were too gaudy for Peggy's taste but Sonia called them cheery.

The kitchen was also the sitting-room. Peggy sat on an orange-coloured chair while Sonia, her hair in curlers, made tea on the gas cooker.

To forestall her hostess's lamentations about the flat Peggy said that she had been to the supermarket and was fixed up to start work at the beginning of July.

'And this,' said Sonia, going over to consult a calendar which had a picture of a sailing-ship, 'is June 15th. If you're going to visit those swanky freen's of yours you'll hae to get a move on.'

'I'm not going.'

Sonia was astonished. 'But she said her family were a' looking forward to meeting you. Ah heard her myself.'

'She was just being polite.'

'Weel, Ah did think it a bit strange, her being sich a lady and them living in a castle, but she did say it, Peggy.'

'They're not my kind of people.'

'That's silly, Peggy. Ah ken it's whit your mum says but it's silly juist the same. They've a' got yin nose and twa ears, juist like you and me. They've got mair money but that's juist their guid luck and we shouldnae grudge them it. You and me could hae cashmere jumpers and Italian shoes if we had mair money, couldn't we?'

'Could we have such good skin?' asked Peggy, teasing her.

'Skin? My skin's as good as hers.' Sonia stroked her cheek. 'It's juist your bad luck, Peggy, that you've go the kind of skin that attracts blackheids and spots.'

'But wouldn't you say eating the best food, living in the country, and having a fine big house with two or three bathrooms — each of them twice the size of this kitchen — wouldn't you say all that makes them a superior kind of people?'

'Maybe it does and maybe it doesnae. Ah prefer to think they're juist luckier. Go and see for yourself. Whitever they are they're the sort you should keep in wi'. Isn't that whit you went to University for? To meet the kind of people who could help you to rise in the work? Weel, you've met them. These Sempills. It would be a shame if you didnae tak advantage. There are times, Peggy, when your brither and me think you're no' very smart at looking efter youself, for a' your brains. Getting a degree's fine but it's only the beginning. It gets you intae the right company, like these Sempills. But you've got to keep in wi' them, even if it means you pushing youself forward. That's where you've got Bobby and me worried, Peggy: you're no good at pushing yourself forward. Even in a bus queue you let people get in front of you. Ah'm being serious. Don't laugh.'

'I'm not laughing, Sonia.'

'When wee Eerchie's born he'll be your blood kin, Peggy. That Diana she'll hae weans, why shouldnae hers and mine and yours tae be freen's? It's no' impossible. Is it impossible, Peggy?'

'No.'

'If it's claes that are the trouble — you should tak

mair pride in your appearance, Ah've telt you that before — then Ah'll be gled to lend you my oatmeal costume Ah was married in and hae worn only twice since, and the hat that goes wi' it. They might be on the big side for you but that wouldnae maitter. Toffs are careless aboot dress.'

'I didn't know that, Sonia. Diana's always very well dressed.'

'Juist as long as you don't go dressed like a tramp.'

'I'm not going at all.'

'You'll regret it, you'll regret it a' your life.'

So I shall, thought Peggy, and with a shudder sought to change the subject.

Unfortunately she happened then to look up.

'So you've noticed it?' cried Sonia.

She was already on to her third chocolate biscuit, while Peggy was still nibbling her first.

There was a patch of damp on the ceiling.

'Slates are missing,' said Sonia. 'It's been reported but naething's been done. When it rains Ah've to put basins underneath to catch the drips.'

'Doesn't Bobby know any slaterers?'

'You ken Bobby. He juist says gie me peace, for You-Ken-Who's sake. This job he has, humphing bags of coal up flights of stairs, it's too much for him. He shouldnae be daeing it for he's really a driver, but Mr Logan says he cannae afford a driver that doesnae dae his share o' humphing. There's something Ah want to ask you, Peggy. Mair tea?'

Peggy held out her cup while Sonia poured.

'Bobby said Ah wasnae to mention it to you, so Ah'd be obliged if you said naething to him. Your faither's a member o' the Labour Party, isn't he?'

Sonia's own father, Archibald Ramsay, was a Tory. He believed that 'Men wi' money' were better equipped to run the country than 'socialists wi' nothing but talk.'

'He'll ken Cooncillor Orr?' said Sonia.

'My father knows several councillors.'

'Orr's the yin Ah'm interested in. You see, he's chairman o' some committee that has to dae wi' housing. Ah ken for a fact that he's got a hoose for people behind me and Robbie on the list. It's true that they've got eight weans but juist the same they'd have had to wait their turn if it hadnae been for Councillor Orr. Whit Ah'm getting at, Peggy, is that Ah want you to ask your faither to speak to Cooncillor Orr, no' for my sake or Bobby's but for wee Eerchie's. Ah ken your faither says he's got principles but surely family comes before principles?'

'Has Bobby asked him?'

'Aye, but he doesn't think much of Bobby. He'd dae onything for you, Peggy. You're the apple o' his ee. Tell him it's being done a' the time.' She lowered her voice. 'I've heard money's changed haun's.'

'Are you saying Councillor Orr takes bribes?'

'Ah've accused naebody, but it's done a' the time.'

'Well, I'm sorry, Sonia, I'd like to help, but I just couldn't ask my father. He'd be insulted.'

She expected Sonia to sulk, for a minute or two anyway, but no, after a long sad sigh, Sonia went back to the subject of the Sempills and Peggy's visit to Poverty Castle.

It would have been far worse if she had had a taste of the tall white house, inside and out, and the four other girls, and their father with the melancholy eyes and their mother with the medieval face. In that case Peggy might have been consumed by a longing so strong that it would have made her ill. As it was her mother remarked on how pale she was.

'You never had rosy cheeks, no' even in your pram, but Ah've never seen you that colour before. It's a' that reading. Maybe you should go and see the doctor.'

Her father was shrewder. 'Are you missing your University freen's?' He meant them all, not Diana in particular. It never occurred to him that Peggy, brought up to take the side of the poor, might be pining for a family which she had never seen, except in a photograph, and which belonged to the parasitical class that enjoyed the best of everything without having to work for it. It amazed Peggy herself. Diana had ideas about class and rank that

Peggy considered absurd and anachronistic. She was never really at ease in Mrs Brownlee's and some of the girls were never at ease with her. They said, half-jokingly, that she was preparing for when she became Lady Campton, mistress of servants. She would be able to claim that she had experience of common people. That was why she travelled in buses when she could afford taxis. All that was true, and yet if next session Diana was absent from Mrs Brownlee's Peggy would be disconsolate. A window through which a richer life than her own could be seen would have gone blank.

Then one morning while she was still in bed her mother brought her in a letter.

'Swanky paper,' she said, with a sniff. 'Must be from your hoi-polloi freen's.'

Her husband had once pointed out to her that hoi-polloi meant the opposite of what she thought, but she still used it.

Peggy almost said: 'Take it away. I don't want it.' She said nothing and took the letter. Her name and address were hand-written but it wasn't Diana's handwriting. It didn't look like a woman's. It couldn't be from Edwin, could it? No, that was daft. She and Edwin had even less in common than she and Diana. Besides, they had never met.

'Aren't you going to read it?' asked her mother.

It was curious, thought Peggy, how her mother accepted with childlike joy the most unlikely circumstances in the romances she read, such as shop girls marrying lords' sons, and yet as regards real life she was hardheaded and sceptical. As a romantic she had enjoyed Diana's visit and had entertained her colleagues in the supermarket with accounts of it, but as a realist she was convinced that association with Diana's family would be harmful to Peggy in that it would make her discontented with her own home and family.

Peggy read the letter.

'Dear Peggy,

I hope you don't mind my calling you that, it would seem pompous addressing Diana's friend and room-mate as Miss Gilchrist. As the nominal head of this household I have been asked, on behalf of everyone, to remind you that you are most cordially invited to spend a few days with us in Kilcalmonell. It is very beautiful here at this time of year. Please come. We shall all be very disappointed if you don't. You see, we all know you and respect you very much, from what Diana has told us about you. Do not, we beg you, deprive us of the pleasure of meeting you in person. Write or telephone and let us know when to expect you. Arrangements will be made to collect you.

Yours most sincerely,
      Edward Sempill.'

After his signature came, in their own handwriting, the names Diana, Effie, Jeanie, Rowena, Rebecca, and Margaret Sempill, who must be Mrs Sempill.

Mrs Gilchrist was impatient. She had her coat on, ready to go off to work. 'Is it frae Miss Sempill?' she asked.

'No. It's from her father.'

'Whit does he want? You've never met him, have you?'

'No. Would you like to read it?'

Her mother took it and read it, with pursed lips. Now and then she uttered a little snort. 'He's being sarcastic,' she said, at last. ''The pleasure of meeting you'. Some hope. They juist want you there to laugh at you.'

'Do you think so?'

'Whit else would they want you for?'

Peggy was silent.

'Don't tell me you're thinking of going?'

Peggy still said nothing.

'You start work, mind, no' this Monday but the next. Ah wouldnae want you to disappoint Mr Stevenson, efter him being so obliging. Maybe they do respect you, Peggy, as they should, but they're no' oor kind. Amang them you'd be naething, amang your ain kind you're somebody. Weel, Ah'll have to be aff.'

When her mother was gone Peggy lay staring up at the ceiling. She wanted very much to read the letter again but she wasn't going to. She was going to put it in the fire, except that there was no fire, the house being all electric. She would put it in the garbage bin under the sink.

When she got up her father was in the kitchen reading his Daily Record. Every morning he went first thing to the newsagent. It was, he admitted, full of trivialities but he couldn't do without it.

'Your mither said you got a letter frae Miss Sempill.'

'From her father.'

'Whit does he want?'

'You can read it if you like?'

'Are you shair it's no' private?'

'Maybe you could advise me, after you've read it.'

'Thanks, Peggy.'

He read at first with frowns and then with smiles and nods. Evidently he thought Mr Sempill was sincere.

'It's a very nice letter,' he said, cautiously. 'Are you going to accept?'

'Do you think I should? Mum thinks I shouldn't.'

'Your mither would be terrified to find herself amang folk like that, but she forgets you're a different generation and you're educated. If you're no' on their social level yet you will be one day.'

He was supposed to believe in a time everyone would be on the same social level. Were his dreams of justice and equality, like her mother's fantasies, merely compensations for the irreducible harshness of real life?

'I'm not going, Dad,' she said.

'If it's money Ah'm shair your mither and me could help.'

'It's not money.'

'He hints in his letter as if he thocht it might be. Why don't you want to go?'

'I want to but I can't.'

'Whit's preventing you?'

It would have taken a long time to sort out the mixture of prejudice, fear, envy, inhibition, and self-distrust that stood in her way. She was used to doing without things that she couldn't afford, but making do a while longer with old jeans or old shoes was hardly to be compared with giving up this opportunity to spend a few days at Poverty Castle. Was her mother right in thinking that when she saw how they lived in their beautiful and comfortable corner she would be sick with discontent?

Better not to go. She would write to Mr Sempill, thanking him and saying she was sorry she could not accept his invitation. She would tell the kind of lie used on such occasions: her mother wasn't well. She would write it at once and go out and post it. Once it was in the letterbox she would be free to concentrate on the book she was reading, which was Prescott's CONQUEST OF MEXICO. Her dropping the letter in the box would be the equivalent of Cortes' burning of his boats on the beach at Vera Cruz!

It took her only ten minutes to write the letter. The notepaper and envelope she used were cheap in comparison with Mr Sempill's. But then hers were coming from a council flat with a view of an abandoned steelwork, his had come from a castle in sight of the sea.

She went through to the living-room to look for a stamp in the little silver dish in the display cabinet.

Her father was still reading the newspaper. 'Are you going to post it right away?' he asked.

'Why not?'

'Shouldn't you wait a day or twa? Second thoughts are often best.'

'I've thought about it too long already.'

It was a bright morning. In Kilcalmonell the sun would be glittering on the sea. Here it shone dully on heaps of litter and some haggard grass. She remembered how Diana had looked at all this unloveliness with pity for those condemned to live amidst it but also with impatience at their failure to tidy it up. She had not realised that living here for years had a paralysing effect. To tidy it up and keep it tidy would need herculean efforts hardly within the capability of people burdened by generations of deprivations. Flowers and bushes had once been planted by the council, only to be torn up within days by children whom everyone, including their parents, had called vandals. But it had seemed to Peggy, herself a child then, that that vicious and exultant destruction had also been an unconscious gesture of revenge. In this television age the children of the poor saw every night how the rich lived.

She came to a letterbox in a wall. She took the letter out of her pocket and held it in the slot but did not let it go. It might not be safe here. Children dropped in lighted matches. Better to find a letterbox in a safer place.

It would be as well to make for the post office in the mainstreet. A letter posted there went faster.

She came to it and walked past. She told herself she must not send a letter that contained a lie. But that itself was a lie. The truth was she had sentenced herself to a kind of death and dreaded to pull the trigger.

She sat in the public park, reading the CON-QUEST OF MEXICO. Young women with babies in prams passed, talking about babies. There had been babies in Montezuma's kingdom. Prescott, that blind admirable man, generously excused the conquistadors, on the grounds that they were men of their time and ought to be judged by the standards of that time. They had believed that cruelties and murders perpetrated by them on heathens in an attempt to win them to Christ were not only pardonable but praiseworthy, and would earn them a place in heaven. But what if, thought Peggy, there was one person, just one, in the sixteenth century who believed in his heart that those cruelties and murders were evil like all other cruelties and murders, that Cortes and his men, for all their endurance, courage, and fame, were brutal murderers, especially as a part of their motive was greed for gold?

She imagined that one person, sitting in the sun in a public park, in Medullin the town in Spain where Cortes was born, not daring to say it but thinking it, that treachery was treachery, greed was greed, cruelty was cruel, and murder murder, no matter what extenuations were offered, religious or patriotic.

In her own day, she thought, such a person might say, in defiance of the vast majority, that the killing of thousands of innocent people at Hiroshima, say, could never be justified. In the twenty-second century, if mankind had not destroyed itself by then, would some historian like Prescott write that it had been the general belief of the twentieth century that such massacres, though unfortunate and lamentable, had none the less been necessary, so that civilisation might be saved. Since all believed it no one was to blame.

'I don't believe it,' she said, aloud.

Two old men passing glanced back at her. One said something and they both laughed. She could guess what had been said. Talking to oneself was to be expected in the old, whose sweethearts were mostly dead, but not in a young girl of twenty with her whole life in front of her. It must be because she

248

was in love. Fifty yards away they were still glancing back and laughing.

She was not being mocked but honoured.

Old men in Cortes' Spain and Montezuma's Mexico had laughed at young girls talking to themselves.

She shut the book and the great problems receded. The small insistent ones returned, as she felt the letter in her pocket.

Her father was still reading the newspaper. He read everything, even the car advertisements, though he couldn't drive and was never likely to buy a car. In the evening he would watch television with the same fixation. He had used to argue back if anyone on the screen said something with which he vehemently disagreed, but his wife had got fed up and ordered him to keep quiet as he was spoiling her enjoyment. Now he just sat and listened to opinions that he detested, without saying a word.

'I didn't post it, Dad,' she said.

'So you took my advice, eh? You're haeing second thochts.'

'I thought I would telephone instead.'

'It's a lot dearer.'

'It's cheaper after six. I'll wait till then. It's not so easy to tell lies on the telephone.'

He had seldom occasion to telephone himself. 'Ah think Ah see whit you mean. Did you tell lies in your letter?'

'I said Mum wasn't well. Don't tell her.'

'Better no'. She wouldnae be pleased.'

Peggy's mother was superstitious about her health.

She didn't like it to be talked about, far less lied about.

At seven Peggy said she was going out to telephone the Sempills.

'Hae you decided whit you're going to tell them?' asked her mother.

'Yes, I have. I'm going to tell them I'm not coming.'

Her mother was satisfied. 'You'd better go then. You micht hae a long walk before you find yin that's working.'

There were two kiosks in the scheme. They were out of order so often the post office no longer bothered to repair them.

'Writing would hae been a lot cheaper,' said her mother. 'But he did put his telephone number on the letter, so maybe he wants you to phone. You ken, Peggy, you mak things a lot mair difficult than they need to be. Is that whit education does?'

'It helps you to see a' sides of a question,' said Peggy's father. 'That's whit it's for.'

'Is that why she can never mak up her mind?'

'About what?' asked Peggy.

'Aboot lots o' things. Aboot who you belang to, us or them.'

'Who are them?'

'Thae Sempills, to start wi'.'

'I said I wasn't going to visit them.'

'So you did, but you didnae soond very happy aboot it. Ah was talking to Mrs Davidson, or to be mair exact she was talking to me. This very day, in the shop. 'Is your lassie blin', Mary? Or does she need new specs?' 'Why dae you ask, Mysie?' 'Because Ah was in the post office for my pension and she cam in and ignored me. Ah said, hello, Peggy, but Ah micht as weel hae been talking to myself. So Ah thocht maybe a' her reading has weakend her eesicht."

'I didn't notice her,' said Peggy. 'It was crowded.'

'Don't worry aboot it, Peggy,' said her father. 'She's an ill-disposed woman. She'd dearly love to hear you'd failed at University.'

'She's no' the only yin,' said his wife, grimly.

But Peggy knew that just as many would be pleased if she succeeded. Like Pauline and Trixie, whom Diana had thought scarcely human. They would see Peggy's success as in a way their own too.

She made for the nearest kiosk, less than two hundred yards away. It might miraculously be working.

There was no miracle. The cord had been cut, the instrument stolen. Panes of glass were broken: a hammer must have been used. Obscene graffiti were scribbled on the wall. Human excrement fouled the floor. It was as if heathens had desecrated a shrine.

She set off to where she knew there would be a kiosk in good order. Broomfield was the most desirable part of the town where the houses were bungalows or semi-detached villas, all with gardens and all owned by the occupiers. The people there paid high rates and voted Tory. Since every house had its own private telephone the public one was seldom used.

It was only five minutes' walk, so close to the poor did the well-off live. The streets were called avenues.

There were flowers in the gardens and full-grown trees. On the footpaths there was no litter, not even dogshit. The dogs were taken to the public park, to shit there.

Two girls came out of a gate. They were well-dressed. They had been at school with Peggy and were now at University where she occasionally saw them.

One walked past without a blink of recognition but the other hesitated and then said: 'Hello, Peggy.'

'Hello, Betty.' said Peggy.

They didn't stop, nor did she.

She felt more encouraged by the greeting than depressed by the snub.

The telephone kiosk, with flower-beds behind it, was not only in working order, it was also whole and undefiled.

Her hands trembled as she put coins in readiness on top of the black box. She remembered the number, for she had been saying it to herself on and off for the past few days.

The telephone went on ringing in the house by the sea. Perhaps on such a fine evening they were out of doors.

Peggy's mouth was dry.

A voice spoke, briskly: 'Kilcalmonell 288. Effie Sempill speaking.'

Peggy could hardly speak. 'This is Peggy Gilchrist. I got a letter from your father this morning.'

The voice became warm and friendly. 'Hello, Peggy. How nice to hear from you. I'm Effie, Diana's sister. Diana's at the Big House where they're back in residence. I hope you're calling to say you're coming. We all very much want you to. We think, well I do anyway, that you would do the Sempills a lot of good.'

'No. I'm sorry. I can't come.'

There was a pause. 'Forgive me for asking but is it money? Fares are very expensive nowadays.'

'It's not money. I'm sorry. I can't explain. Good-bye.'

She hung up, with difficulty. All her strength had left her. She had pulled the trigger.

She was dead and had to bring herself to life again. It would be a painful resurrection and God knew what the risen Peggy Gilchrist would be like. Human company would be needed, but not that of people who knew her or rather had known her.

In a quiet side-street there was a cafe which did not have a juke-box and therefore was not patronised by her contemporaries. She went there. It was empty save for an elderly couple who paid her no heed. She ordered coffee and took it to a table in a corner. It was a dull little place with chocolate-coloured walls and tinny chairs and tables painted dark green. The proprietor, an Italian, kept glancing at her in puzzlement. Girls of her age seldom came in and when they did they had boy-friends with them.

This, thought Peggy, is the kind of place that mediums with mundane minds picture the after-world to be. She imagined such a medium in the Spiritualist hall in Tobago Street saying to Peggy's mother who sometimes went there (Peggy had once accompanied her for fun) hoping to receive a message from her mother: 'You have a loved one who has just passed on. She was rather fond of being on her own, wasn't she? Well, you'll be pleased to know that she's got her own little corner now and is content. She says you've not to worry about her. She understands now lots of things that weren't clear to her before.'

So do I, said Peggy, to herself.

She understood for instance what Effie had meant by saying: 'We think, well I do anyway, that you would do the Sempills a lot of good.' Diana had once said: 'My sister Effie thinks she's a revolutionary. She's very naive.' But surely it was Diana herself, with her feudalistic views who was naive. Effie had seen what Diana never could have: that their good fortune in always having plenty of money and living in a fine big house in a beautiful place might have caused them to become self-sufficient and in some respects false, needing someone from outside, someone poor whose home was in a run-down housing scheme close to a derelict steelwork, someone like Peggy, to enable them to see their self-sufficiency and falseness, so that they could, before too late, remedy it.

The old couple got up, with an effort, he helping her and went out slowly into the sunshine and disappeared.

For a few seconds Peggy almost believed her pretence. There was about the old man and woman an uncomplaining resignation that mediums would have recognised. It was as if they were saying to each other, telepathically, for ghosts had powers not given to the living: 'Well, whatever it was we believed in or hoped for this is what we have got and we shall have to put up with it because it's going to last for eternity; at least we're together.'

Yes, she understood better now.

She had told Effie that she couldn't explain why she didn't want to visit Poverty Castle, and it was true, she hadn't had the courage to delve deep enough to find the explanation. She had found it now. She had been afraid of being subverted. There was a part of her only too ready to give in and go over to the enemy. The Sempills would have made her defection too easy and pleasant.

She realised now how unfair she had been, not to herself but to them.

That telephone call had been cowardly and rude. She ought to make another, if only to apologise.

She got up and went out. Behind the counter, in his apron, the Guardian Angel, picking his nose, wished her good-night.

There was a telephone box outside the police station. Surely it had not been wrecked. She might not have enough coins left. The call would have to be very short.

There was someone telephoning. Peggy waited, patiently and unobtrusively.

Soon the woman came out, smiling. She was happier than she had been before she telephoned. It could be seen in the way she walked. Some weight had been taken off her mind.

It was a different voice this time, younger and less intense. 'Kilcalmonell 288. The Sempills' house. Who is calling, please?'

'Peggy. Peggy Gilchrist. Are you Rowena?'

'No, I'm Rebecca. Didn't you call earlier? Effie said

you did.'

'Yes. Will you tell her I've changed my mind. I'd like to come.'

'Good! Just a minute and I'll get her.'

What if Effie was at the bottom of the garden? What if the three minutes expired before she came? Peggy had no more suitable coins left. She had spent them on the coffee. Her connection with the Sempills might be ended not because she or they had broken it off but because she didn't have a tenpenny piece. It would be like something in a Hardy novel.

Then she heard Effie, panting. 'Rebecca tells me you've changed your mind. That's marvellous. When can you come?'

'It would have to be this weekend. I start work a week on Monday.'

Was there on Effie's part a momentary hesitation? Her voice was as hospitable as ever. 'That's fine. Can you make it Friday? A train will take you to Gourock where you catch the Dunoon ferry. We'll meet you on the pier. Do you think you can manage the five past six ferry?'

'Yes, I think so.'

Then they were cut off. Still, all that needed to be said had been said.

12

Peggy's mother was convinced — 'naething will mak me think different' — that she had changed her mind out of spite and it was that same spite which caused her to refuse offers to buy her a new outfit, especially of underclothes. 'If you don't mind shaming yourself Ah mind you shaming me.'

'As long as what I've got is clean, Mum.'

'I should hope what you wear's always clean, Peggy Gilchrist.'

Peggy's father gave her a wink and three pound notes.

Sonia brought along the oatmeal costume, hat, and high-heeled shoes. 'At least try them on, Peggy.'

To humour her Peggy did. Sonia had to laugh.

'We're no used to seeing you dressed up, Peggy. You'll hae to learn to be for when you become a teacher, though, mind you, nooadays teachers dress like workmen.'

'It's an adventure, Sonia. How can anybody have an adventure on high heels?'

'Was it an adventure for Miss Sempill when she visited us?' asked Sonia, shrewdly. 'Look how beautiful she was dressed.'

'She didn't have high heels, though.'

'Ah don't want to hurt your feelings, Peggy, but if Ah speak frankly it's for your ain good. You're supposed to hae brains and yet you cannae see that anybody that's not been lucky enough to be born wi' a good appearance has to make up for it by claes and make-up. Look at you, no' even lipstick.' Sonia was almost tearful.

Peggy liked her: she had a kind heart. If the Sempills were as kind they would do.

'Whit present are you taking them, Peggy?'

'Should I take them a present?'

'Shairly you ken it's bad manners not to. Ah suggest a bunch of roses.'

'They'll have lots of roses in their garden.'

'You ken, Peggy, a' thae books you read learn you nothing. It's no' the present itself, it's the thocht that counts.'

Peggy suspected that upper-class people might regard the bringing of presents as vulgar.

'A box of chocolates wad dae,' said Sonia. 'You're always safe wi' a box of chocolates. But no' too big a one. That wad be bad taste.'

In the station, waiting for her train Peggy looked at the boxes of chocolates on sale. She did not intend to buy one. They were to remind her where her loyalties lay, with her parents and Sonia, not with the Sempills.

In the train she found herself beside a man about her father's age, reading the Daily Record and taking his time to move from Page Three. Her mother tried to censor that page in her father's copy, 'accidentally' tearing it or mislaying it or spilling jam on it or using it prematurely to wrap tea leaves in. The joke was that her father, like many working class socialists, was at heart a puritan.

She sighed, happily. Remembered with affection and humour, her parents, like Sonia, would help her to hold her own with the Sempills...

She had the CONQUEST OF MEXICO in her knapsack but she preferred just to look out of the window, to make sure she did not miss Dumbarton Rock.

This was not the first time she had travelled to Dunoon by train and ferry. Last year she had gone on a CND pilgrimage to the Holy loch. Unlike today it had been pouring with rain. Her sharpest memory wasn't of the silent vigil with the massed police impatient to make arrests, but of an incident in a tearoom in Dunoon afterwards. An elderly woman appeared and furiously harangued the proprietor for allowing 'such scum' into his premises. She hoped he would have the place fumigated. When she had gone one of the demonstrators, a young woman with a child in her arms, both of them sodden, had asked what was the matter with the old woman. His reply had been a shrug of his shoulders. Peggy had thought that it wouldn't be with a bang or whimper that the world would end but a shrug. Thus everyone disowned responsibility.

Peggy had often wondered what could have caused the old woman's malevolence. Had she been ill and in pain? Had she been too poor to afford the sausages and chips that the 'scum' were eating? Had her husband or brother been killed in the last war? Even so, why that vicious hatred of people who were trying to prevent another war in which countless millions would die? It was that hatred which one day would cause the missiles to be launched.

But she had not come this time as a dutiful act but for an adventure, to refresh her spirit and perhaps make discoveries. She took her cue from a little girl of three or four, with a red ribbon in her hair, whom she saw in the queue to board the ferry. Everything was wonderful to her: the Jupiter with the flat red funnels, the yellow-eyed gulls perched on masts, and the sea beyond. She said nothing but contained her rapture. Her mother, burdened with a baby, was not able to give her much attention, but she did not mind.

For the first time in her life Peggy thought that she might have a little girl of her own one day.

It was joy out of all proportion to the act to take the little girl's hand and help her along the gangway.

As a discoverer should, Peggy went up on to the top deck, heedless of the strong cool breeze, and stood as near the bow as she could get.

That must be the Cloch Lighthouse. Were those mountains in the distance the Isle of Arran? And was that great lump on the horizon further off still Ailsa Craig? These were strange seas. Like Cortes and his men she did not know what awaited her on land.

As the ferry approached Dunoon she found a place, still on the top deck, from where she could watch people on the pier without being seen by them. Loudspeakers bellowed 'Scotland the Brave', played by a pipe band.

There was Diana, accompanied by the twins and also by a tall young man in white flannels and striped blazer. He must be Edwin. Even at that range

260

his nose was seen to be big.

The four of them were being gazed at with fascination. Edwin would be speaking that loud posh upper-class English accent that Scots of the lower orders found impressive but comic; also his blazer was an oddity; but it was really his companions who were drawing the mesmerised stares. As always Diana was ladylike and elegant, in a blue dress with a white scarf over her hair. Effie and Jeanie were tall too, with lovely long fair hair: one wore red cords, the other yellow. But it was above all their self-assurance that attracted the beholders, themselves beset with all the usual worries and doubts. The Sempill girls weren't aware of it themselves. It was natural to them. It would never become arrogance.

Peggy had instructed herself how she should behave as a guest. Though grateful for the hospitality she should treat her hosts as equals. Now she was afraid she would not be able to do it. An inbred servility towards wealth and rank would prevent her. In theory she could give reasons why she should not humble herself even to the Queen, but in practice, confronted by the Sempills and Edwin, she might find herself mumbling and hanging her head.

She had come to make discoveries. Here she was making one about herself that dismayed her.

Effie and Jeanie had come forward to have a closer look at the passengers disembarking. On their handsome faces was eagerness to welcome her but also alarm that she might not have come after all.

She hurried down the stairs and was the last to come off.

They were at the foot of the gangway to greet her. They towered over her. Jeanie shook her hand but Effie kissed her on the cheek. Diana and Edwin came forward. Diana patted her shoulder. Edwin gave her a little bow and a big grin.

As alert as a cat in a strange situation Peggy noticed people wondering what the relationship could be between these tall well-dressed, well-spoken members of the upper-class and the small scruffy girl in the cheap clothes. Perhaps they were thinking that she had come to be their servant. But a servant wouldn't have had her knapsack carried for her, nor would she have been led to the big blue car and given the place of honour beside the driver.

Other motorists might have been anxious about parking their car in such a congested place, with cars coming off and on the ferry, but not the Sempills. If they had been challenged they would have been polite but unconcerned. They would never have cringed with embarrassment.

Money gave courage, thought Peggy. But there was Edwin with more money than they, ready to blush and look sheepish.

Effie was to drive as far as Lochgilphead where Jeanie would take over. Evidently they did not think much of Edwin as a driver. He wasn't huffed or crestfallen. He sat contentedly in the back, holding Diana's hand.

'We'll go by the high road,' said Effie, as they set off. 'It's quicker.'

It would also mean their avoiding the Holy Loch and the American nuclear submarines. Peggy remembered that Effie was a revolutionary, at least according to Diana.

'How are your parents, Peggy?' asked Diana.

'Fine, thanks.'

'Has Sonia had her baby yet?'

'Some time next month.'

'How old is Sonia?' asked Jeanie.

'Nineteen.'

'I want children but not next year, thank you very much.'

'I hope not until you've finished your course.' said Diana. 'Jeanie's going to be a vet, Peggy, and Effie a doctor.'

'And Di's going to be a lady wife,' said Effie. 'As for children I'm never going to have any.'

'So you say,' said her twin. 'Probably you'll have half a dozen. Won't she, Edwin?'

He guffawed. 'At least.'

He had all the upper-class characteristics and yet Peggy found herself liking him more and more, and trusting him too. He would never try to make her or anyone feel small. She could see why his parents were willing that he should marry Diana.

'What about you, Peggy?' asked Effie. 'Are you looking forward to having children?'

Peggy told them about the little girl with the red ribbon.

'That's when children are at their best,' said Effie, 'when they're three or four. They're absolutely delightful then. By the time they're ten they've become egocentric little beasts. It happened to us Sempills. Didn't it, Edwin?'

'It certainly did not. At ten you were still

delightful, all of you.'

'What about the famous cricket match? We were horrible then.'

'My father didn't think so. He thought you were marvellous. So you were. Especially Di.'

'Nigel didn't think so.'

They laughed. Peggy thought she remembered Diana saying that Edwin had a brother called Nigel.

Ahead now were mountains, to Peggy unknown territory. Like the conquistadors she was being escorted by natives of the country. She did not, like Cortes, fear treachery and physical attack but she did feel in danger.

Effie noticed her smile. 'What's the joke?'

Peggy shook her head.

'If you're thinking that the Sempills are a self-sufficient conceited lot you're right. For years and years we've thought we didn't need anyone but ourselves. Outsiders must have found us insufferable.'

'I never did,' said Edwin.

'We're just beginning to concede that there are other people in the world besides ourselves. Now and then we still slide back into our old bad ways. Don't be afraid, Peggy, to tell us off.'

'The speed limit on this road is sixty miles an hour,' said Diana. 'You are doing seventy.'

'This car could do a hundred with ease.'

'We could end up in Loch Eck with even greater ease,' said Jeanie.

The loch was long and narrow. It was dark with shadow, though the hills above it were bright with sun. It looked cold and deep.

'We promised we'd be home for dinner,' said Effie.

Peggy's heart sank. They probably dressed for dinner. She had brought a change of blouse but no dress. She should have heeded Sonia's advice, or better still her mother's and not come at all.

A few minutes later when they were passing Cairndow, Keat's country, Jeanie said: 'Do you know any of Keats' poetry, Peggy?'

This was the Sempills' way of claiming Peggy as a friend. They had driven Edinburgh relatives along this road without ever mentioning Keats. Only the elect were honoured. It would not have mattered if Peggy had not been able to supply a quotation.

'I used to be able to say whole poems by heart,' said Peggy. 'Why?'

Effie explained that Keats had walked along this road a hundred and fifty years ago. 'It ruined his health.'

'Isn't Keats old-fashioned?' asked Diana. 'Shouldn't we be quoting T. S. Eliot?'

'He never stayed at the Cairndow Inn,' said Effie.

'Keats didn't like Scots people,' said Peggy. 'He rhymed 'wakened' and with 'spike end' because he was a Cockney and that was how he spoke. He was hardly any taller than me.'

They weren't sure whether or not she was being ironical.

'But he wrote beautiful poetry,' said Jeanie.

'Yes. 'Now more than ever seems it rich to die,
To cease upon the midnight with no pain,
While thou art pouring forth thy soul abroad,

In such an ecstasy."

She spoke it quietly but with feeling.

There was a silence in the car.

She should have remembered that the Sempills would be worried about their mother.

They had passed Tarbeg, with Jeanie driving, and were on the single-track twisty road that led to Kilcalmonell when Effie, now seated in the back, suddenly said: 'I think we should warn Peggy about Nigel.'

'Who's Nigel?' asked Peggy.

'Edwin's brother. He's younger than Edwin and not nearly as nice.'

'He's an outrageous snob, and proud of it,' said Jeanie. 'He's at Oxford and has a very low opinion of all other Universities. Except Cambridge of course.'

'He's not as bad as that,' said Edwin. 'Is he, Di?'

'It's a pose with him,' said Diana.

'That's a change of tune, Di,' said Effie. 'You used to agree that he was awful.'

'I know him better now.'

'Then you must know he's worse than awful. Sorry, Edwin.'

'Don't mind me.'

'Jeanie and I were afraid that you wouldn't be a match for him, Peggy. We know better now.'

'Don't listen to them, Peggy,' said Diana. 'Nigel's young — '

'He's older than Effie and me,' said Jeanie.

'And he may have an unfortunate way of expressing himself at times — '

'Unfortunate?' cried Effie. 'Obnoxious, you mean.'

'At times!' cried Jeanie. 'All the time!'

'I assure you, Peggy, he can be very charming when he likes.'

Her sisters yelled.

If Nigel speaks to me, thought Peggy, whether charmingly or obnoxiously, I shall say as little as possible in return.

13

Born and brought up in drab places Peggy had been conditioned to find interest and pleasure in people rather than scenery. She kept quiet therefore when her companions were enthusiastic about this or that view of sunlit peak or sapphire loch, but when she came into Kilcalmonell parish she thought it was beautiful and said so several times. Here was a harmony between people and nature. There were farms, houses with large gardens, a church, a shop, a village hall, and a little harbour, all set in the midst of green fields with cows and sheep in them, and magnificent trees. All the time there were views of the sea and the far-off Paps of Jura.

'We're not looking forward to having to live in Edinburgh,' said Jeanie. 'Are we, Effie?'

'No. We're coming home every weekend.'

Peggy doubted it. These two lovely and lively girls would have too good a time in Edinburgh.

They came to a large black iron gate. Effie got out and opened it.

They then drove along a tarred road through a thick wood. I really am an outsider, thought Peggy. I can't tell an oak from an ash or an elm from a beech.

A bird with beautiful feathers and a long tail flew up off the road, with a loud harsh cry.

'A pheasant,' said Jeanie. 'Edwin's people come north every summer to massacre them.'

'And deer,' added Effie.

'Not me,' said Edwin.

'If we're given venison tomorrow I'll refuse it,' said Jeanie.

'Don't worry, Jeanie,' said Diana. 'Everyone knows you're a vegetarian.'

'I'm not,' said Effie, 'but I won't want venison. I prefer deer alive in the wood to deer dead on a plate.'

Peggy wondered who might offer them venison tomorrow night.

Jeanie explained. 'We're invited to dinner to-morrow at the Big House.'

So that was the reason for Effie's hesitation during the telephone conversation. Peggy had proposed coming at an inconvenient time.

Before she could start feeling dismayed by this news she saw in front through the trees the high white house, which she had seen so often in the photograph. Then they were in the large cobbled courtyard, all round which were coloured flower-pots containing what she learned later were geraniums. They drove past a small red sports car to the front of the house.

Peggy Cortes had arrived at Montezuma's palace.

Montezuma, alias Mr Sempill, was seated in a deck chair on the lawn, with a glass in his hand: he smiled jollily and yet still looked sad. Mrs Sempill sat beside him, in a white hat and multicoloured dress. Two persons were playing badminton languidly, a young man in white shirt and flannels with a red tie round his waist: this must be Nigel, and a girl of about sixteen, of breathtaking beauty: she must be Rowena. Rebecca, the youngest, knelt on the grass, restraining a dog that wanted to chase the shuttlecock.

'Well, here she is!' cried Effie.

Each of them had his or her own way of greeting the newcomer.

Mr Sempill raised his glass in salute: 'Welcome to Poverty Castle, my dear!' he cried.

Mrs Sempill, thin-faced and long-necked, turned and smiled, not all that cordially, Peggy thought.

Rowena's wave was flaccid. She did not believe in energetic movements.

Nigel just ignored her. It was deliberate, so in a way it was a greeting. Nigel was being awful.

Rebecca jumped up and ran over to Peggy. Though she was the smallest of the Sempills she was still inches taller than Peggy. Diana had said that Rebecca was the best-hearted of them all, and here she was proving it. She would always do more than her share and never grumble. Her sisters, though they were all older, depended on her. Her opinion would often be the one that settled an argument.

She kissed Peggy's cheek. 'You must be tired after your journey.' she said. 'I'm sure you'd like to wash and rest before dinner.'

Peggy also needed to be by herself for a few minutes.

'Yes, I would,' she said. 'Thanks.'

Rebecca called to the others. 'I'm taking Peggy up to her room.'

Carrying the knapsack, she led the way.

Peggy pretended to see the house through Sonia's house-proud eyes. The spaciousness and the many rooms, especially the three bathrooms, would have had Sonia speechless and perhaps tearful with envy. The carpets would have been too muted in colour for her taste but she would have loved their soft thick pile. Though she could never afford it herself she knew the best quality when she saw it. The numerous pictures would have disappointed her, in that there were no spotted Bambis or golden-curled infants, but the gilt frames would have compensated. She would have pointed with triumph to the flowers which were everywhere, in a variety of bowls and vases. Many were roses. The house was fragrant with them.

Peggy's room was on the second floor, at the front,

so that the window looked down on to the garden and beyond to the sea. It struck her that it was adoration, not just plain ordinary love, that Mrs Sempill was demanding from her family. They all gave it too, even Diana. Peggy felt compunction as she thought how she and Bobby showed their love for their mother, and how she showed hers for them. Like most members of the working class they distrusted excessive displays of affection: it was part of their puritanism. But there was something else: a lack of refinement. Generations of living in small cheap houses in dreary crowded ghettos, of working hard at boring tasks for long hours in ugly places for little pay, and of being taught in utilitarian schools only enough to enable them to do the work their masters required of them, all that had inevitably resulted in coarseness, spiritual and physical. Peggy should know for she was herself a specimen. Nor could it be claimed, as her mother and Sonia would do indignantly, that the working class made up for their lack of grace by being more genuine in their feelings. The Sempills' fondness for one another was as genuine as roses.

Rebecca joined her at the window. 'Did Diana tell you that Mama's going to have a baby?'

'Yes, she told me. She looks very well.'

'The doctors say it should be all right. She's so keen to have a boy, after having five girls.'

Not too confident of her own chances of surviving the ordeal nineteen-year-old Sonia would consider forty-eight-year-old Mrs Sempill as good as doomed.

Suddenly Peggy caught sight of the peacock. It had its gorgeous tail outspread.

'Where's the Big House?' she asked.

'Over there, but you can't see it for the trees.'

'They were saying in the car that you've been invited to dinner tomorrow night.'

'Yes. You're included of course.'

'I didn't bring a suitable dress.'

'You can borrow one of mine.'

'I don't think it would fit me. I'm what's called a smout.'

'We'll make what adjustments are necessary.'

Peggy left it at that. Later she would find some excuse for declining.

Mr Sempill was wearing a kilt, rarest of garments in Netherlee Park. Even at that distance the purple of his cheeks and the redness of his nose could be seen, the consequence of too much alcohol, a very common occurrence in Netherlee Park. In the photograph he had looked lonely. He still did, in the midst of his family.

Mrs Sempill was now walking about the garden, making gestures with her arms as if warding off flies or evil spirits. Didn't pregnant women often act oddly? And think that the world revolved round them and their unborn child? If she isn't as nice to me as the others, thought Peggy, I must make allowances.

Edwin and Nigel seemed to taking their leave. Edwin kissed Diana. Nigel exchanged banter with the twins.

In appearance he was the kind of young man Peggy admired: the very opposite of Sadie Meiklejohn's beefy burly heavy-footed rugby players. His hair, neither too long nor too short, was neatly arranged.

Rebecca showed her to a bathroom. Dinner would be in twenty minutes, she said. She had to go and help Mrs McDougall. They would eat in the kitchen as they always did when it was only family. With that compliment she left.

The untidiness of the bathroom would have affronted Peggy's mother. In hers even the tooth-brushes had always to be in their proper place. Here jars of cream, tins of talcum, bottles of perfume, deodorants, razors, tissues, and miscellaneous cosmetic aids, were scattered over every counter and on the carpet, many with their tops or stoppers off. 'That's not a reading-room, Rab,' her mother would say, rapping on the door, and her father would soon creep out, with his Daily Record folded under his oxter. Here it was like a library, with bundles of books and magazines. One book lay on the floor, open: MANSFIELD PARK by Jane Austen. Which of the sisters was reading it? Not Diana: she was too ladylike to read such a well-bred book while seated on the lavatory. Not Effie: Jane Austen's characters would be too genteel for her. Not Jeanie: she would read these veterinarian magazines. Rebecca perhaps? But she probably didn't use this bathroom, which was why it was in such a mess. Rowena then? Yes, she would appreciate the indolent ladies and gentlemen.

With your face and hands clean, and your bladder empty, you could face anyone. That was a saying of her father's which always provoked a reproof from her mother, who called it vulgar. Well, thought Peggy, as she went downstairs, I'll soon see if it's true.

Alas, never had she felt so stunted and scruffy

than when Mrs Sempill came up to her, took both her hands, and thanked her for having been so helpful to Diana. Peggy wondered how she or anyone could have helped capable, self-sufficient Diana. In Mrs Sempill's blue eyes, all the brighter because of the dark patches under them, she saw, not gratitude or sympathy, but gladness that *her* girls were so much more beautiful than this waif from the slums. All her life Mrs Sempill had been pampered. When she was a little girl her doll would have had longer lashes than any other girls. To get the attention she craved she must have resorted to many wiles and tricks. Was becoming pregnant one of them?

14

The big stone-floored kitchen with the sideboard adorned with blue delf, the bright blue cooker irradiating warmth, the pleasant smells of baking and cooking, and the five relaxed cats would have looked a lot more homely if it hadn't been for Mrs Sempill.

She had put on so much make-up and jewellery that she was more like a high-class tart than a housewife, especially as she was wearing a red dress cut so low at the front that most of her breasts could be seen. They were passable breasts for a woman nearly fifty, though not of Page Three quality, and she was proud of them. Now and then she would stare at flat-chested Peggy in pity it seemed and forgot her name. Whether this was mischievous pretence or genuine loss of memory, Peggy could not be sure. Sometimes when spoken to she did not seem to hear. Her family took care not to confuse or startle her by repeating what they had said in a louder voice: they just let it pass. It must have been that same protectiveness which had prevented the girls from objecting to her mouth absurdly enlarged by lipstick and her exposed bosom. She cried out once, suddenly and shrilly, that she had to remember that she was eating for two; but for all that she did not eat much.

They are making me very welcome, thought Peggy, and are talking to me almost as if I was one of them, but I am not to be told the truth about Mrs Sempill's state of health, mental and physical. It doesn't mean that there is anything seriously wrong with her like suspected cancer or imminent miscarriage or incipient insanity, it's just that they're willing to share everything, except their mother.

Mrs McDougall, the housekeeper, a fresh-faced, white-haired competent woman of about forty five, was also excluded in this respect, though none of them, except Diana, treated her as a servant. All of them, again with the exception of Diana, called her Morag, and she used their first names, including Mr

Sempill's. A stranger would have thought she was his sister or Mrs Sempill's, and not a housekeeper not long in their employ. Nevertheless, she was not let into the secrets concerning Mrs Sempill, whatever they were. Perhaps they were not deliberately kept from her, or from Peggy. Perhaps they were of a kind that were felt and could not be told. Only Mrs Sempill's children could feel them. At times her husband looked shut out and left in the dark.

Peggy was already fond of Mr Sempill, with his mournful Montezuma eyes. Whatever private griefs he had and whatever dooms he foresaw, he did not let them turn him sour or peevish. On the contrary he was always gentlemanly and good-natured. Wine doubtless helped, for he drank a great deal, but Peggy had seen men made morose, not to say belligerent, by too much drink. He was particularly affable to her and it was more to please him than indulge herself that she consented to have her glass refilled by him four or five times: by the end of the meal she had lost count. It was the first time in her life that she had drunk wine. To her consternation she found that it was making her talkative and boastful. When Mr Sempill asked her what historical book she was reading at the moment she should have answered vaguely and modestly, instead she said, pertly: 'THE CONQUEST OF MEXICO by WH Prescott,' and proceeded to give a not very coherent exposition of its theme.

'Nonetheless,' said Mr Sempill, 'it is one of the great adventures of history, the invasion by Cortes and his conquistadors of the Kingdom of Montezuma'.

'But they destroyed it, didn't they?' cried Effie,

bitterly. 'They murdered Montezuma.'

'No, they didn't,' said Peggy. 'It was an Aztec killed him.'

'Alas, Effie,' said Mr Sempill, 'it has always been a characteristic of the human race to expend great courage and fortitude on wicked causes.'

'A characteristic of men, Papa,' asked Diana. 'Didn't they want to bring the benefits of Christianity to heathens?'

'What benefits, for heaven's sake?' cried Effie.

'You heard Peggy say that the Aztecs sacrificed human beings.'

'What about the Spanish Inquisition? And bloody Mary Tudor, who burned hundreds of people alive? Religion brings out the cruelty in people.'

'Is that because God's cruel?' asked Rowena. She might have been asking for the brussel sprouts to be passed, so casually did she say it. 'Well, I mean, look at famines and earthquakes. Aren't they called Acts of God?'

'And there's Hell,' said Effie, 'where God's supposed to torture sinners until the end of time.'

'There's nothing in the whole Bible about being kind to animals,' said Jeanie.

Mrs Sempill shook her head and rattled her earrings. 'You are all being too morbid,' she cried. 'Whoever or whatever it is that gives us the miracle of life should we not be grateful? Please let us talk about something more uplifting.' She smiled at Peggy as if to forgive her for bringing up such an unpleasant subject.

'You must read us something out of Prescott, Peggy,' said Mr Sempill. 'In this house, you see, we do not sit like zombies in front of a television set. We read to one another, we sing, we play records, we discuss like intelligent individuals. There *is* a set upstairs, for the lazy-minded.'

'Black and white,' said Jeanie.

'Who needs colour television, when we have sunsets like that?' He pointed to the window.

A few minutes later they were all out in the garden, except Mrs McDougall who had the clearing up to do and the cats on the look-out for scraps.

The sea was blood-red. Clouds, seagulls, and faces were pink. Probably so were the midges, if they could have been seen. They were certainly felt. Appreciation of the cosmic beauty had to be stoical and brief because of those infinitesimal predators.

Mrs Sempill must have regretted showing so much bosom, Mr Sempill that he was wearing a kilt. Effie cursed. Jeanie, lover of animals, found it hard not to join in the abuse of their tormentors. Indolent Rowena led the rush into the house: hers were the biggest and itchiest blotches.

15

Next morning Effie and Jeanie were to drive Mrs McDougall to Tarbeg. She was to have the weekend off. Peggy was invited to accompany them. The alternative would have been to help Rebecca and Mrs Sempill tidy up and prepare lunch. If it had been just Rebecca, Peggy would have enjoyed it. Diana and Rowena were to spend the morning at Kilcalmonell House, horse-riding. Peggy wasn't asked.

Peggy liked strolling about the bright busy little town, though her companions seemed moody. She put it down to worry about their mother. On the way back they surprised her by discussing Diana hostilely; at any rate Effie did, Jeanie being more restrained.

Peggy quickly gathered that Diana had recently let her family know that she had given in to Lady Campton's demand that the wedding should take place in church, on the Campton's estate in the South of England. It would mean her becoming an Anglican.

Effie saw it as a great treachery. 'She'd do anything to be mistress of Kilcalmonell House,' she said, bitterly. 'It's been her ambition from the day she first saw it.'

'That's not fair, Effie,' said Jeanie. 'She loves Edwin.'

'How could anyone with a scrap of intelligence love Edwin? Edwin's not there. He's a nonentity. All right, a nice nonentity. Do you think his mother would let him marry Di if he wasn't a nonentity? She knows Di will run the show for him. Not that she likes Di much. They're too alike for that'.

'That's ridiculous, Effie. Di's not a bit like Lady Campton.'

'Give her time'. Effie's anguish was genuine. 'When we were kids, Peggy, we thought Di was marvellous. We worshipped her. She was our heroine. We all wanted to be like her. She was afraid of nothing or if she was she never let it show. She treated everyone alike. Papa used to call her the world's best democrat. She would never have spoken to Mrs McDougall then the way she does now.'

So I wasn't imagining it, thought Peggy.

'You remember, Jeanie, how shattered we all were when we thought she had gone over to the grownups? Now she's gone over to the useless rich. We've really lost her this time.'

'She's still our sister.'

'No. She's already a Campton. What do you think, Peggy? You must know her pretty well.'

It seemed to Peggy none of them did. She shook her head. 'I'd rather keep out of it, Effie, if you don't mind. Diana invited me. She's my friend.'

'Quite right, Peggy,' said Jeanie, and changed the subject. 'Rebecca was saying you're going to borrow one of her dresses for tonight.'

'She suggested it, but I don't think I should go. I'll stay and look after the cats.'

'If it's Nigel, don't worry about him,' said Effie,

grimly. 'We'll keep him at bay.'

'It's not Nigel.' Indeed, Nigel was a reason for going, not for staying away. It would have been interesting to examine his awfulness. 'I'd feel like an interloper.'

'But you're invited,' said Jeanie. 'Lady Campton said we had to bring you.'

'Di's sung your praises,' said Effie sarcastically. 'You might find yourself being invited to the wedding.'

'Who will all be there?' asked Peggy.

'Lady Campton. She's a bitch but I suppose her bark's worse than her bite. It's some bark, though. She's got a voice like a female bobby and her language's not always ladylike. Sir Edwin. He's all right. Tickle his stomach and he rolls over on his back. In other words flatter him and he'll like you. Edwin. You've met him. If anyone's cross with him he's miserable. Give him a kind word and he'll lick your hand. Nigel's just as ready to bite it. That's the lot, except for Lady Campton's sister, Lady Angela, whom Jeanie and I haven't met. Rowena says she's always slobbering over an obscene little dog.'

'No dog's obscene,' said Jeanie.

'Well, it's always licking its private parts, according to Rowena. Then it licks Lady Angela's face. Come on, Peggy, what's to be frightened of in that lot?'

As soon as they got home they fetched Rebecca from the kitchen and went up to her room where she selected three dresses from a wardrobe full of them and spread them on the bed.

Jeanie took charge. Effie stood aside. This business was too trivial for her.

One dress was red, another pink, and the third green.

'Which do you prefer, Peggy?' asked Jeanie.

'I've been told I suit red.'

'Try it on then.'

So Peggy had to strip to cheap panties and bra in order to put on the expensive silk dress. With its white cuffs and collar it looked more suitable for a girl of fourteen than a young woman of twenty. It was tight at the chest.

'Just as well you've got small boobs,' remarked Effie. It was also too long.

On her knees Rebecca was about to turn it up with pins for subsequent sewing.

'Don't bother,' said Peggy. 'It'll hide my legs.' Like her boobs they were deficient.

She studied herself in the long mirror. 'Well, at least I'll be safe from Nigel. He wouldn't be nasty to a nice wee girl like that, would he?' She put a finger in her mouth.

It was also on the loose side.

Jeanie rushed off and returned with a red-and-white belt.

'What about some jewellery?' asked Rebecca.

'Just a moment.' Effie marched off and soon came back with red beads and an assortment of earrings. She let Jeanie and Rebecca help Peggy to put them on.

'What about your hair?' asked Jeanie.

I never realised what a freak I am, thought Peggy: puny boobs, skinny legs, meagre hips and thin dry hair.

'What about red ribbons?' asked Jeanie.

Rebecca found some in a drawer. She and Jeanie tied up Peggy's hair with them.

There remained shoes. None of the Sempills had shoes that would fit her.

'I've always had small feet,' she said. 'My mother says it's a sign of high pedigree.'

She laughed and the others joined in.

'Lady Campton's are huge,' said Effie.

They all laughed again.

'I'll sit where my feet will be in shadow,' said Peggy.

'You don't have thermal underwear, do you?' asked Effie.

'No.' It was June, after all.

'Their central heating's ancient. It's always breaking down. The drawing-room's usually freezing.'

'And smoky,' said Rebecca. 'Remember the last time? Everybody was in tears.'

Their laughter this time came out in shrieks. Peggy did not have the same comic memories but she laughed too. She very much felt that she was one of them.

After lunch they went for a walk to the beach and the ruins of the castle. Mrs Sempill not only insisted on going but danced on ahead across the machair, though there were many rabbit holes to cause stumble or fall. With her multicolored silk scarf she waved away their cries of caution.

They were all present. Diana and Rowena had come back from Kilcalmonell House with a reminder from Lady Campton that Peggy was included in the invitation.

Diana had taken Peggy aside. 'I don't know what Effie and Jeanie may have been telling you.'

'What about?'

'The Camptons. Kilcalmonell House.'

Peggy played the innocent. 'They said the drawing-room was smoky.'

'It depends on which way the wind is blowing.'

Peggy kept her face straight. Diana never had much humour. On the subject of the Camptons and Kilcalmonell House she had none.

'Just be your usual honest self, Peggy, and you will have nothing to worry about.'

As if I was being warned not to steal the teaspoons, thought Peggy, finding it hard not to laugh.

On the walk she was in what she called a Sempillish mood: confident, reckless, and defiant. She was not in awe of them any more, not even of Mrs Sempill. As for Lady Campton and Nigel she was looking forward to encountering their snobberies.

Walking across the machair to the beach she listened appreciatively to the information given her, now by one of them and now by another. These bushes with the sharp thorns and yellow flowers were whins. 'Gorse is the English name,' said Mr Sempill. Pointing his stick up at the sky he shouted:

"When thou from hence away are past

Every night and all

To whinny muir thou comest at last

And Christ receive thy saul.

If ever thou gavest hosen and shoon

Every night and all

Sit thee down and put them on

And Christ receive thy saul.
If hosen and shoon thou ne'er gavest nane
Every night and all
The whins sall prick thee to the bare bane
And Christ receive thy saul."

'Don't be so morbid, Papa,' cried Diana.

This little white flower, it seemed, was eye-bright, that yellow one tormentil. Those black and white birds with the red chopstick beaks were oyster-catchers. Did she know there were more red deer on Jura than sheep? Whales had been seen here last summer. The sand was shell-sand, which was why it was so white. These flowers on the shore were thrift, sea-campion, and wild iris. This was an urchin, those anemones. Kilcalmonell Castle dated from the four-teenth century. It had been sacked several times, the last being in 1644. Men, women, and children had been treacherously slaughtered then and their bodies thrown into the well.

It was Mr Sempill who told the story of the castle, standing on the bright turf within the broken walls. He held his stick as if it was a sword and he was protecting his family from the violence of the past. Rowena and Rebecca came running and placed a wreath of laurel over his brow. They themselves were wearing wreaths. Soon they all were. What victory, thought Peggy, do they think they're celebrating.

Suddenly Mama was weeping. They sat her down on a mossy stone and comforted her. Peggy was shut out. It was a Sempill occasion. She wandered off and stood under the laurel tree. Above her a bird screamed and oyster-catchers piped, as they had done that day hundreds of years ago, heedless of the cries of killers and slain.

Within the walls the Sempills were happy again. Mama could be heard hysterically chiding them for being so concerned just because she had felt overcome for a moment, not by weariness or weakness, they were not to think that, but by the wonderful feeling which all women in her condition had, that it had been given to them to replenish the earth.

Peggy's blood turned cold. She was no spaewife but it seemed to her that in Mrs Sempill's voice there was another ancestral note besides that of exultant motherhood. It was fear that if she died her child would die with her.

Peggy went back. They were still wearing their wreaths.

Mrs Sempill stared at her, as if demanding why she was so impertinent as to invade the privacy of the Sempill family. Suddenly she came towards Peggy, with her arms outstretched.

'While you are with us, my dear,' she cried, embracing her, 'you are one of us. Is that not so, girls?'

They all cried yes it was. None of them seemed to be aware that their mother was not being quite sincere.

16

Papa wore Highland evening dress and looked, Effie said, like a chieftain in a Raeburn painting. But where, thought Peggy, was the arrogant strut, the haughty stare?

Mama was swathed in swirls of pale-blue muslin. She tinkled and glittered with jewellery all over her person. She had at least five rings: her hands weren't still long enough for Peggy to count. Her make-up was not so clownish, thanks to Diana, who, to the twins' annoyance, had inspected its putting on.

The twins were dressed alike, in white blouses and long tartan skirts.

Rebecca's dress was green with a flared skirt, Rowena's white with a red sash, and Diana's unrelieved black.

The twins again had protested. It made her too old, too severe, too dutiful. That last was Effie's scornful word. Rather mischievously, Peggy had said it made her look aristocratic.

They left Poverty Castle at twenty-five past seven. It was a bright warm evening. In the Daimler were Papa, Mama, Diana and Rowena. The twins, Rebecca, and Peggy followed in the white Escort.

'What do I call them?' asked Peggy. 'My host and hostess, I mean.'

'Lady Campton and Sir Edwin, I suppose,' said Jeanie.

'Yes, but you see I'm a member of a society at the University, whose members are pledged never to acknowledge titles, which they consider to be anachronistic.'

Effie, who was driving, turned her head. 'Are you serious?' She sounded not only astonished but disapproving.

'Yes. The founder is a friend of mine.' He wasn't really, though he had once tried to seduce her, saying that he wanted to do her a good turn. 'I'll tell you something, wee Gilchrist. You know a hell of a lot about the lives of other people, most of them dead, but your own life's empty.'

'Are titles bad things?' asked Rebecca.

'Other countries think so, for they don't have them. In a democracy they're ridiculous.'

Effie and Jeanie exchanged glances. The little bolshy was at last showing her colours.

'How many are in your society?' asked Jeanie.

'Seven, so far.'

'Seven!'

They laughed.

'Many great and noble enterprises have small beginnings' said Peggy.

'But, Peggy, we can't be rude to our host and hostess, can we?' asked Jeanie.

'That's why I asked. It wouldn't do to be rude.'

Again Jeanie and Effie looked at each other. Listen to her, those looks said, coming from a ghastly housing scheme, and having the cheek to be ironical at the expense of people who, whatever they were personally, were rich, owned two large estates, and were acquainted with members of the Royal Family. They liked her but, not knowing her well, could they trust her not to disgrace them? It wasn't her fault, it was the way she had been brought up. She was intelligent, which made it worse, for a stupid person's gaffes wouldn't matter, whereas a clever person's, being not altogether unintentional, could cause offence.

Peggy smiled. Effie the revolutionary was as naive as Diana had said. She was prepared to champion the poor, provided they behaved themselves and were respectful to their betters.

The house was now in sight, through the trees. Cortes would have been escorted by a picked bodyguard of cavalry. She was on her own. The Sempills were really on the other side. Besides, it was Mama they would rally round to protect.

As the car drew up at the front door Peggy heard in her mind Sonia's awed voice: 'Jeez, Peggy, it's as big as a church.'

Edwin was waiting on the steps, dressed in evening clothes. He ran down to open the door for Mrs Sempill and then for Diana.

Peggy had once paid to see through a stately home outside Edinburgh, but this time she was here as a guest, she would be on the privileged side of the silken ropes.

The moon could be seen though it was not yet

shining. It wasn't all that far away. All you needed to reach it were powerful enough rockets. For Peggy to reach the level of the Camptons a far greater distance would have to be traversed. The whole system of society, perhaps human nature itself, would have to be changed. Since this hadn't happened in the past four or five thousand years it wasn't likely to happen in the next two or three minutes.

The Sempills were about to enter the house.

'Coming, Peggy?' called Effie.

For a few moments Peggy felt like running away.

She went up the steps slowly, past a stone nymph green with moss. 'Sorry,' she said. 'I was looking at the moon.'

The hall really *was* a hall, you could have played badminton in it; in Peggy's at home you couldn't have swung a cat, far less a racket. It had a parquet floor and a lofty ornate ceiling. On the walls were animals' heads. A bear had tears in its eyes. There were two suits of armour and some murky paintings.

A stony-faced middle-aged maid took their stoles. She was at her stoniest when attending Peggy. She had served the gentry long enough not to be taken in by an impostor.

Peggy remembered her father saying: 'The working class don't grudge the rich being rich. Whit they hate is for one of themselves to rise in the world. You should ken, Peggy.' Yes, she knew. Many people in Netherlee Park thought she should be working in the supermarket. They would have been more outraged than the maid if they had seen her here, pretending to be upsides with toffs.

The twins were unaware of the servant's contempt.

Why not, since she was treating them most respect-
fully. Only Rebecca noticed. She gave Peggy a smile
that was sympathetic and uneasy.

Few women could have come into a room with the
Sempill girls and taken the limelight. Peggy wasn't
one. She kept behind them, thankfully, ready to
creep to a chair in a corner.

The drawing-room was huge, not very warm,
smelling faintly of woodsmoke, and, thank goodness,
not very well lit. In the big fireplace logs smouldered.
On her tour of the stately home near Edinburgh,
Peggy had thought that aristocrats seemed to go in
for style rather than comfort, but she had been
judging by the staterooms, not the living quarters.
She had been told that the Camptons had bought the
furnishings with the house. Nothing was new or
very valuable. If there were any rare pieces of
antique furniture in the house they were kept in a
statelier part. The loose covers were faded, the carpet
was worn in places, the once white ceiling with its
elaborate cornices was darkened with smoke; but
there was plenty of comfort. It was not unlike,
though on a grander scale, the sitting-room in
Peggy's home, but there was a noticeable difference,
in that everything here, from the fire-irons to the
pictures, from the vases to the curtains, was solider,
better designed, and composed of superior materials.

Did that also apply to the owners? Yes, it did. The
reading of history had trained Peggy to accept truths
abhorrent to her. She had to admit therefore that
these people did have a distinction, or style, or class,
or polish, or quality — none of these words really
described it — that was never to be found among the
denizens of Netherlee Park. Could it be that,

overawed by the size of the house, and conditioned by her own upbringing in much humbler and coarser circumstances, she was imagining what did not exist? Was she tamely attributing to these not very clever and not very handsome people something they did not really possess? She would have liked to think so but honesty prevented her. From birth they had enjoyed the best of everything, had never known the degradations and humiliations of poverty, and had taken for granted that they were the elite. All that was bound to have had an effect. Who, asked to tell between two dogs which one was owned by a rich man in a mansion and which by a poor man in a room-and-kitchen, would choose wrongly?

The Sempills had this distinction too, to a lesser degree. They more than made up for it by being handsomer, cleverer, and more mannerly.

For, paradoxically, the Camptons were by no means good looking or courteous. Lady Campton had a big nose as well as big feet, and a loud unpleasant voice. Sir Edwin was bald and fat, with an amiable but obtuse face. Lady Angela was blue-haired, raddle-faced, and scraggy-necked. Edwin was gawky. That left Nigel. Seen closer, his slimness was still to Peggy's taste but his superciliousness wasn't.

They showed their lack of courtesy when Diana stood beside Peggy and announced: 'This is Peggy.'

Lady Campton gave an incredulous stare: could this insignificant little creature be the girl Diana had praised? Lady Angela, who was nursing a small rat-faced dog she called Horatio, whispered into his ear. He showed his agreement by snarling. Nigel, on his stomach reading a book, didn't look up. Sir

Edwin, however, came forward and shook Peggy's hand. 'So you're the brainy young lady from Glasgow.'

It would have made a good opening for a limerick, she thought, and indeed that was how he had sung it out, but she liked him. He wasn't trying to make amends for the churlishness of his family, he was too used to this to notice it, he was just being himself, cheerful, decent, and hospitable.

Peggy crept off to the chair in the corner. It was going to be an ordeal but if she said nothing and kept out of the way she could thole it. She had discovered though that she had a great deal more pride than she had thought. She might have difficulty in subduing it, if any of them, Nigel most likely, tried deliberately to humiliate her.

She should have avoided alcohol lest it made her talkative, but when Edwin brought her a sherry she took it, encouraged by his friendly grin.

Sir Edwin proposed a toast. 'To the Sempill ladies, as bonny a bunch of gals as a man could ever wish to see in his house. Especially you, my dear.' That was said to Mrs Sempill. 'I am sure none of your daughters will be offended if I say you are the bonniest of all.'

His wife was offended. What she was drinking couldn't have been vinegar, though her expression couldn't have been sourer if it had.

The compliment, alas, caused Mama to forget her promise to be discreet.

'Thank you, Sir Edwin,' she cried. 'If I am blooming it is because, as you know, I am going to have another child, a boy this time.'

The Sempills waited apprehensively, not knowing what Mama might say next. None of them, not even Diana, looked cross with her. They loved her too much.

The Camptons reacted more individually. Sir Edwin was delighted, though he might not have been able to say why, for if his own wife had just said she was pregnant he would have been appalled, especially as, Peggy suspected, they had long ago given up what produced pregnancy. Lady Campton sulked, though she too couldn't have said why, for the only time she looked happy was when she was gazing at Nigel, *her* baby. Lady Angela was lewdly amused and told Horatio so. Nigel showed himself to be a prude as well as a prig, by scowling in disgust. Evidently like Sir Thomas Browne he would have preferred human beings to propagate like trees, without any messy contact.

'I would have thought,' said Lady Angela, 'that you were a bit too old for the breeding game. Like darling Horatio. He used to sire champions, you know.'

'I am the happiest woman in the world,' said Mrs Sempill.

'May I say you look it, dear lady?' cried Sir Edwin.

'Thank you, Sir Edwin. I feel young again. It is as if my whole body is being renewed. Look, Lady Angela, hardly a wrinkle.' She stroked her cheek and neck.

Her daughters who knew she was being brave as well as proud smiled at her with love and then frowned at Lady Angela with indignation. Even gentle Rebecca was indignant.

294

The dining-room was worse-lit and not much warmer. The table could have accommodated twenty with room to spare, so fourteen, Horatio being allowed to avoid unlucky thirteen, had either to be crowded cosily at one end or spaced out. Lady Campton had opted for the latter arrangement, for some reason of her own. The guests were not permitted to sit where they wished. Lady Angela was placed between Edwin and Diana, to the former's chagrin. Peggy herself had Nigel as her nearest neighbour. She wondered why, never guessing that it had been his suggestion. She didn't mind. It wasn't every day she had dinner with, at her elbow, a baronet's son. She might want to boast about it to her children one day, pointing out to them that it outdid walking on the moon.

The stoney-faced maid and a footman attended the table. Had the butler been left in England or couldn't the rich afford butlers any more?

It was no banquet. The food reminded Peggy of that served at Sonia's wedding: meagre portions, fancily dressed up, and tepid. There was, however, plenty of wine.

At the outset Nigel called to his mother. 'Shouldn't we say grace, Mother?'

'Don't be silly, Nigel. You know we never say grace.'

'Neither do we,' said Mr Sempill.

'But perhaps Miss Gilchrist's people do?'

'They don't,' said Peggy.

He lowered his voice: 'I was under the impression that Scots of the lower orders were all Calvinists.'

She lowered hers: 'Just as I was under the

impression that the English of the higher orders were well-mannered.'

First goal to me, she thought.

She let her wine glass be filled. She needed all the help she could get.

Horatio was eating off Lady Angela's plate. Peggy's mother would have been horrified.

'What's so amusing?' asked Nigel.

'It's private.'

'It's not the done thing, you know, to indulge in private thoughts on a public occasion.'

She looked about her and saw that others too were having private thoughts. Lady Campton's seemed to involve Peggy, judging from the looks she was giving her. The Sempill girls were unusually quiet: they still hadn't forgiven Lady Angela, who didn't give a damn. Mrs Sempill seemed to be in a dwam. She didn't look all that young.

Sir Edwin and Mr Sempill at opposite ends of the table had begun a conversation or rather an argument about the names of their houses. Sir Edwin contended that if Ardmore could be changed to Poverty Castle then Kilcalmonell House could be changed to Kilcalmonell Castle. There already was a Kilcalmonell Castle, said Mr Sempill. Just a heap of old stones, said Sir Edwin. They were both quite tipsy.

'Isn't it extraordinary,' whispered Nigel, 'that a girl from your background should be at University, even if it is red brick?'

'What do you mean, my background?'

'Are you not from the working class? Proud of it too, I've been told.'

'Glasgow University is not red brick. It was founded in 14--. It isn't extraordinary. Not in Scotland. It's a tradition here for clever young men and nowadays clever young girls to go to University, whatever their position in society. As a nation the Scots have always been more democratic that the English. At school we laughed at LOOK BACK IN ANGER. All that fuss about a working class man with a degree. In Scotland they've always been ten a penny.'

Lady Campton was looking puzzled. Nigel seemed to be quite interested in that awful little girl.

Edwin was casting lovelorn glances at Diana, past snarling Horatio.

'Isn't my brother an ass?' asked Nigel.

'Yes, but a nice ass. Is that oxymoron?' The wine was beginning to talk. 'I had a teacher once who was daft about figures of speech. He made us learn them all. Oxymoron, synecdoche, paronomasia, metonymy, and the rest. I bet you couldn't give me an example of synecdoche.'

'Are you trying to pull my leg?'

'Succeeding too.'

During dessert — ice-cream and tinned peaches — he leaned towards her. 'Tell me, Miss Gilchrist, are you a virgin?'

She giggled. 'To tell the truth Mr Campton, I'm not sure.'

She had gone one Sunday afternoon with Tom Moncrieff, founder of the Anti-Titles Society, in a borrowed car to Loch Lomond. All she had wanted was to admire the bonny banks but he was determined to fill her empty life, not to mention her womb. She had kept remembering her mother's admonition: 'Time enough for that nonsense when you're married.' Tom had complained about her lack of co-operation. He had got her tights and panties down and was poking at her when an old woman wearing a white woolly hat had knocked on the car window with her stick.

Meanwhile, Sir Edwin and Mr Sempill were having another argument. Sir Edwin had been informed by a member of his club — 'fellow in a responsible position in the Government' — that if the distances were properly measured it would be found that most of the North Sea oil fields were in English, not Scottish waters. Like most people Sempill made the mistake of forgetting that the world was round not flat. After dinner, if Sempill was game, they could go to the library where there was a globe.

Peggy and no one else could tell if Sir Edwin was joking. Perhaps he didn't know himself. That dubious jocularity, she thought, so peculiar to the English ruling class had brought them an Empire. So often they had proclaimed jovially to the citizens of this or that country that they would be much better off under English rule. While they were laughing at the joke they were taken over. It had happened to the Scots in 1707, with some help from the venal Scots' nobility.

She turned round. Nigel was staring at her, 'Do you know,' he whispered, 'you and I are alike.'

She was astonished. Given a minute she could have named a dozen differences. The wine wasn't just talking in him, it was havering. 'How do you make that out?' she asked.

'You are always on your own. So am I.'

She was about to say, speak for yourself, and point out that she had her parents, her brother, her sister-in-law, her neighbours, and her University acquaintances, but of course he was right. The private and ambitious Peggy Gilchrist had been alone since birth.

She would have thought though that he had plenty of friends. Surely he wasn't awful to everybody? If he was he deserved some credit for consistency.

After dinner Edwin offered to show the Sempill girls and Peggy round the house, but just when they were about to set off Mrs Sempill felt ill. Mr Sempill had to be summoned from the library.

Edwin was the only one who came out to wave them off. Peggy felt sorry that Nigel hadn't appeared to say goodbye. It wasn't likely she would ever see or hear from him again.

When they got back to Poverty Castle, Mama fainted when being helped out of the car and had to be carried into the house. An outsider might have suspected that she had had too much to drink and found it rather funny, but her family and Peggy, who had been made one of them, knew differently and were very upset.

A n extract from a letter from the novelist's wife to her daughter. 'He's absolutely worn out but refuses to rest. When I tell him that it doesn't matter a button whether or not he finishes his book — all his previous ones having been more or less ignored — do you know what he says? That it isn't simply a matter of finishing a book, it has to do with not leaving his characters in the lurch. No doubt he's being ironical as he often is, but he's serious too. He really does think he has a responsibility to those people who don't exist. It's useless telling him they don't exist. He just says I give them existence by denying their existence. I haven't looked at his manuscript for some time, so God knows what's happening to his precious Sempills.

Another thing, he now wants to be buried in Kilmory cemetery; Kilcalmonell in his book. You know how he's always said he wanted to be cremated, with as little fuss as possible. Yet he now asks to be buried in a place at least a hundred miles from here, at the back of beyond, when there's a perfectly suitable cemetery in Dunoon just eight miles away, not to mention another very picturesque one at Inverchaolin even nearer, though it's a kirkyard and the minister might have objections to an atheist being buried in it. I suppose I could promise for the sake of peace, and then do the sensible thing and have him buried locally or cremated. How could it matter to him? He believes there's nothing at all after death. But I couldn't do that, so if he doesn't change his mind again he'll get his wish and be buried in Kilcalmonell or Kilmory I should say. After all, that's where his parents are buried. Would you come, Morag? I'd very much like you to but considering the distance and expense I would understand if you didn't. So would he. He doesn't want anyone else to be there. If I'm alone, except for the gravediggers and undertaker I don't think I could stand it. It would be like a scene in one of his books. Only he would have made it in some way funny! After forty years of marriage I still don't know him. I can't forgive him either for during his last weeks giving far more time to these characters of his, these Sempills, than to me. You never thought your mother was such a crybaby, did you?'

300

Part Three

Diana and the twins, seeing Peggy off on Dunoon pier, had promised to send her a postcard from Spain, but weeks went by without her hearing from them. She was more disappointed than she would admit, even to herself. In the supermarket she proved so dexterous and quick on the uptake that her mother and some of the other women who worked there advised her to make it her career and forget the University. Weren't they always reading about people with degrees who couldn't get jobs? She could easily work her way up to be a manageress and earn more money than most school teachers. It was more interesting too, meeting real people instead of reading about imaginary or dead ones in books.

Sonia had her baby, a boy, and every day pushed him in a second-hand pram to her mother-in-law's where she breast fed him and changed his nappies while Auntie Peggy read CIVILISATION ON TRIAL.

Then one day towards the end of August she came

home from work and found a postcard waiting for her. It was from Spain and showed a view of orange groves against the background of a thumb-shaped mountain. On the back Effie had scribbled; 'Enjoying our holiday here, in a village called Jesus Pobre (Poor Jesus!) We all send our love.' That was all. There was no mention of Mama.

Sonia took it and read it without asking permission. Postcards weren't private, she said.

'Huh! Enjoying their holiday, are they? It was mean of them not asking you to go with them, Peggy.'

'They knew I would be working.'

'You'd have thought, wi' that big hoose lying empty they'd have offered it to us for a holiday.'

'It's not empty. Mrs McDougall their housekeeper will be living in it and looking after the animals.'

Peggy often revisited Poverty Castle in her imagination. She remembered with particular pleasure the ceremony, that was Mr Sempill's word for it, when he carved her name on the trunk of the rowan tree, among the names of his family. It was, Effie had said, the equivalent of Red Indians mixing blood. Edwin was the only other person outside the family to be given the honour. They had all watched Papa carving and when he was finished had applauded.

About two weeks later another postcard came, not from Spain this time but Greece. It had a picture of the Acropolis in Athens. On the back was neatly written: Give us this day our daily bread. The sender's name wasn't given. It had been sent her care of Poverty Castle, and at the foot was a note from Effie saying that they thought it must be from

Nigel who was on holiday in Greece. They had no idea what the message meant. Was it some kind of code?

Peggy had said nothing about her visit to Kilcalmonell House.

Sonia was puzzled therefore. 'Who's Nigel?' she asked.

'A neighbour of the Sempills.'

'Did you meet him when you visited them?'

'Yes.'

'Who is he? Why should he send you a postcaird?'

'I've no idea.'

'Is there something going on between you and him, Peggy, that you're keeping to yoursel'.'

'Not that I know of.'

'Whit age is he?'

'About twenty.'

'Whit does he do?'

'He's a student at Oxford University.'

'Anither toff! Do you ken whit Ah'm going to tell you, Peggy? Things went on during that visit that you've never telt us.'

'Didn't I come back just the same as I went? Did you notice any difference?'

'Right away Ah noticed it. You're sadder. Weel, Ah suppose that was to be expected, for you got a taste of how the rich live and then you'd to come back here. This Nigel, is he a minister's son? Gie us oor daily bread. That's part of the Lord's Prayer, isn't it?'

'I think so.'

'It's a funny thing to write on a postcaird.'

'So it is.'

'And you don't ken whit it means?'

Peggy shook her head.

'Does he fancy you, Peggy?' Sonia spoke doubt-fully. It was her belief that no man was ever likely to fall in love with Peggy, who was too well-educated for working class men and too lowly born for upper class ones.

'No, Sonia, he doesn't.'

'Do you fancy him?'

'No.'

'You don't sound awfully sure. Ah'm like this Effie. Ah think it could be some secret message.'

The solution came to Peggy one day in the supermarket, as she was working at a check-out counter. It was a slack spell and she was thinking of the dinner in the Big House when she suddenly realised the 'Give us each day our daily bread' was an example of synecdoche.

2

A week before the new term was to start Diana wrote to say that she would not be returning to

Mrs Brownlee's. She had found new lodgings where she would have a room to herself and, what was more important, a telephone of her own, which would enable her to keep in touch with home during the next two or three critical weeks. She knew Peggy would understand. They would see each other at the University and she hoped Peggy would visit her often. She did not give her new Glasgow address.

Peggy was hurt more than she had any right to be. She wasn't really Diana's friend. Didn't friends have to be social equals? They had little in common. Like the other girls she had sometimes wondered why Diana had stayed on in Mrs Brownlee's when she could have afforded better. Her point about the telephone made sense. In Mrs Brownlee's if a call came in the middle of the night it might not be heard by anyone. The other girls would be relieved that she had gone. Without wanting to, in some cases resenting it, they had acted deferentially towards her.

All that was true, and yet Peggy felt forsaken. She had let herself take too seriously Mrs Sempill's invitation to regard herself as one of them. They had all urged her to visit them whenever she felt like it, and no doubt they had meant it at the time, but that had been several weeks ago. Her only contact with them since was that postcard. It hadn't been an oversight which had caused Diana not to give the address of her new lodgings. She had been letting Peggy know she mustn't drop in any time she pleased.

Peggy's mother noticed that she was downcast.

'Ah'm no' surprised you're no' looking forward to going back to University. Didn't Ah tell you it was a big mistake?'

Her father guessed the true reason. 'You'll meet ither freen's juist as interesting.'

What other friends would live in so beautiful a place, in such a splendid house? What other friends would consist of five lovely clever sisters?

Sonia would have been more inquisitive if the colour of wee Archie's stools and a rash on his stomach hadn't absorbed all her attention and concern.

So in October Peggy returned to Mrs Brownlee's where her new room-mate was a first-year student from Oban, a big ruddy-faced sturdy blatherskite with a Highland accent. Fiona soon heard from the other girls about her illustrious predecessor and asked more questions about her than Peggy was willing to answer. Was it true that Diana was engaged to a baronet's son and heir? Did she really live in a house called Poverty Castle? Did she have four beautiful sisters? Had Peggy once gone to stay with them? What had it been like?

'You must find me awfully ordinary compared with her.'

'I find you awfully talkative compared with her, Fiona.'

'Sorry.' But a few minutes later Fiona would be enquiring again. To be told once wasn't enough for her. Yet she must have done well enough at school to be admitted to University.

One day for fun but also with a little spite Peggy suddenly asked her what synecdoche was.

'Syn-what?'

'Synecdoche.'

'God, how would I know? Is it some kind of

disease?'

'It's a figure of speech.'

'Never heard of it.'

One Wednesday evening there was a telephone call for Peggy. The girl who came to tell her said it was from Diana Sempill. Peggy tried hard not to run going down the stairs.

She paused for a few seconds to recover her breath and self-respect before lifting the telephone. She spoke quietly: 'Hello. Peggy Gilchrist speaking.'

Was there a hint of haughtiness in Diana's voice? Was the future Lady Campton displeased at being kept waiting? That was ridiculous and unfair. Diana never found it easy to put into her voice the friendliness she was feeling.

'Why haven't I heard from you, Peggy? Why haven't you visited me?'

'I don't know your new address.'

'Good heavens, didn't I give it to you? How stupid of me. I was anxious about Mama when I wrote to you, Peggy. I still am. We all are. I'm afraid she's not well.'

Peggy remembered the tall fair-headed woman weeping in the ruins of the castle. She remembered her too stroking her cheek and neck and crying. 'Look, Lady Angela, no wrinkles.' Had the miracle gone wrong?

'I'm very sorry,' said Peggy. 'She looked so well and happy.'

'She was happy but not well. She's still happy but very far from well. I may have to take a few weeks' absence and go home to help look after her. The twins are in Edinburgh, and Rowena and Rebecca are at school all day. There's a nurse and Mrs McDougall but the twins and I think one of us should be there too. They've agreed it should be me.'

Peggy would have liked to say, 'I'll come with you, Diana,' but what she did say was, 'I hope it turns out all right. When is the baby expected?'

'About three weeks. We're all going home this weekend. Could you come and see me tomorrow? About four? For tea.'

'I don't know your address.'

'Of course. How silly of me. If you have a pencil handy-'

'Yes.' Peggy took down the address and the telephone number.

'I'm looking forward to seeing you again, Peggy. You're a great encouragement to us all.'

'Me?'

'We all think you're indomitable. Nigel too. See you tomorrow then.'

As Peggy went upstairs to her room she saw herself in a mirror on the wall. A more ordinary-looking girl she had never seen. There were thousands like her out there in the streets of Glasgow. Indomitable? What nonsense. Look, there were tears in her eyes. Like a child she was crying because she had been left out.

Next day when she came back from lectures there was a message from Diana. It had been received that morning about seven o'clock. The visit was off. Diana had had to leave at once for home. She had said that Peggy would understand.

3

Diana's telephone had rung at fifteen minutes to five. It roused her from sleep.

It was Rebecca, frightened. 'It's Mama, Diana. It's happening. We've been up all night. It's terrible. Dr Grant's here. I don't think he knows what to do. He's sent for another doctor, a specialist in obstetrics. Poor Papa's blaming himself. He's talking about getting a helicopter to fly Mama to Glasgow, but Dr Grant doesn't think that would do any good and Mama doesn't want to be moved.'

Diana strove to keep calm and think clearly. 'How is Mama?'

'She looks awful, Diana. She just keeps moaning that the baby must be saved, it doesn't matter what happens to her. But it does. I'm afraid, Diana.'

So was Diana afraid but she must not show it. 'It'll be all right. We knew it would be difficult. I'd like to speak to Papa.'

'He won't leave Mama's side. He asked me to let you know. Will you telephone the twins? Dr Grant

313

says it would be as well if we were all here.'

'Yes, I'll telephone them immediately. But I'll have to find out if Papa's serious about getting a helicopter. It would be awful if we arrived in Kilcalmonell to find that Mama was in Glasgow. Where is Rowena?'

'In her room. She won't come out.'

'Please go and tell Papa I want to speak to him.'

'All right.'

As Diana waited she thought about what had to be done. The twins had the Escort in Edinburgh. They could pick her up. It might be advisable to go all the way by road, via Loch Lomond. Ferries could be delayed.

It wasn't Papa speaking but Dr Grant. She pictured him, grey-haired, stooped, worried-looking.

'Your father asked me to speak to you, Diana. He's with your mother.'

'How is she, Doctor?'

'It's her heart. The strain's been too much for it.'

'Is she having a miscarriage?'

'No, but it's not the easiest of deliveries. I've sent for Dr Hislop. He's the best obstetrician in these parts.'

'Rebecca said Papa was talking about getting a helicopter to fly Mama to Glasgow. Would that help?'

'I don't think so. We can do all that's required, if her heart stands the strain. We may have to move her to Tarbeg Hospital.' He refrained from pointing out that just a week ago he had suggested that Mrs Sempill ought to spend the last two or three weeks of her pregnancy in a Glasgow nursing home. 'I may say, she doesn't want to be moved.'

'Is she in a condition to decide what's best for her?'

'Your father says her wishes must be respected. He wants you all here as soon as possible.'

'Tell him we'll be there by eleven o'clock at the latest.'

'Good. Don't drive dangerously, though.'

Still in her night-dress she telephoned the twins. They too had a telephone in their room. She would try to keep calm though Effie might misinterpret it. There was no help in panic or hysterics. If, she thought, as she listened to the telephone ringing in the room in Edinburgh, if Papa had brought us up to go to church and believe in God we could have prayed. It could still be done, but not honestly.

Effie muttered, sleepily. 'Do you know what time it is, whoever you are?'

'Sorry, Effie. It's Diana. I've just had a call from Rebecca to say that Mama's having her baby and is very ill. We've got to get home as soon as we can.'

'Oh Christ!' Effie could be heard wakening Jeanie and giving her the news. Then she was shouting into the telephone. 'How does Rebecca know? She's just a kid.'

'Dr Grant's there. I was speaking to him. Another doctor's on his way.'

'So it's the baby?'

'Yes. Dr Grant's afraid Mama's heart might not be able to stand the strain.'

'We were all warned, weren't we?' Tough Effie

was weeping.

'We're not giving up hope, Effie. But we mustn't waste time. Come in the car and pick me up. We'll go all the way by road, I think, and not depend on the ferry.'

'It's just as fast anyway. What time is it now?'

'Five o'clock.'

'We'll be at your door soon after six. We should be in Poverty by nine.'

'Yes, but don't take risks.'

'We won't. The roads will be quiet at this time.'

'But you'll still be sleepy.'

'No, Di, we're both thoroughly and horribly awake. Thanks for keeping calm. I know like me and Jeanie you feel like wailing and screaming. If you gave way so would we. Like old times. See you soon.'

As Diana put the telephone down her hand was sore with the tightness of her grip.

Before the twins arrived at a quarter past six she had telephoned Mrs Brownlee's and left a message for Peggy Gilchrist with a yawning maid. She had also been in touch with home again. Dr Hislop had arrived and was confident that the baby so far had come to no harm. He would not commit himself about Mama. Rowena had spoken too. She was crying. For the first time in her life she did not know how to play the part she had been given.

It was too early to ring Edwin. It could be done from Poverty Castle, if it was necessary.

It was still dark when the twins arrived at her door. She got into the back of the car. It was almost a minute before any of them spoke.

'Any later news?' asked Jeanie. Her voice was hoarse.

'Dr Hislop's there now. He thinks the baby's safe.'

'That bloody baby!' muttered Effie. 'Well, it shouldn't have happened, should it? And if it hadn't happened Mama's life wouldn't be in danger, would it?'

'It's not the baby's fault,' said Jeanie.

'As if, for Christ's sake, there weren't enough in the world already, millions upon millions more than are needed.'

'Needed for what?' asked Jeanie, irritably. 'Shut up, Effie.'

Jeanie's right and Effie's wrong, thought Diana. But what if Mama dies and the baby survives, will we be able to love it as we should?

Only once during the two and a half hours' journey was Peggy Gilchrist mentioned.

'Do you see much of Peggy?' asked Effie.

'I haven't seen her at all. We don't attend the same lectures.'

'Haven't you been to visit her?'

'She was coming to see me this afternoon.'

'I wonder if she did spend the summer working in the supermarket.'

'I expect so.'

That was all that was said about Peggy.

4

Peggy waited until the evening before telephoning. This wasn't so that she could use the cheap rate but because she shrank from intruding and had kept hoping that Diana would call and tell her what had happened.

It was Effie who replied. Her voice was hard and cold and did not change when she knew it was Peggy she was speaking to. 'My mother's dead.'

Peggy felt tears in her eyes. She could not stem them. They ran down her cheeks. She could not remember ever having shed tears before.

Mrs Sempill had loved bright colours and jewellery, she had been so proud of her daughters, and she had asked Peggy to regard herself as one of them.

Peggy could not bring herself to ask how the baby was.

'We didn't see her alive. We were too late.'

'I'm sorry, Effie.'

'It's a boy. So she got her wish. So she was happy at the end. That's what they're saying. They're saying too that it's not the baby's fault. I know it isn't but I've got to blame something.'

Peggy wanted to say, 'Can I come and share your grief, Effie?' but she just said that she was sorry.

'Papa's devastated. We all are. Who said the Sempills were lucky? Thanks for telephoning, Peggy.'

That was it. Peggy was left staring at the notice which requested users of the telephone to show consideration for others, but in her imagination she saw the tall white house by the sea, whose name yesterday was a misnomer but today was not.

She was trembling as she went upstairs. She could not have been more distressed if it had been her own mother who had died. This was Thursday, the funeral would probably be on Monday. They had taken her to see the cemetery at Kilcalmonell, where some of the gravestones had skulls and crossbones and eighteenth century dates. Unlike most cemeteries it was untidy, with bushes, trees, and wild flowers. Birds sang in it. Now in October there would be many fallen leaves. She wanted to be there on Monday. She felt she had a right.

Fiona, munching an apple, did not at first notice her damp eyes. When she did she stopped in the middle of a bite. She had told her parents that her room-mate was a wee Glasgow hard case. 'Bad news?' she asked.

'Yes.'

'Your family?'

'Yes, my family,' said Peggy inwardly. Aloud she said, 'Diana Sempill's mother is dead.'

Fiona's eyes grew large. This was big news. 'She's the girl that was here before me? The one that lives in a castle?'

'Yes.'

'Was she ill?'

'Yes.'

'What was wrong with her?'

The baby was a family secret. 'Her heart.'

'That's terrible. She couldn't have been very old.'

'She wasn't fifty.'

'That's not old today, is it?'

Fiona then went off to spread the news.

If they wanted me to come, thought Peggy, Effie would have said so. Funerals are family affairs. Their Edinburgh relatives will be there.

All the same she could not bear to go home that weekend where no message could reach her.

On Saturday afternoon she went for a walk in the Botanic Gardens and sat among the withering chrysanthemums, trying to read CIVILISATION ON TRIAL.

She had a cup of tea and a chocolate biscuit in a Wimpey's and then hurried back to the boarding-house. There had been no message from Kilcalmonell.

Several times she was on the point of telephoning herself. Perhaps they wanted her to come but in the turmoil of grief had forgotten to ask her, or perhaps they thought she would come without having to be asked. When they remembered, too late, they would be upset.

When she went to bed she left her door open so

that she might hear the telephone ringing below in the hall. At weekends the house was almost deserted. Once it did ring, at half-past twelve, and she was on her way downstairs when a very annoyed Mrs Brownlee shouted up: 'It's for Sadie Meiklejohn. You might have guessed.'

On Sunday afternoon Peggy walked to the Art Galleries and sat with her book, in the company of aristocratic ladies who had lived hundreds of years ago but somehow were still alive. One resembled Mrs Sempill, in having fair hair, eager hands, and especially a look of adoration as she gazed at her husband, a haughty grandee more interested in his wolfhounds than in her. He was very different from Mr Sempill, who would have looked back adoringly.

When she got back to the boarding-house about six there was still no message. She gave up hope then.

The girls began to arrive back, boisterous and cheerful with tales of their adventures. Fiona was enthusiastic about a shinty match she had seen. One of the star players was a boy-friend of hers. Afterwards they had gone to a disco. On their way home the moon had been shining on Oban bay.

Fiona was asleep and Peggy trying to sleep when a girl came and said Peggy was wanted on the telephone. It was ten minutes to twelve.

'Who is it?' asked Peggy.

'No idea. Somebody yelled up it was for you. Hope it's not bad news.'

It could be Peggy's mother anxious to know that she was all right. Peggy felt ashamed. All that weekend she had scarcely given her mother a thought.

It was Effie Sempill. Her voice was not so cold and hard. She was more reconciled. 'It's just occurred to us, Peggy, that we haven't asked you if you would like to come to Mama's funeral.'

'I would like very much to come.'

'She would have wanted you to be there. She said you had the gift of silence.'

A typical Mrs Sempill way of describing dour reticence!

'Unlike herself, she said.' Effie was weeping, quietly. 'She was always talking, like a bird is always singing.'

Just as her hands were as busy as wings.

'Sorry we've left it so late, Peggy. The funeral's at three tomorrow. There's to be no church service and no minister. Mama's relatives wanted her to be buried in Edinburgh but she wanted to remain her in Kilcalmonell, to be close to us, for she knew that, wherever we were in the world, we would always come back to Poverty Castle. Do you know how to get here?'

'Yes.' After all, she had been there before.

'A bus leaves Glasgow for Tarbeg early in the morning and arrives about twelve. Someone will meet you there. By the way Nigel's here. He flew up with Edwin. So maybe he's not so awful after all.'

Peggy wondered if she should ask how the baby was. She would see for herself tomorrow.

'You'll be staying the night of course.'

'I don't want to be in the way.'

'You'll never be that. You're very good at effacing yourself. Too good, some of us think. See you tomorrow then.'

It was only then, as she put down the telephone, with tears of relief and joy and sorrow running down her cheeks, that Peggy realised she didn't have any clothes suitable for a funeral. Did it matter? The Sempills themselves, some of them anyway, might not be wearing mourning clothes. Any dark coat would do, dark stockings, and a dark headscarf, but she had none of these.

Who were the girls with the most varied wardrobes? Sadie Meiklejohn and Paula Johnston, who were room-mates. They were obliging and generous but both of them were inches taller than she.

She knocked on their door, hoping they weren't asleep.

'Come in,' called Sadie.

They weren't in bed. Sadie was wearing only purple briefs: her breasts were big and brazen; like rugby footballs, one of the girls had said. Paula's red nightie was short and transparent. Their faces were plastered with cold cream.

There was a reek of cigarette smoke and scent. It was rumoured that they smoked pot.

They stared in astonishment at the Wee Swot, as they called her.

'Sorry to bother you,' she said. 'But maybe you've heard that Diana Sempill's mother is dead.'

'Yes, we heard. Too bad.' They hadn't cared much for Diana but their sympathy was genuine while it lasted.

'I've been asked to go to the funeral.'

'Are you going?' asked Sadie. 'I always refuse. Funerals are ghastly.'

'Yes I'm going, but I haven't any suitable clothes.'

They had to smile. Her wardrobe was pitiful. They were University students themselves but even so couldn't understand how any girl would rather spend her money on books.

'Do you have a coat I could borrow, please?'

They smiled again, at this absurd and cheeky request. Why should she think they had clothes suitable for a funeral? And surely she knew they were both at least two sizes bigger than she?

'You're welcome to anything I have that you think might suit you,' said Sadie.

'Me too,' said Paula.

'I know they'll be too big for me but it won't matter at a funeral, will it?'

Was this, they wondered, exchanging glances, a sample of the Wee Swot's irony, which they had heard about?

'Any dark-coloured coat would do.'

Sadie brought out a dark-blue coat with red cuffs and collar. Paula's was olive-green with yellow buttons. Peggy asked if she could try them on.

Both coats were too long and wide.

Rummaging among a bundle of belts Sadie found a blue one. Tightly drawn, it made the dark-blue coat look less long and wide.

'This would do,' said Peggy. 'Do you mind if I borrow it, Sadie?'

'Not a bit,' said Sadie, amazed that a girl of twenty-one would go to a function, even a funeral, dressed like that. The Sempills and their relatives would be most properly dressed. 'You're welcome to it, Peggy, but surely there's a coat in the house nearer your size?'

'It's too late to go round asking. I'm leaving first thing tomorrow morning.'

Paula had looked out a mauve headscarf and beige stockings.

'What about shoes?' asked Sadie.

'I've got a black pair that will do.'

They let in but perhaps tomorrow would be dry.

'What did Mrs Sempill die of?' asked Sadie.

They didn't know about the baby. Peggy felt mean about keeping them in the dark and yet borrowing their clothes.

'Her heart,' she said.

'For all their money,' muttered Sadie.

For all their beauty. For all their pleasure in life. For all their love for one another. For all their luck.

'Thanks very much,' said Peggy, at the door. 'I'll take good care of them.'

'Good luck anyway,' said Sadie, and added, more to herself than to Peggy, 'and I don't just mean at the funeral.' She couldn't help giving her blessing for what it was worth to a girl who had nothing and didn't seem to mind.

He had once written that of all the mean tricks death played on people the worst was to take them by surprise, giving them no time to prepare with courage and dignity. In one of his stories an elderly man was struck down in the lavatory, in the act of wiping himself. Therefore Jessie, though shocked and grieved, was pleased too, for his sake, when, after calling three times that lunch was ready, she went to his study and found him, not busy at his desk, but seated in the armchair, with his hands clasped on his lap and the remnants of a smile on his face. She would have thought he had fallen asleep if his eyes hadn't been open. Harvey the cat, which usually lay on the desk, undisturbed by the typewriter, had vanished. He didn't like trouble and kept out of the way till it was over.

There was a sheet of paper in the typewriter. She glanced at it. He had managed to finish the sentence before the warning came, perhaps a stab of pain or dizziness. He had struggled into the armchair to prepare himself, for the grimmest of all interviewers. She hoped that he had been able to finish his novel, though she did not think he had. Perhaps death had tricked him meanly after all.

For a day in October the weather was fine. There was blue sky. In the mountains of Arran the warrior slept.

She thought of the table set for two.

She was composed now. Later it would not be so easy. She had telephone calls to make, one to the doctor, and one to Morag in Milwaukee.

The doctor at first was displeased at being disturbed at his lunch after a hard morning's work, but when she told him what had happened he was sympathetic and regretful. He had been proud of having as a patient one of the country's leading novelists. He would come immediately. Was she all right? Was she alone? Yes, she was all right and she would rather be alone in the meantime.

By bedtime the doctor and undertaker had been and gone, Donald had been carried upstairs and put on a bed, with help from the farmer and his son, Harvey had come back but not to the study, she had read the book from the beginning and found that the last chapter had not been written, and she had been in touch with Morag.

It had not been an emotional conversation. Neither of them was that kind of woman.

'I'm sorry to tell you, Morag, your father's dead.'

'Good heavens! When did it happen?'

'About two hours ago. This is the third time I've tried to reach you. The funeral's to be on Friday, in Kilmory, or Kilcalmonell as he calls it in his book. That's where he was born and where his father and mother are buried. That's what he wanted. Will you be able to come?'

'It'll not be convenient but I'll certainly come. How did it happen? Was he found in a wood?'

'No. I found him, in the armchair in his study. He didn't manage to finish his book after all.'

'At least he didn't suffer.'

'We don't know that. It would trouble him, during that last minute, knowing that it wasn't finished.'

'Surely he should have been thinking of you, then?'

'He would be, in his way. It's a pity. He worked so hard at it.'

'And killed himself doing it. How stupid.'

'It was his life, writing his books.'

'God knows why. It's not as if he ever made much money out of them.'

'He didn't do it for money.'

'What other reason makes sense? I could see the point of wearing yourself out finishing a book if it was going to make a lot of money but not if it was going to be a financial flop like all the others.'

'He didn't want to leave his characters in the lurch.'

There was a pause. 'Are you sure you're all right, mother? It must have have been a terrible shock.'

'Yes, it was, and yet I suppose I was expecting it. My husband whom I married more than forty years ago has just died. Is it any wonder then if I say peculiar things?'

'I'm sorry, mother. I didn't mean it like that. It's just that, well, we both know his characters never existed, except in his mind.'

'And in mine. If you can come, Morag, I'll be very pleased to have your company. I don't suppose William will come with you.'

'He's at a conference in Los Angeles at the moment.'

'It doesn't matter. Your father wanted just you and me to be present.'

'Aren't any of his literary friends to be there?'

'He left instructions that there was to be no public notice of his death until after the funeral, so only the people around here know. I expect you'll fly to London and then to Glasgow. Do you want me to meet you at Glasgow airport?'

'There's no need. I can find my way to Dunoon. Perhaps you could meet me at the pier.'

'There's been quite a lot of meetings there recently.'

'What do you mean?'

'Nothing. When you know the times of your flights will you let me know?'

'I'll telephone you later today. In the meantime look after yourself.'

That was the trouble, she had only herself to look after now.

The hearse was to set off with the coffin at eleven so that it could make the one hundred mile journey at a seemly speed. Mr McClure the undertaker was already perturbed by there being no minister and only two mourners who in addition were not to be conveyed in one of his opulent chauffeured limousines but were driving themselves in a seven-year-old dented yellow Mini. He had made it plain that he was more concerned about propriety than profit. Morag too was upset by the lack of a service but she said nothing. She had arrived tight-lipped, dry-eyed and edgy. Her mother had explained that she was going to take the opportunity to have a look at Kilmory or Kilcalmonell which she hadn't visited for more than twenty years. She did not mention that she wanted to see places associated with the Sempills. Morag would never have understood and her incomprehension would have been increased if she had been told that for her mother there would be two funerals that afternoon, one real, and the other happening in her mother's imagination. For Jessie would see in her mind the mourners who, that other October, had gathered round Mrs Sempill's grave.

Jessie had to do all the driving, Morag being accustomed only to cars with automatic transmission. Luckily it was a fine day, with good driving conditions.

'We'd better not be late,' muttered Morag, as they ambled alongside Loch Eck at a steady thirty-five miles an hour.

'Aren't the rowans beautiful?'

Morag was no enthusiastic admirer of nature. 'All those berries, doesn't it mean a severe winter?'

'So they say.'

'I still think you should come and live with us: for a while anyway. I don't like to think of you all by yourself in that lonely house, with only sheep for neighbours.'

'I won't be alone. I've got Harvey and my neighbours are deer, rabbits, cows and birds. A hawk comes every day and sits on the telephone pole.'

'I'm not joking, mother. At your age you shouldn't be on your own.'

'Wouldn't I be on my own in Milwaukee most of the

time, when you and William were out at work? It would have been different if you had children.'

That put Morag into a huff. She shed tears.

'They drove along this road lots of times,' said Jessie.

'Who did?'

'The Sempills.'

Morag had forgotten. 'Who are they?'

'Characters in your father's book.'

'For heaven's sake, mother, please stop talking about them as if they were real people. It's crazy.'

So Jessie didn't talk about the Sempills but she thought about them more than she did about Morag.

At Cairndow she quoted Keats, to herself, vaguely: 'Truth is beauty, beauty truth.'

In some ways, she thought, Morag's like Diana. She has the same habit of tightening her lips to show disapproval, lacks humour, and distrusts imagination.

After two and a half hours they drove down the brae into Tarbeg. The harbour was crammed with fishing boats. There were hundreds of gulls and five swans.

'Let's have lunch here,' said Jessie, and she parked the car in front of the Royal Hotel.

'Have we time?'

'Plenty. It's only half an hour from here to Kilcalmonell.'

'All right.' Morag felt she needed a rest from her mother's driving.

'We'll have a sherry in the lounge first,' said Jessie, leading the way.

'Mother, this is father's funeral, remember.'

'I remember.' In the lounge, was it at that table the Sempills had sat, when Diana had chatted to the waitress about a school-friend keen on dancing who had married a shepherd and gone to live in a cottage among the hills? Was *that* the waitress? And was it in that corner, among

330

the potted plants, that Mr and Mrs Sempill had sat before going for their stroll in the moonlight?

'What's the matter?' asked Morag. You're looking funny again.'

'Your father and I once spent a weekend in this hotel. Before you were born. We were visiting Kilcalmonell.'

'You mean Kilmory.'

An hour later they were on their way again.

As they turned off the main road and headed for Kilmory, Morag was impressed by the beauty of the countryside. 'But it's miles from anywhere,' she added.

'Your father used to be cross when I said that. Where's anywhere, he would ask. Is it Glasgow? Edinburgh? London? Timbuktu?'

'He must have known what you meant. Miles from decent shops, theatres, cinemas, busy streets. Was that a seal I saw on that rock?'

Jessie looked back. It was a seal. Why not the Sempills' seal?

'I wonder,' she said, 'if your father when he was at Glasgow University ever met anyone like Peggy Gilchrist?'

'Who's she? Don't tell me, a character in his book.'

'I wonder what happened to her. I like to think she married Nigel. But then, like Mrs Gilchrist, I'm a romantic at heart.'

'This is becoming an obsession, mother.'

'It's my way of remembering your father.'

They came to the highest part of the road before it began the descent into Kilmory. Jessie got out of the car and looked through binoculars at the village below her.

Yonder, among trees, was Kilmory House. To the right of it shone a beach of white sand. That was where Poverty Castle ought to be, and there it was, high and splendid in the sunshine. It was really a massive rock.

'We'll be late, mother,' called Morag.

Yonder was the cemetery. The hearse was there, glittering. A number of people were gathered at the gate. The news must have got out. At Mrs Sempill's funeral, how many had come to watch?

They arrived at the cemetery gate at five minutes to three. Mr McClure, displeased at what he considered their disrespect, informed them in a whisper that since the gate was too narrow to admit a vehicle the coffin had to be carried to the grave. This would be done by men from Tarbeg whom he had engaged. It ought, his tone implied, to have been done by friends or relatives of the deceased.

None of the local people approached to speak to Jessie. One or two were old. They might well have been at school with Donald.

Morag and Jessie followed the coffin through the gate and into the cemetery.

'I've never seen such untidy graves,' muttered Morag. 'We'll have to hire somebody to look after father's.'

'He preferred untended graves and ruined churches.'

Morag did not say it but her face showed it: her father was now no doubt paying for his sacrilegious prejudices. She and William were members of an Evangelical church in Milwaukee.

As the coffin was lowered into the grave curlews on the shore called mournfully. Donald after all was having his funeral service.

Jessie closed her eyes.

She saw Effie in a red jerkin with a black band round her arm. Both hands were thrust into her pockets and her shoulders were hunched. She had vowed not to weep at the graveside and she wasn't weeping. Beside her Jeanie was, quietly: she too wore a black armband. Diana stood beside Edwin, she in a black coat and hat, he in a dark suit with a black tie. Once he tried to take her hand but she

withdrew it. In Rowena's pocket was a brooch taken from her mother's jewel box, just as she had years ago taken the glass cat from the shelf in the shop. She held Rebecca's hand, not to give comfort but to receive it. Rebecca, the youngest and gentlest, was also the bravest. Both of them wore coats that bright but cool day, Rebecca's red and Rowena's green. Their tokens of mourning were black ribbons in their hair.

Beside Peggy Gilchrist in her borrowed clothes stood Nigel. Did he, once, offer to hold her hand?

Mr Sempill's eyes, wet even on the happiest occasions, streamed tears. He could not subdue his grief: it had him by the throat. He thought of himself as his wife's murderer and at the graveside was desperately but hopelessly contrite.

A nurse was looking after the baby in Poverty Castle.

Mrs McDougall was present, and several anonymous Edinburgh relatives.

Had there been a piper, in that corner over there, behind the whins, playing a lament?

Had Mr Sempill composed an elegy for his wife? Unable to speak it himself, which of his daughters had done it for him? Rowena, so clever at reciting? Diana, the most resolute?

Only the dead man in the coffin could have answered those questions.

Jessie felt her arm being tugged. It was Morag, impatient to leave a scene of sorrow and shame. She would complain about it to William for years.

Jessie was in confusion as she walked towards the gate. They were all going, to the blue Daimler, the white Escort, and the black limousines of the undertaker. There would be refreshments at Poverty Castle. Would the baby be kept discreetly in the background, or would he be brought into their midst triumphantly? Would they all, including Effie and Peggy, take turns at holding him?

They were all gone.

'You're on your own now,' murmured Jessie. 'He's done all he could for you. Good luck.'

'What did you say, mother?' asked Morag.

'Nothing.'

'You did say something, mother.'

'I must have been talking to myself.'

'Not for the first time, I must say. I think we should go straight home.'

'No. Let's go to the shop and find out if they still serve tea in October. The robins, you know, are very tame.'